Something of the Night

RICHARD NEER

A RILEY KING MYSTERY

RICHARD NEER

ALSO BY RICHARD NEER:

FM: THE RISE AND FALL OF ROCK RADIO
THE MASTER BUILDERS
INDIAN SUMMER
THE LAST RESORT
THE PUNCH LIST
AN AMERICAN STORM
WRECKING BALL

SOMETHING OF THE NIGHT

For Vicky

One

I sat in the office playing solitaire on my laptop when my three thirty appointment showed up precisely on time. Her name was Paige White and she was some sort of agent. Her assistant had set up the meeting with my guy, and I had no idea what it was about or what or who Ms. White agented.

Paige White seemed to be in her late forties, like me, but unlike me, she put some effort into her wardrobe. She wore a tailored pants suit, in white linen that showed her tall lean form to great advantage. Her dirty blond shag was streaked with sun-drenched highlights, and combined with her robust color; I assumed she'd spent time in the tropics lately.

"Mr. King. Paige White. Just call me Paige."

"I'm Riley. Sounds like a last name, but it's a first. Pleasure."

"Have a seat, Paige. Can I get you anything? Coffee? Water?"

"Evian would be fine if you have it. If not, any sparkling water will do."

"Long ride?" I vaguely remember my assistant telling me she was from up north, but I couldn't recall where exactly as I buzzed him to fetch her water (Toms River, New Jersey's finest tap) and a diet Dr. Pepper for me.

"Drove down from Fort Lee. It's about an hour and a half up the Parkway."

"You live there?"

"My office is there. I live in Englewood. Next town. Actually, I have the same type of setup that you have here. Less than ten people working for me but we're pretty tight knit. Kind of family, in a way."

Who was the detective here? She'd done some homework on me.

"And what do you do exactly? In your work that is."

"I'm a literary agent. I represent authors."

"Anyone I'd be aware of?"

"That depends on your level of awareness, doesn't it? I represent Lars Himmelman, the man who wrote the biography of Man o' War. Spent ten months on the Times bestseller list. The liberal answer to Rush Limbaugh's book by Allin Harris was mine. John Peterson, the detective writer is our biggie…. Elton Spicer's the character. Clint Eastwood played him in a movie this winter. Those are the major ones plus a few others."

I finally got it. Paige White. White Page. That couldn't be her real name, could it? I was curious about the name but I stayed vanilla with, "Impressive list."

Clearly, she was interviewing me for the job, and I'd already indicated a lack of interest about why she needed the services of an investigator. This could be nothing or a financial windfall. It wasn't as if I couldn't use an infusion of cash at the moment.

"How can I help you then?"

She withdrew an SD card from her Coach briefcase – a little accessory item that would cover my expenses for a month. "Ever hear of a Paul Geist? From Toms River?"

"It's a small town but not so small that I know everybody in it."

"Of course. Just took a stab."

"Uh huh."

"I want you to find him for me."

"Why?"

"He's got some money coming to him. Perhaps a great deal."

This was the oldest scam in the book, something I hoped a literary agent could improve upon. How many noire movies were plotted around killers who locate their prey by telling an unsuspecting friend that he'd hit the jackpot on a forgotten business venture years ago and was suddenly rich? How many Nigerian princes needed just a small loan so that they could come to America and return the favor tenfold?

I asked Paige White to explain.

"I told you that ours was a small business. We started up about ten years ago. I'd been an account executive at an ad agency in New York and I became friends with a writer. Well, more than friends really, you know. In any case, he'd written this really good first novel and he just couldn't get it in the right doors. I knew a few people in publishing through my advertising contacts so I told him I'd go directly to the editors. Well, long story short, I got him a deal and his book did very well, better than our relationship I'm afraid. But he honored his commitment and his success gave me a stake to start my own business."

My cynicism intruded. Better than the relationship? Had this guy treated her badly and maybe Ms. White wanted a little revenge? "So now you've made it and you want to pay him back for starting you out but you can't find him."

"No. He's on my speed dial. Let me explain. Like any new business, we had to establish credibility. Top authors weren't exactly flocking to us for representation. We had to pore through a lot of manuscripts in hopes discovering fresh talent. If you find one winner in a thousand you're lucky. But my ex's books kept us afloat and eventually we built the business into what it is now."

"Very inspiring, Paige. So who's Peter Geist?"

"Paul Geist. He is an English teacher from Toms River who years ago discovered I was a new agent looking for talent, so he sent me a manuscript. It wasn't bad ---- not ready for prime time though. I just encouraged him to work at it and keep sending me stuff. Geist was prolific. I must have gotten a book every year from him for five or six years. Each one was a little better than the last, but he still couldn't get over the bar. But as our business grew and we signed more established writers, I didn't really have as much time for the Paul Geists of the world, so the last one he sent gathered dust on my shelf for months. Anyway, his manuscript caught my eye and I was bored cleaning so I decided to read a few pages. I couldn't put it down. I mean, it was riveting. Whether he just needed time to grow or some epiphany happened in his writing, I don't know. I think we might be talking a decent-sized advance. But when I called the number I had for Geist to share the good news, it'd been disconnected. Tried email, no response."

"Try directory assistance? Google?"

"Of course, I did a Google search. Nothing helpful there. I called the school where he taught. I even sent an intern down here a couple weeks ago to the address he'd put on the manuscript. Some woman answered the door and said that Geist was a previous tenant and had moved out almost a year ago. She was still getting some of his junk mail and there was no forwarding address. He'd just vanished."

"You call the police?"

"I did. But they had no missing persons report on him. They said that people relocate all the time, retire or whatever and leave no forwarding address. They wouldn't spend time looking for a guy who might've moved to Florida or something."

Paige was savvy enough to search in all the conventional places available to civilians. But I had other sources through my old friends at the FBI. "I'll need a retainer. I can't say exactly how much this'll cost you overall, but I will give you periodic progress reports and a rough idea of the hours already expended."

"Like I said, business has been good. If we exceed your retainer, you bill me and you'll be paid. I may charge some of it back to Mr. Geist, depending on the advance, but either way, it will be taken care of."

Over the last few minutes, I'd warmed to Paige White. Looking at her a bit closer, I revised my estimate of her age upwards a few years. But she was still very attractive, smart, owned her own business. She was taking pains to do the right thing for a struggling author, even if it meant shelling out from her own pocket. No doubt if there was a large audience for this book, her commission might be substantial, so this wasn't entirely done out of altruism but she did seem to care about the man and his work.

"Paige, gut instinct. Any thoughts as to where this guy went? You're not thinking anything bad happened to him?"

"I'm not sure. His book has a very authentic feel, almost like a diary. He might have been writing from actual experiences. My fear is that the book hit someone a little too close to home and that ... well, that's silly."

"No, please go on. Anything you might feel, no matter how trivial or far-fetched it might seem, could be helpful."

"I guess because I rep so many of John Peterson's thrillers, it's probably just my imagination. But given the nature of the text, someone may want to do Paul some harm."

"Why?"

"It's about a small town English teacher and a priest who have a three way with one of his students. It reads like a diary. She winds up killing them both."

Two

As Paige sketched out the scenario, I flashed on Kubrick's *Lolita* and that Nicole Kidman flick *To Die For* where she recruits a couple of high school kids to knock off Matt Dillon for her. Toms River wasn't exactly a hotbed for murder, but had made national news over the last three years with a couple of ex-cops who had gone on a killing spree.

"I think maybe you need to read it for yourself to get the full impact. I'll trust your discretion. I haven't shared it with anyone, even my office people. Maybe I'm just being paranoid but in case someone *is* trying to quash it, God knows what lengths they'd go to, especially if they caused Paul Geist to vanish. The priest's involvement is particularly troubling. The description of the molestation, if I can call it that, is so vivid that it's hard to believe someone just made it up from whole cloth."

"So you're thinking that this guy is chronicling his life? That's what writers do, I suppose."

"To an extent. Obviously, you write what you know. It's a jumping off point. But very few writers actually live the life of their characters. Hemingway supposedly wasn't quite the he-man one would think from reading his work. Even detective stuff, like Parker's *Spenser* books. Bob liked the same food and music as his protagonist, but he'd never fired a gun in anger."

7

"But if it's as true to life as you say, and this writer was into molesting children, wouldn't this guy be risking one of his victims coming forward if it sees the light of day?"

"I'm not a lawyer, but I don't think any laws were broken. Age of consent is sixteen here."

"Whether they technically broke any laws or not, I can't imagine a three way with a priest would go down very well in the community."

"As an artist, he might not care. I mean, Roman Polanski is still respected as a filmmaker, and he was convicted of statutory rape and had to leave the country. The Woody Allen situation is another. If Paul Geist is alive, he may not be welcome in Toms River anymore, but the artistic community might take a different view."

"You say *if* he's alive? You think he may not be?"

"That's why I'm hiring you."

"Sounds like I start by trying to separate fact from fiction."

"You're the professional, you do what you feel is best. There might be some clues in the book. I don't know Toms River all that well. Geist might have just turned into a better writer from all those years of trying. But this work represents a great leap forward, stylistically."

"How so?"

"The book will remind readers of Strelnikov. You know, that Russian writer who was so acclaimed in the seventies based on that one huge novel. They made it into a blockbuster movie. Strelnikov was imprisoned in the USSR, as you may recall. After Glasnost came, he was able to emigrate to the states. But after a couple of years, he went into seclusion because he hated being famous."

Strelnikov --- sounded like a boutique vodka. I wasn't familiar with this Commie scribe but I nodded thoughtfully so the sophisticated Ms. White would think she wasn't hiring a member of the illiterati.

Prologue completed, she extracted her checkbook, asked for a number and who it was payable to. I gave her my opening gambit, prepared to negotiate, but she didn't flinch --- just started writing.

"How can I get in touch with you, Paige?"

She scribbled a number on the back of her business card. "Here's my personal cell number. Please keep it private; I've got another one for business. When can you get started?"

"How about tomorrow? I'll read some tonight, and then start at the school in the morning. You say you already talked to someone there?"

"Just the personnel lady and she didn't tell me much --- only that Geist left last June after the school year ended. It's a fairly small Catholic school. Sacred Cross."

"I know it. Over near the Parkway. It's not too big. Enrollment around three hundred, I think. I've done some fundraising work with them and I know the headmaster well enough to say hello --- Father Gregory Salieri. I might be able to make some headway. Where will you be tomorrow?"

"Friday the publishing biz usually shuts down by noon ---- in the summer they often aren't around at all. Hamptons, you know. So I plan to make a weekend out of it.

One of my authors, John Peterson, has a place on the ocean on Long Beach Island. He's in his West Coast digs until July so he's given me the run of the house 'til then. I loaded up a bunch of books I've been neglecting. I plan to light a fire, snuggle in and read all weekend."

The fantasy of the delectable Ms. White, wrapped in a blanket in front of a roaring fire with a snifter of brandy was appealing to my more prurient instincts. "I'll call you there. It's supposed to get cool tonight but the forecast is for a warm weekend. This is a good time to be on the island."

Three

In an earlier life, I was a basketball player at Georgetown, even though much of it was spent on the bench. And now, being a single guy with an FBI background enjoying the mysterious and sexy life of a private investigator, I've always been pretty active physically.

I've let my appearance suffer. I need to work through this, I know. I blame the weather--- after bundling up and jogging slowly a couple of times, battling the biting winds off Barnegat Bay and the sub zero chill factors, I gave up. I contemplated buying a treadmill. I know of a friend on the Dover Township police force who was selling his, but when I thought of the two thousand dollar coat rack it had become in his basement, I decided against it.

I was running out of excuses. This Paige White case intrigued me. Her buttoned down professionalism had embarrassed me into realizing how far down I'd come.

I could easily block out an hour a day to work out at *something*. And hopefully, the endorphin rush (or whatever the hell they call it these days) would push aside my recriminations and make me into a fully functioning human being again. If spring truly was a time for rebirth, maybe it was time to regenerate Riley King into the man he once was. Or a piece of him anyway.

The first step on my road to self-discipline would be to call my buddy Rick Stone and cancel our drinking plans for the evening. I rang his cell.

"Yo, Ricky man, got some bad news. Well, like not really bad, actually, you know, like it's good but, in a way, it's not...."

"Jeez, you sound like some high school girl from the valley. Out with it, man."

"Have to cancel tonight. Got an interesting case and I need to do some research. It's a real interesting case, Stone. I need to do some reading to get up to speed."

"Tell me about it, Riles."

I laid out the basics for him, sanitizing the storyline a bit. "So I want to check out some of that manuscript before I go charging into Sacred Cross tomorrow. You know Father Salieri pretty well, no?"

"A little. He's a good man. We did a fundraiser golf tournament for the school last year. Although with that basketball program they've got going, they could do one for us."

I said, "Yeah, they keep sending me newsletters, usually with personal notes from the padre himself. Wanted my take on some of his recruits. Told him I was flattered but too busy."

"You should, might do you some good. Although I don't know how some obscure Georgetown bench rider could teach these kids anything. They're already playing at a level you couldn't touch in your heyday, whenever that was."

Stone was always belittling my athletic career, and I usually give it right back to him.

All in all, life seemed good for Rick Stone. His midday sports show on a local powerhouse radio station was doing well. He had stayed in great shape and was now involved with a gorgeous blond "football sideline reporter" (is this a *real* job description?), who makes more in her four hours of work a week than Rick does in a month.

Whether it was his time in the Marines, (which he is loath to discuss), or just his native curiosity, he was a great sounding board when it comes to the criminal behavior I encounter.

"Seriously, Ricky, you think Salieri would tell me anything useful about something that could be damned embarrassing? I mean, a priest in a three way? Apparently the personnel chick at the academy wasn't too forthcoming with Paige White."

"That 'chick' you're referring to is a sixty year old nun. Although the way you've been moping around, she might be just your speed. Call Salieri in the morning and ask for a few minutes of his time."

"I need to bite the bullet and ask Father Salieri about a teacher-student-preacher affair. My client even fears he might have something to do with Geist disappearing."

"Good luck pal. Call me afterwards. Maybe we can have lunch after I get off the air."

I live in Bayville, just south of Toms River, most noted for having produced the Leiter brothers of big league pitching fame. My house is on a finger of Barnegat Bay that

13

was far enough inland to be spared the major wrath of superstorm Sandy, but like me, it needs work.

After I fed Bosco, my golden retriever, I waded into the mess I call a closet and extracted my nylon shorts and a faded Georgetown sweatshirt. I put on my New Balance cross trainers, let the dog out into the fenced back yard to do his business, and took off at a leisurely pace, not bothering to set my Seiko to zero, just casually noting my start time. I figured twenty minutes would be a good starting point, and I wouldn't even think of how much ground I covered. A couple of years ago, I could do three miles in that time.

I was wheezing before I got off my street. Although it didn't seem like I was moving that quickly, I slowed even more until I could get into a comfortable groove. Another runner passed me in the opposite direction and we gave each other respectful nods, although I detected a smirk as he eyed my pitiful pace and makeshift outfit. His ensemble was coordinated to the nines and he sported the pasty skin and anorexic frame of a serious devotee that I never have coveted. *Whatever.* I was determined to ignore my competitive juices for now and slowly work up to the point where I would time myself and try to better my splits.

I went as far as I could in ten minutes and then retraced my steps, although by the time I reached my door, twenty-three minutes had passed. That meant my weak pace going out had slowed by three minutes coming in. And to top it off, I felt horrible, like I wanted to vomit but couldn't. My knees ached. Sweat was pouring off me, dripping onto the kitchen floor as I let Bosco back in. He looked at me with disdain. He didn't say, but he seemed to know that he could have covered the same distance in a third of the time without even panting.

"Yeah, dude, dogs don't sweat, I know. I probably stink, too, to your super sensitive nose. Get used to it." I could barely get the words out through labored breathing.

He thought I was really mad and yelling at him and he started to slink away. Dogs don't get sarcasm. "Hey, wait, Bosco. Come here. *Cookie.*"

The magic word. His tail wagged and his ears perked up as he followed me to the dog-cookie jar. He inhaled the MilkBone I offered and sat obediently in anticipation of another. I petted the top of his head instead and he trotted away happily.

If only people were so easily pleased.

Four

I wasn't hungry after the run and I was looking forward to chillin' in my boxers with a bit of light reading. I could put the ball game on as background and make it an early night after taking care of one last piece of business. I'd call my old Georgetown teammate Tommy Smith. After a brief stint in the NBA, cut short by injury, he became an agent for some of his fellow hoopsters. His influence expanded into the hip-hop world, and within a few years, he'd become a *major playa*, now calling himself Yusef LaBomb.

"Tommy?" I said, after his assistant put me through.

"It's Yusef. You one of the few I allow to call me by my slave name. Riley, dog, what up?"

"Yeah, it's me Tommy so you can drop the drama. King's English spoken here."

"You wound me, dog. Cut me to the very quick."

Tommy Smith is based in L.A. and was still in the office at 3:30 --- his time. He is a street kid from Portsmouth, Virginia who'd played when I was a senior and he was a freshman. He'd come to see me as a big brother in the short time we knew each other, and sought my help when he was in early danger of flunking out of school. Against my better judgment, I'd bailed him out by ghost writing a paper and he never forgot the favor. He was a much better player than I was --- drafted by the Washington

Wizards in the second round after graduating with a 3.2 GPA. His street cred served him well when he started his agency. He was a master at tailoring his rap to the audience, simultaneously talking trash with a brother on one line while discussing high finance and opera with a corporate CEO on the other. I suppose he's viewed as a lower case Jay-Z, but I never shared that appraisal of him.

"Business cool?" I asked.

"Never better. Yo dog, never got to tell how sorry I was that we never clicked on that Ivan Alderson deal. Dude was just too wild. Got nothin' for you in New York now but you know you got a standing offer out here you ever decide to go West, old man."

"Thanks." Tommy had talked vaguely about starting an East Coast branch with me running the office but his clientele was still largely in California. With my qualms about the weather here and the shaky nature of my own business, it was reassuring to know that Tommy provided an attractive fallback if things deteriorated.

"Tommy, reason I called was I've been approached by a woman in your line of work named Paige White. Literary agent wants me to find a missing author. Know anything about her? She's based in Jersey. Fort Lee."

"Paige White. Wait a minute, she repping that race horse dude? Man who penned that tome on that century dead beast?"

"Penned that tome? What, are you writing headlines for *Variety* now? Yeah, that's her. What do you know?"

"Not much. Small agency. We could eat her for breakfast and still have room for a short stack. But she got juice. They be making a flick 'bout that pony. Dig it, try doing dialogue for that one. I hear Eastwood's got the hots for one of her guys. Already done one of his books, based on some ancient white private dick, now he's looking to do a series. Sound like *Matlock* shit to me. Who was that dude ol' Buddy Ebsen play on TV, Barney Fife? Barney Miller, Google, I can't recollect. Old fart couldn't get out of his own way, tripping over his Depends, but he be catching up with brothers running circles round him. And that fat-ass mustachio dude --- deep voice. Will Conway, Cannon, whatever. We need to bring back *Shaft*. Now there's a brother we can be proud of."

"Your expertise on television and film history astounds me, Tommy. But do you know anything about Paige White?"

"Met up with her once. Fine looking as I recall. Tell you what, you at home? Let me make a call, be right back at you."

Ten minutes later, he was back, good as his word. "Yo, dog, axed a friend of mine who did some business with her last year. Shopping a book on J.J. Stokes's life story. Never quite worked out but he spent some quality time with her."

"And?"

"Said she was a tough lady. Good thing J.J. wasn't with him at the time, cause she ripped him a new one. Said if he didn't get his ass in gear, he be looking for a new team,

18

not a publisher. No bullshitting this lady. Knows when someone be running a scam on her. All business, real professional. Drives a hard bargain."

"Anything about her personal life?"

"Dude says he came on to her, she having none of it. Thinks she's a dyke."

"You believe him?"

"My man think any woman a dyke who don't go down on him first ten minutes. Take it for what it's worth."

"She crooked in any way? Hooked up with bad people?"

"Can't say that. Seems straight, working with them high rollers in the movie business. Ain't got many authors, but ones she has are the shit. That means good, case your street sense be all suburban now."

"Okay Tommy, thanks. Let me know if you hear anything else."

"Dude."

Tommy knew the underbelly of his business and if there were any red flags, he'd stumble onto them sooner or later. His networking instincts were now activated, and he was a master at connecting the most seemingly unrelated dots into a pattern. He'd have made a great detective.

Paige White outwardly appeared to be what she said she was. With her penchant for turning books into movies, I didn't feel guilty in the least about taking her retainer check. If she had identified this manuscript, *Julie and James,* as a hot commodity, there could be major dollars in it.

19

I flicked on the game, poured a drink, kicked up the recliner, and began *Julie and James* on my tablet.

I skimmed through the text quickly. The quality of the writing seemed proficient to my uneducated tastes, but after a half hour I felt like I needed another shower. This was simply one of the vilest concepts I'd ever come across. If the story bore any relation to the real life of its author and his colleagues, I wasn't sure I wanted to find him. And if some harm had come to him as a result, it wasn't hard to side with the offended parties.

Five

I decided not to announce my visit to Sacred Cross Academy, just in case Paige's earlier inquiries had raised the principal's *def-com* rating regarding his ex-English teacher. A few cases I'd handled over the last couple of years involved parents who suspected their kids were up to serious no good. Most of the time, their concerns were unjustified, but I could sympathize with their worries. Sandy Hook could happen anywhere. Public schools now have security gates and metal detectors.

On a less tragic level, girls in public schools wear midriff-revealing tops and low-slung jeans that ride below their visible thong underwear. Any part of the body that can be pierced or tattooed is. Old fashioned as I am, I'd have a hard time sending my kid out in the morning looking like that.

My first impression of Sacred Cross was that parochial schools hadn't changed nearly as much as their public counterparts. The structure had been built as a town school in the fifties, and still retained the one level, blue panel and light brick look of that era. Approaching from the west, a vast expanse of lawn surrounded the recently paved asphalt parking lot, and wide concrete walkways branched out toward the main entrance. From the northern side, it took on a more dissonant appearance, like a rambling suburban ranch that had a three-story addition grafted artlessly onto one side. The addition took the form of an enormous field house capable of holding six thousand spectators. Despite the outward ungainliness of the arena, connected to the flat-roofed school building by a squat glass-enclosed tunnel, its interior was state of the art.

I'd been there a couple of times, approaching from the grand eastern entrance where a 10 acre parking lot dwarfed the school's main access. Indeed, if you came from that direction, you couldn't see the schoolhouse itself, which huddled behind like some bastard outbuilding.

The gym bore no resemblance to the wooden-bleachered, smelly environs where I'd learned the game. There were brightly colored cushioned seats and sprawling concession stands that not only served standard stadium fare but also sold school logo-ed shirts, hats, key chains, duffel bags, and any other item they could slap their distinctive blue and gold colors onto. The locker rooms compared favorably to those of the pro teams. There were plush carpeted weight rooms with hi-def televisions, stainless steel whirlpools for soaking away minor aches (and luring unsuspecting cheerleaders after hours, I imagined). The lockers were roomy cherry cubicles with Ethernet connections. I had often wondered where a small Catholic school got the money to pay for this opulence, but I knew that high school hoops had become big business. Clearly the modest tuition the parish charged couldn't support an edifice of this magnitude, but the state finals were held here every five years, regionals every two and there was talk of the national championship game in the near future.

I parked my black Audi A5 in the main lot on the opposite side of the campus from the gym. The traffic whine was a constant reminder of its proximity to the Garden State Parkway, but the trees planted by the state fifty years ago had matured enough to shield the highway from view. It was a few minutes after ten, and the place seemed placid, with the students already in class or on athletic fields that were blocked from my sight by the field house. There were no security checks as I strode through the main entrance, inhaling the familiar smell that haunts all Catholic schools. I had always thought it was incense or some other rare ecclesiastical herb; maybe the less metaphysical explanation is that their cleaning supplies are purchased in bulk from the some lapsed Catholic distributor, hoping to buy his way into paradise. The aroma brought me back to my own childhood, and unpleasant memories of my Catholic school upbringing.

The principal's office stood to the left. The outer chamber was encased by a glass partition, which afforded the proctor a full view of the incoming students. Through the window I saw a dated wooden counter fronting an old metal edged desk, where a modestly dressed woman sat busily typing away at something that seemed important to her. She was peering into a computer monitor, the only indicator that I hadn't passed through some wormhole that propelled me fifty years into the past. Back then the secretary would have been a Sister of Charity with a starched-white splayed bonnet, but the way nuns dress today, it's hard to tell them from lay workers.

As a nod to the respect I once carried for the institution, I wore a dark blazer over my black tee and jeans, opting for grownup shoes instead of the Nikes now resting in the trunk of the Audi. In the principal's antechamber, no door guarded the entry. Aside from the desk, the only furnishing was an old scotch plaid sofa, which I assumed had seated many reprobates like myself as they awaited scholarly justice. The terrazzo floors were waxed to a high gleam, and my silent entrance went unnoticed by the woman behind the desk until I meekly cleared my throat.

"Oh, you startled me. Can I help you Mr. ...?" she said.

She wore a red plastic nametag --- Patricia Murphy, Administrative Assistant --- the only color enlivening her drab gray outfit. Whether she'd officially received the orders of the sisterhood or not, her life probably mirrored that of the nuns of yesteryear. I saw no wedding ring on her stubby fingers, and no vanity in the unpolished square cut nails.

"King. Riley King. I'm here to see Father Salieri."

"I don't see you on his appointment calendar," she asked, consulting the ancient cathode-ray monitor. "May I ask what this is in reference to?"

"I think the good Father knows who I am. Just a casual visit, if he's busy I can come back later." The last thing I wanted was to appear threatening, and I didn't see the need to outright lie about why I was there. Not yet, at least.

"I'll see if he's available." She knocked softly on the only door in the room, an undistinguished heavy commercial slab with a plain pewter lever handle. I felt a stab of anxiety course through my torso that had nothing to do with Father Salieri or the questions I was about to ask. The whole scene was conjuring up disagreeable memories of the numerous times I had been called down to Sister Beatrice's office for some horrible crime against humanity I'd committed while in algebra class. It generally was a wiseass answer, or some silly sexual double entendre that struck my adolescent fancy.

I heard a muffled basso bidding the nun to enter, and a moment later Salieri emerged, all bonhomie and handshakes.

"Riley King. Good to see you again. When was the last time? Our fundraiser last winter? Come in, come in. Care for some coffee?"

"No, I'm fine. Nice to see you, Father."

I followed him into his inner sanctum, which was a bit more put together than the rest of the place. Walnut attorney bookcases surrounded the room's only window fronted by a massive antique desk. There were a couple of aged leather wing chairs, and the walls were lined with photos of Salieri and celebrities from the sports world, a couple with the Archbishop and a particularly prominent one with Bing Crosby, featuring the then-young priest with the Groaner at what appeared to be a golf outing.

"What brings you out on this fine morning?" Salieri was doing his best Barry Fitzgerald, but that's where the resemblance ended. Unlike the old time character actor, Salieri was a former chaplain who'd served in Vietnam. His military crew cut was now all gray, and his sun-weathered features reminded me of a thinner Nick Nolte. His voice was a low rumble, punctuated by a persistent cough but graced by a friendly lilt that I imagined could turn ominous if some student transgressed his regulations. Despite the megawatt smile, he didn't look altogether healthy. His skin bore an ashen tint, and he'd lost weight since the last time I'd seen him.

"I've just been hired to look into the disappearance of a former teacher here. I was hoping you could point me in the right direction. Fellow by the name of Paul Geist."

"Hmmn." Salieri looked down at his desk and rearranged the stapler and the pencil holder. "I don't know what I can tell you. He left us last June, almost a year ago. Haven't heard from him since."

"Did he leave on his own or was there some kind of problem?"

He responded quickly, too quickly, "Oh, no problem. None at all. He'd been here twenty some years and apparently decided that teaching no longer suited him. He and I talked about it several times but his mind was made up."

"So you tried to convince him to stay?"

"I tried to help him find what it was that he really wanted in life. Paul was in his late-forties, you know, the time when a man might go through a mid-life crisis. He had divorced a couple of years prior and I think he lost his way. In addition to the Church's objections toward dissolving Matrimony by civil authority, it often sets one or both partners adrift. They lose their compass, so to speak."

"Did he tell you what he wanted to do after he left?"

He bobbed his head back and forth in an equivocating manner. "He wanted to be a writer. That was in his heart. But he had doubts as to whether he could make a living doing that."

"So he didn't think he was good enough. Ever read any of his work?"

"Paul truly believed he was the next Saul Bellow, but he thought that the literary establishment was blind to the fact. He was convinced he was good, he just believed that without some kind of gimmick or entrée into the business, he doubted he could ever succeed."

I wasn't sure if he'd deliberately avoided my question. "What about you, Father? Did you think he had the talent to make it?"

"Frankly, he never shared his work with me."

"Any idea why?"

"Not really, although I did get the feeling that he wrote of worldly matters that he felt wouldn't be appropriate for a man of the cloth."

"You mean sex? I feel a little awkward, you being a priest and all, but let me tell you a few things about this book." I proceeded to give him the most sanitary version of the tale I could, but it was like finding the cleanest dumpster to sleep in. I surprised myself that I'd even been able to actually utter the "S" word in a principal's office, much less describe the more salacious aspects of Geist's work.

Salieri fidgeted "He never showed me any of his work, other than the occasional article for the school paper. I find it shocking that a teacher I've employed for over two decades could write anything that vile."

I didn't enjoy seeing this man squirm. He did seem legitimately taken aback when I described the contents of the book. But I had to consider the possibility that his discomfort wasn't caused by perverse nature of the material, but that he'd been discovered as one who had participated in it.

"What were your impressions of him as a man? I mean, was he materialistic, greedy? Did you sense any hint of sexual involvement with one of his students? "

"I would not have tolerated that. No. Nor did he seem preoccupied with money. A lay teacher in a Catholic school is not a high paying position. I took it that he used his time off in the summer to write. His wife worked --- at what, I don't know. When he decided to leave, he asked that his pension be paid in a lump sum, even though it would dramatically decrease the total amount he'd receive. The monthly payout at sixty five wouldn't have been a lot. Supplemented with Social Security a man of modest appetites could survive on it but little more. But by taking all the money this early, I'm afraid it wouldn't sustain even a monk for more than a year."

"Any idea why he wanted it all at once?"

He stroked his meticulously shaven chin with his thumb and forefinger. "No. If he was serious about writing, perhaps he wanted to travel and take a stab at it. You say he's missing? Isn't it possible that he just took off in search of his muse and that he'll turn up sometime?" He began to cough, and reached for the water glass that he kept beside his desk.

"I suppose." We sat silent for a moment as I assessed the possibility. Salieri broke the spell.

He said, "Mr. King, if you don't mind my asking, who hired you to find him?"

"I'm afraid that's confidential. Let's just say that this latest manuscript has attracted some attention in the publishing world and it could provide a considerable opportunity for him, if he can be located, that is."

He showed no reaction so I continued. "You know, Father, I don't even know what Paul Geist looks like. Makes it a little tough when you're trying to find someone. Do you happen to know where I could find a picture?"

He seemed to have drifted off into his own thoughts and it took him a second to snap back to the present. "No, I don't, but I don't know that it would help much. You see, Paul was quite the chameleon. He'd go away for the summer and very often we wouldn't recognize him when he came back. His hair could be long or clipped shorter than mine. He shaved his head on more than one occasion. His face was alternately clean-shaven, or had a moustache, a Van Dyke, or a full beard. His natural coloring was dark, but he came back as a blonde one semester."

"Interesting. What about things he couldn't easily change? Height and weight. Distinguishing features."

"He must've been around five eight. Not a tall man, but he went through a phase of wearing boots that I suspect had lifts in them to make him seem taller. And his weight varied. I wouldn't ever have called him fat, but he went up and down --- from maybe two hundred to as little as one forty. That was during his running phase. Ran a couple of New York marathons, oh, around five years ago. And he was average looking. Not what I'd call handsome but not unpleasant to look at. Brown eyes, nothing distinguishing, really."

"I suppose you *do* have his last address."

"Oh certainly. Patricia can give that to you on your way out."

He started coughing again, but less severely this time.

He said, "I'm afraid I have another matter to attend to now. I hope I was somewhat helpful." He shuffled some papers on the desk and glanced at his telephone. "You know, I really doubt he's actually missing. I'm sure that Paul is on one of his little sabbaticals and will turn up sometime. He talked about traveling to Italy someday. Maybe he's lost in some lovely little village in Tuscany, enjoying the grape and laughing at our cold weather. Ah, that we could all retreat thus. Now if you'll excuse me."

He rose and shook my hand, a bit gingerly. I gave him my card with the cell number on it and told him to call anytime if he remembered something that might help and he said he would. After initially seeming to be interested, he was now hustling me out of his office, throwing in a bit of old world whimsy to appear gracious. His assistant gave me Geist's last known addressand she almost pushed me out of her space after handing me the slip of paper.

30

On the way out, I noticed that the extension on Salieri's phone was lit and I hadn't heard the phone ring. I would have loved to know who he had called.

Six

A less cynical man would have written off Salieri's lie of omission, but I chose to view it as intentional. The school *had* to have numerous photos of Geist on file somewhere, but short of breaking and entering after hours, the easiest pathway was the library.

As I expected, there were yearbooks in the neatly arranged stacks. I asked the librarian but was told that no digital copies existed prior to last year. In the early nineties, Paul Geist began to show up. I found many photos of the former English teacher who also headed the theatre club. They had a scanner that allowed me to copy some of them onto a flash drive.

I called Stone and arranged to pick him up at the station after he got off the air. We headed for the nearest diner and found a quiet booth in the back.

Rick said, "Did you see Salieri this morning?"

"I did. Got next to nothing. I got some yearbook photos --- Paul Geist, in his many incarnations. He taught at Sacred Cross for over twenty years. Salieri says he was a chameleon."

"I suppose. But you'd be surprised how we all change in twenty years. Lisa and I were going through some old photos the other night."

Stone was in his late forties, but looked ten years younger and could still model for GQ. The only insecurity I could detect about his appearance is that he's very self-conscious of his once thick blond hair, which was beginning its inevitable recession. He was trying every regimen and solution on the market to halt its progress.

I changed the subject. "Digging out old pictures, huh? Getting serious, I'd say."

He unconsciously ran his fingers over his hair, pushing it down toward his eyes.

He said, "Don't know, really. She can be hard to read. I mean, she loves sports as much as I do and she's very athletic. But sometimes, I feel like the guy in Steely Dan's *Hey Nineteen* with her. It's not like she's stupid or anything; her grades put mine to shame. She's just from a different generation."

"Don't knock it. She's gorgeous, and after Erin Andrews, she's every adolescent's wet dream. Think of all the fun you'll have teaching her."

"There's that. But come on, tell me about this case. What did Salieri say?"

I ran through my meeting with the priest for him. "I'm thinking he knows a lot more than he's telling. I bet he saw that manuscript. Maybe he even knows what happened to Geist."

"Riley, Riley. You never got over what the nuns did to you in high school, did you? Try this on for size. You told me last night the book dealt with a teacher and a priest and their obsession with a young girl. At least it's a girl. You're

33

aware of the scandals the Church has been dealing with over the last few years. If Salieri knew what was in the book, wouldn't he naturally want not to talk about it? Think of the harm it could do to Sacred Cross if it ever got published."

"Exactly. So he arranges for Geist to disappear so that it doesn't see the light of day."

Stone leaned back in the booth and shook his head. "Man, you really think a priest would kill somebody to keep a novel from being published? And since the agent *already* had the manuscript, what good would that do?"

"Maybe Salieri didn't know that. Look, the guy served in 'Nam. I bet he knew all sorts of natural born killers during his tour. Probably heard confessions from a lot of them. How hard would it be for him to contact one of those guys and arrange a hit?"

"*I* know a lot of tough guys. I've never been tempted to call one of them up and ask them to pull a wet job for me. Salieri was a founding member this school. Look at the basketball program he's built. Kids from all over the state are coming there. They've got a six thousand seat arena. They give poor kids scholarships, run food banks, clothing drives. The man has been a godsend to this town. And you're thinking he's a killer just because he doesn't volunteer information about an ex-employee? I think *his* theory holds more water. This weirdo Geist was having a mid-life crisis and went off somewhere to write the great American novel."

"Maybe he already has, according to Paige White. I haven't read the whole thing, but I don't get the appeal. It's thinly veiled porn."

"So?"

"So --- the school in the book is called Holy Cross and the principal *is* a priest named Salvano. Got your attention?"

Seven

After lunch, which turned out to be a veggie burger for me, (Weight Watcher Special, 340 calories, just 5 grams of fat, but all the taste of the real thing --$7.99), I went back to the office to check messages and make a few calls. The first was to an old FBI buddy of mine who'd risen to be agent in charge in St. Louis.

Daniel Logan is a beefy guy from Williamsburg, Virginia who'd come up through the ranks at the same time I had. His unruly shock of red hair had long since given way to a close-cropped layer of fuzz around the fringes, but his florid face was as smooth as melamine. We saw each other annually when he'd fly into New York to indulge his one odd habit --- the dude loved musical comedy and reserved a week of his yearly vacation to catch the latest shows.

He answered his own phone. "Riles, you old coot, how are you? Don't tell me, you got orchestra seats for *Les Miz* and you need a date."

"Not on a bet. I thought the movie was unwatchable. The last great musical was *Man of La Mancha*."

"There's no hope for you. I'll be in town in August. I'm going to check out all the latest shows. *Kinky Boots* sounds fabulous."

I didn't know too many straight guys who used the word *fabulous* very often but Dan was one of them. I said,

"Need a favor, bubba. I just scored a missing persons case and I need to see if the guy just left the country or if some harm has come to him. Think you can help?"

"Ever since the Patriot Act we have a pretty tight lid on foreign travel. Computers are a whole lot better than they were before 9/11."

"That's comforting, NSA boy. I guess. Guy's name was Paul Geist, out of Toms River, New Jersey, although I suppose he may have an alias."

"Is the guy a big time felon? You know, it's not as easy to create a new identity as it once was. Guys who're connected or have big bucks can still manage it, but it's not like you can grab some dead baby's birth certificate from public records anymore and build a new persona."

"Wow. You guys must've finally seen *Day of The Jackal*. Hey, for the bureau, that's real progress."

"Things have changed since you were here, Riles. I'll admit, they're not perfect, but it's getting there."

"And you guys wouldn't let a little thing like civil rights get in the way of law enforcement, would you?"

"Do you want my help or not? You East Coast liberals have a short memory. I don't think anyone wants to see planes crashing into buildings again, or am I just being a hard-ass here?"

"Point taken. First time anyone's called me an east coast liberal, though. Anyway, you think you can run this guy Geist for me? Might get you house seats for *Book of Mormon* next time you're in town, if it's still running."

"Sold. Give me a day. Call you tomorrow."

"Saturday?"

"Criminals don't take weekends off. Why should we? But seriously, give me a day, maybe two at most."

"Danny, you're talking to me. But I am impressed by your dedication. If this is being monitored somewhere, I can't think of a more dedicated public servant than Dan Logan."

"Screw you. I'll call you." I'd halfway been hoping Dan could give me an instant answer and tell me that Geist was safely ensconced in some fishing village in Scotland but it was not to be.

Geist's ex was next on my list. Finding her wasn't hard --- she was listed under her married name in the phone book --- but I was doubtful as to what I might get from her. Either she'd clam up entirely, not wanting to recall a painful period in her life or prattle on endlessly about what a schmuck her former husband was, citing every last time he hadn't lowered the toilet seat or farted in bed.

Paula Geist lived in a neat little condo complex just off the river. It was advertised as 'river vu", and indeed in the dead of winter with every last tree exfoliated, you could climb on the roof of the most elevated building and catch a glimpse of some ice. The development was modeled after a Nantucket fishing village with flickering electric street lamps that looked like gaslights from a distance. The interior streets were stamped concrete, vaguely resembling cobblestones and the vinyl shakes cladding each unit approximated old cedar until you got close enough. The windows had plastic grills but the exterior doors were actually made of wood, the one authentic nod to the Cape.

I took the Audi around back, and knocked on the door bearing a large brass "4", the address listed for the ex Mrs. Geist

A slender woman answered, dressed in a blue hospital smock. She had deep-set brown eyes, a full mouth and was almost pretty. The one feature that tipped the balance the other way was a bumpy nose, disproportionately large given her other features.

"Can I help you?"

"Yes, Ms. Geist? I'm Riley King. I'm a private investigator. I'd like to ask you a few questions."

"Regarding?" She seemed guarded but not altogether unwilling.

"Your former husband. You *are* Paula Geist, right?"

"Is he in some sort of trouble?"

"That's what I've been hired to find out. Do you have a few minutes?"

"Do you have some sort of identification."

I flashed my license but she grabbed my hand before I could put my wallet away and checked the ID carefully. "All right. Come in, Mr. King."

The interior was immaculate. There was a small tiled entryway, leading directly into a tidy living room with a gas fireplace crowned by a white wooden mantel. I could see a dining area through an arched opening. The furniture wasn't expensive but was upholstered in heavy fabric with tasteful floral patterns in deep red and muted cerulean. A few magazines lay carefully stacked on the pine coffee table, across from a pickled armoire that I assumed hid the television.

"Very nice place, Ms. Geist."

"Paula. I'd offer you something but I just got home from work. I'm headed out fairly soon so if you could just get down to business. I'd appreciate it."

Everything about this woman screamed "organization"--- from the crisply ironed nurse's outfit to the seamless manner in which the decor was pulled together. Given what I suspected of Paul Geist's rather Bohemian outlook, I suppose he might have seen her as a necessary counterpoint to curb his native excesses.

"Do you know where Paul is, I mean, where he's living now?"

"He's not on Oak Street anymore?"

"Apparently not."

"Then no, I have no idea."

I could see that she wasn't going to elaborate. Bitter divorce?

"When was the last time you spoke to him or saw him?"

"Since a few days before our divorce was finalized. He called, we spoke for a minute or so and that was it. That was about two years ago,"

"You say *before* the divorce was finalized?"

"Mr. King, as a private investigator, you must know the way New Jersey divorce procedures work. We went the no-fault route. There was little in the way of marital assets.

So you live apart a year, hire some low rent attorney to file the paperwork and you don't even need to show up in court."

"And no contact with him since?"

"Where are we going with this exactly? Why do you want to know where Paul is?"

There was no finessing this woman. But since she'd told me that the divorce was final and that money wasn't a factor, I could be honest.

"Okay, I won't beat around the bush. I'm sure you know that Paul was submitting manuscripts to a publishing agent over the years. Well, one of them shows some promise and we're trying to locate him. He left Sacred Cross last year and no one at the school knows where he is, at least the people I've talked to so far. I figured you might have some idea."

"No, I don't. Now if that's all…"

I made no move as she rose, showing little concern that her husband might be missing or worse. This was a woman determined to move on and not look back.

"Paula, please. I don't know anything about your marriage, and frankly, it's none of my business. But the man's just disappeared without a trace and a major player in the publishing world thinks he's got a best seller on his hands. Can you at least point me toward his friends, somebody who might still be in contact with him?"

"Paul thought he was some sort of tortured artist who wasn't appreciated and maybe wouldn't be in his lifetime. He always used to say that if John Grisham turned in the same work he had, it'd be hailed as genius but that those New York snobs in the book business wouldn't recognize talent if it bit them in the ass. We were doing okay, you know, until Paul got this idea that he could be some kind of suffering writer. He changed. He closed me off. He closed everybody off. You asked before about friends. He didn't have any. The few people we did socialize with --- he turned off like a spigot. He kept refusing invitations, saying that he needed to write. Then in the summer he insisted on taking these extended trips without me, up to Vermont or someplace up north. He said he needed the time in solitude to write, or commune with other creative types. Claimed he didn't want to take a cell phone because he needed absolute silence with no distractions. The man built a wall around himself."

Just talking about her husband's writing brought emotion bubbling to the surface. The muse clearly was his phantom mistress. What was also clear is that the guy *often* disappeared from view, reinforcing the theory that he'd merely taken off on a writer's retreat and would re-emerge in his own time.

I said, "You wouldn't happen to know exactly where he was in Vermont?"

"No. He never really even talked about it with me. If I asked, he'd dismiss it. Wouldn't even talk about the town or the weather. Cripes, for all I know he could have been camping out in the Pine Barrens."

"You say no friends, but did he have any relationships at school --- any mentors or confidants?"

"The only one he ever mentioned was the principal, Salieri. But Paul even turned on him in the end. Said that hypocrite priest talked a good game, but when it came to love versus gold, Salieri always went for the money."

This Paul Geist was turning out to be quite a cipher. After a couple of follow-ups that led nowhere, I gave his ex my card and extricated myself as gracefully as possible. For now, she had created more questions than answers. I took the back way out toward Route 37 and headed inland.

Traffic was light in my direction at three on a Friday, but the causeway toward the barrier island was already becoming congested, and as summer neared, it would only get worse.

I had a weird sensation as I took the cloverleaf toward my office. I felt like I wasn't alone, like there was someone tailing me. There was some kind of SUV a few lengths behind me, with a green license plate my old eyes couldn't make out in any detail. I turned south on Hooper; and the SUV took the cloverleaf with me, discretely staying a few cars back.

Church Police? I almost laughed aloud at my paranoia, but at the first opportunity, executed a right on yellow and left the car in my dust.

Eight

It was close to five by the time I got home. I debated calling Paige with a progress report while the interviews were still top of mind, but decided to let it simmer as I took my evening run, which would commence immediately after feeding and jousting with Bosco. Some science indicates that dogs have no emotional capacity, but whether it's simply the joy of knowing the food provider has returned or some pure version of unconditional love, I can't imagine any human companion expressing the exuberant displays of affection Bosco always shows whenever I walk through the door.

I went out for a run, hoping I'd do better than I had yesterday. Triggered by my visit to Sacred Cross this morning, I couldn't stop thinking about my Catholic upbringing. When I was in school, corporal punishment was still in vogue. I can still feel the sting of the metal edged rulers that cut my knuckles whenever I transgressed their rigid doctrines. To the young Riley King, nuns all seemed mean and bitter witches.

The trauma that forever tipped the balance for me was inflicted in the tenth grade. I was locked in a dark closet for an entire school day because I had the temerity to misbehave by armpit-farting during the morning's class prayer. As I stood in the blackness, the air grew foul with my own sweat in the ninety-five degree heat of that late summer's day. Despite my desperate pleadings to be released to use the bathroom, swearing I'd never diss the Lord again, my entreaties fell on deaf ears. Unable to contain myself, I urinated down my leg and wallowed in the damp stench for several hours. When the principal opened the door at the end of the day, I bolted from the room and didn't stop running until I reached home. Luckily, my mom was out with friends, so I hastily stripped off my soiled pants and underwear and washed them in the bathroom sink. I feigned illness and skipped school the following day, dreading the call from the nuns that never came. When I returned to class the following Monday, they acted as if nothing had happened. Maybe deep down they knew that they'd crossed the line.

I felt a pang of remorse for not thinking at all about the Geist case as I jogged. I'd call Paige after my shower and at least feed her my first impressions and then delve into a little more detail on her relationship with the missing author. Maybe watch some baseball and turn in early.

Ah, the exciting life of a hunky detective in a seaside paradise on a Friday night.

Nine

After my shower, I stood in the kitchen with a
towel wrapped around my now trimmer
waist. I know it's all water weight but the
scale indicated I had dropped four pounds in the last couple
of days --- a good start. I shooed Bosco away from sticking
his nose under the towel where it didn't belong. I don't
know why dogs do that --- maybe it's their strange attempt
at showing intimacy. Licking water off the leg is one thing
but when he puts that cold snout near my privates, I call him
names that would make a longshoreman blush. He just takes
it in stride and walks away, sighing deeply as if I just don't
understand his needs.

I dialed Paige's cell number and she answered on the
second ring.

"It's Riley King."

"Riley. Nice to hear your voice again."

"Figured I'd call and let you know what I've found
out today."

"Oh, okay. I've been on the beach here. This place is
gorgeous. Not too many people. I guess you don't get many
days in the eighties this early. They still have all the stop
lights flashing yellow."

"Yeah, things don't usually start hopping on Long
Beach Island until Memorial Day. After that it'll take you an
hour to get off the island on a Sunday night."

She exhaled deeply. She sounded dreamy, seductive. Or was it my imagination?

"How far are you from here, Mr. King?"

"About twenty miles driving. I can see the lighthouse on the northern tip of the island from my window. If you're in Loveladies, it's probably only ten miles as the crow flies."

She let the silence linger and I was about to get to business when she spoke. She was so relaxed and mellow, unlike the driven-efficient businesswoman she presented yesterday. "I have an idea. Why don't you drive down and we can talk in person. We can grab a bite and talk a little. I can order in. I've got a nice Beaujolais and the view from this place is stunning. If you don't already have plans, that is."

I could easily tell Paige everything about the day in the next two minutes over the phone, but the idea of a nice ride to LBI to a secluded beach house to drink wine with an attractive woman was tempting. Or was I misinterpreting the signals?

"I don't really have that much to tell you actually. Hate to tie you up for an evening for the little I have to offer."

"Not at all, Riley. You're an interesting man, and I could use the company instead of rattling around this big house all alone. Consider it a service call."

Was I reading too much into her choice of words? So far, Paige just wanted to locate a missing person. I was a little lonely tonight and maybe I needed to test myself to see if I was really ready to dip my toe in the dark waters of relations with the opposite sex.

"All right. I'll need to get dressed first. I'm just out of the shower."

"Don't get dressed on my account." She *was* flirting, had to be. "I mean, let's keep this casual. I'm only wearing shorts. I don't want to dress up." She gave me her address and began to describe how to get there but I stopped her. I'm familiar enough with LBI. Hell, the whole island is only eighteen miles long and less than a mile wide for most of that.

As I drove down Route Nine through Lacey Township and Forked River, I tried to suppress the idea that this evening was anything more than a client update, but part of my anatomy was stirring to tell me otherwise. Paige was smart, accomplished, and unattached as far as I could tell. Maybe my recollections of earlier conquests during the jog had awakened something.

Staring me in the face was that crowding fifty, my options involving women were becoming limited. I'd like to think of myself as the same stud muffin I was at twenty five, but when department store counter-babes that I used to hit on now reference me in terms of *what their dad would like*, the real world intrudes.

When I look in the mirror, the reflection appears only slightly more mature than the one that once scored 21 and grabbed six boards against St. John's a few decades ago.

I flipped on the Audi's Harmon Kardon system, one of the main things that attracted me to the car. My dial was preset to a local classic rocker that billed itself as "The Hawk". I didn't even know what the real call letters were. They were playing Springsteen's *Bobby Jean* and I instinctively cranked up the volume. For the hundredth time, I tried to ferret out clues as to why Bobby Jean was really guitarist Steven Van Zandt, who had left the E Street Band at around the time the song was written. This listen I decided it was really about an old girlfriend, and scuttlebutt around the Jersey shore was that Bruce had left plenty of those in his wake.

I wasn't so into the music that I failed to notice the green SUV following me at a safe distance. At first, I pulled some mild evasive tactics, but the truck still hung around. I marked it as a late model Ford Explorer, very much like the one I thought was tailing me earlier. Forest Green was a popular color and there must be hundreds of identical vehicles on the road in Ocean County. The shadows were growing too long to make out the plates.

I drove normally the rest of the way so as not to let the other driver know I was onto him. But why would anyone follow me? The Sacred Cross visit? If Salieri did have a guilty secret regarding Geist, might he have co-conspirators willing to take the next step to cover up their misdeeds? Or did the ex-Mrs. Geist have a bigger stake in this than she presented?

My Beretta was in the glove box. As I glided over the causeway on Route 72 to the island, I reached in and placed it on the seat beside me. My fears were probably groundless, but there was no harm in being prepared, especially since I was too early into this to know whom I was dealing with.

On the northern end of Loveladies, a mile before it gives way to the middle-class full time residents of Barnegat Light, I approached the address Paige had given me. I turned into the narrow unpaved cove without signaling and the green SUV went roaring by. I got out, grabbed the gun and waited behind a copse of pines for the Explorer to return. After several minutes, there was no sign of it. Just to be sure I walked north through the trees along the edge of the boulevard. Nothing looked out of place. Maybe the lack of action lately had given me to paranoia.

Ten

Long Beach Island is pretty calm this early in the season and actually it's my favorite time to be there. South of the causeway which enters the island at Ship Bottom, older houses are clustered together on small sandy lots that command exorbitant rental fees given their original five figure purchase prices. These tiny houses are packed throughout the summer, often with several groups at once in an attempt to keep the cost affordable. Most of these low-end renters only use the houses to sleep anyway, preferring to spend most of their waking hours at the beaches and arcades. They attract a lot of students and young families, seeking sun and hedonism at a modest price.

But turning left on Long Beach Boulevard, the business districts in Surf City soon give way to the upscale nabes of North Beach and Harvey Cedars, followed by the island's crown jewel, Loveladies. The homes west of the Boulevard face Barnegat Bay; the east side the Atlantic, though most of the borough is narrow enough to provide access to both. Here the plots are more spacious and the architecture has been described as "contemporary on steroids", odd pastiches that attempt to meld several styles and periods with mixed success.

Wealthy residents, mostly summer dwellers, have erected these huge paeans to flaunt their prosperity. A

51

quarter acre lot on the ocean could cost upwards of a million dollars, and high end digs often encompass as many as four of these parcels. There are virtually no lawns: most of the ground is garnished with orange river rock. Many of the buildings are clad in traditional gray cedar shakes, although some have opted for neon colors in some feckless homage to Victoriana. But their asymmetric shapes either succeed as dramatic pieces of modern art or fail as gaudy displays of how money accompanied by too little taste can despoil the natural beauty of even this chosen place. These blights upon the seascape are becoming more prevalent as local zoning ordinances fail to compete with wealth and the political clout it buys.

That being said, I was mightily impressed by the sprawling tinted glass and steel structure that author John Peterson called home, or at least one of his homes. It arose three stories over the dunes, providing panoramic views of the bay and ocean from every window. Girded by sundecks springing from every orifice, the entire structure opened graciously to its environs. Tall pines provided privacy on the landward side of this acre on the ocean, and the home's height shielded its occupants from the beach crowd. Arriving just in time to catch the beginnings of a magnificent sunset from the western entry, I again marveled at the splendor of this grand island. I tapped on the frosted glass door, and Paige appeared instantly.

"Eight million dollars."

"What?"

"Come on Riley, you were wondering what it cost. Everybody does when they first see it. John Peterson bought it for seven and put a million dollars worth of renovations into it. Probably could fetch ten on the open market today."

"And this is his second home?"

"Fourth actually. He lives in the Holmby Hills area in L.A. most of the time. You could put two of these into that house. And he's got a place in Vail, right on the mountain. Plus another beach house somewhere in the Caribbean, I forget the name of the island. Now I hear he's looking for a little chateau in the South of France."

From what I could see as she ushered me in, the interior was every bit as impressive as the outside. A travertine entry gave way to more limestone surfaces in what I'd call a living room but undoubtedly had been dubbed *the gathering room* or *the grand room* by some pretentious architect. The ceilings varied from coffered twelve-foot heights in the more formal areas to soaring redwood slopes stretching towards the purple and orange tinted sky. An expanse of Palladian windows and arched French doors led out to a huge flagstone patio. The endless ocean view was uninterrupted by balusters and railings; in their place were large transparent plates of Lexan suspended between unobtrusive copper posts. A glimpse into the open kitchen featured the requisite stainless steel Sub-Zero, Miele and Viking restaurant quality appliances, although I doubted a man like Peterson ever fired up anything but the microwave.

"And how many bestsellers has he had, Paige?"

"John's had twenty or so on his own, but lately he hasn't been writing solo very much."

"Oh?"

"Yeah, he travels a lot these days and writes with collaborators. He'll come up with a plot and some characters, give some young writer a detailed outline and the other guy does all the research and heavy lifting. Then John looks it over, makes a few suggestions, rewrites to reflect his own style, and voila, instant best seller."

"Doesn't that offend you at all? I mean, the guy's name is on a book he didn't write?"

She laughed softly at my naiveté. "Let me get you a glass of wine. I ordered in Chinese. A lot of different things because I didn't know what you liked." She had at least six different dishes spread across the granite island that stood like a battleship in the center of the kitchen. Although I was glad that I was here, food wasn't why I'd come. I didn't want to wake up tomorrow and find those four pounds had returned along with a couple of their brothers, so I begged off.

Paige busied herself preparing a plate and didn't argue when I demurred. "I'm sorry, Riley. I didn't mean to sound like I was ducking your question before. It was just something I made peace with a long time ago. The other author's name *is* on the dust jacket, albeit in smaller print."

"But isn't it deceiving the public? They think they're getting a John Peterson novel and they're really getting the work of Joe Blow?"

"It's not like they're buying a forged piece of art. Lots of big authors use collaborators; historians and political pundits have teams of researchers that do most of the writing. People don't care, as long as the work is entertaining."

"But how can a patched together book like that be equal the work of the original author?"

"Believe me, if John was turning out trash I'd be the first one to scream at him. Our relationship has had its ups and downs, but he respects my evaluation of his work. If his sales start dipping or the studios aren't optioning his newer stuff, it would be addressed. Sure you don't want anything? It's really good."

She scooped some boiled vegetable and tofu glop onto a thin pancake and dipped it in soy sauce. There was an easy sensuality in her movements, nothing studied or contrived, just a naturally graceful way of performing the most mundane tasks.

"Thanks, but I'm okay. You enjoy it, don't let me stop you. But seriously, I just wonder how Peterson feels with all this money, knowing that he's not really doing the work."

"He *is* doing the work, Riley. His stuff has always been character driven. I'll admit it can be a bit formulaic at times, but he has developed a curmudgeonly old detective that people are comfortable with, like an old shoe. He's a good observer of current trends and he puts Spicer in the middle of something loosely based on today's headlines and things take off from there."

"But what about you? Aren't you just putting out pap for money? Is that why you got into the business?"

I was offended by all this wealth bestowed on someone who didn't seem to work hard, leaving the real labor to an underpaid vassal. Of course, if I was hoping to get laid, insulting Paige's main meal ticket probably wasn't the wisest course.

"I've always loved great literature. But I learned early on that selling books isn't about literature. It's like anything else. You represent the John Petersons so that every few years, you can help get a *Julie and James* published. Let me be honest with you. I exaggerated when I told you that Paul Geist's book *will* be a best seller. It probably won't be. First time novelists are lucky if they crack a few thousand in sales. But the work is important and there's a chance it'll be recognized and be the start of a fruitful career. And that'll be very satisfying to me."

"But what about Peterson? Doesn't he want more than just money? Isn't respect part of it?"

"Johnny knows what he is. Maybe in a few years, he'll want to write *literature*, but for now, he's content to be what he is --- a successful commercial writer. Come on, let's go out on the bayside deck and catch what's left of the sunset."

I poured myself a glass of wine and followed her out through the tall glass doors. Comfortable wrought iron chaises awaited us there, and glass topped tables with legs mimicking the patina of aged copper. The sun was fading, throwing dull streaks of painted pastel toward the Atlantic to

56

the east, which was gently returning lazy amethyst waves to the shoreline. I could get used to this.

"Riley, look at what *you* do. How many of your cases have any real importance and how many are just about petty squabbles between spouses? But those trivial disputes pay the rent and allow you to put time in on the things that really matter to you. And if I hadn't been willing to pay you out of my own pocket, would you be looking for Paul Geist gratis? That's my contribution to literature."

I was willing to let the whole thing drop and watch the sunset but I'd evidently struck a chord with her. I shrugged. "I'm not so sure that what I read last night was great literature. I skimmed the first few chapters and it struck me as pretty perverted, to tell the truth."

I hadn't gotten very far in the text but it certainly added fuel to Father Salieri's motive to make Paul Geist and his manuscript go away, especially if Geist was writing from life. I told Paige about my interview with the priest.

We let the night air bask over us as we talked and I found myself warming to her again. She was wearing white shorts, her long tanned legs curled under her on the chaise. Up top, a white bikini bra covered by a mesh wrap revealed the outline of small but nicely formed breasts. Her face wasn't as severe as it seemed in my office yesterday; it had softened around the edges without her city makeup. Even her hair relaxed, hanging loose and finger-combed down her elegant neck. I forced myself to concentrate on business.

"Paige, yesterday, you gave the impression that you didn't really know him well."

"I never met him in person or even saw a picture. I have no idea what he looks like. I spoke to him on the phone a few times, never about anything other than his writing."

"Maybe he was banging a student, like in the book. How sick is that?"

Again, Paige gave me a patronizing look. "That's like the third time you've criticized the content of the manuscript. Loosen up, man. Kids today aren't carrying the old morality into this century."

"You can't tell me you approve of the guy's behavior in the book."

"Riley, Riley. They were experimenting with sexual taboos, searching for their own sense of morality, not buying the rules some eighty-year-old virgin in Rome tells them. That's what's so refreshing about this book. It's about two generations seeking truth in their own way. And it doesn't cop out with some Hollywood moralistic ending."

I had doubts about my role in presenting this stuff to the public. But as Paige's iconoclastic mind laid it out, it was provocative, and I suppose that's one of the hallmarks of worthy literature.

"Yeah, but there's stuff you just don't do. Rules you have to follow or things turn chaotic. You have to admit, there's stuff in this book that's just wrong." Not the most intelligent of answers but the best I could come up with.

"Why are they wrong? Because they've been drilled into your head from an early age. I imagine growing up that your parents told you to stay away from loose women. Women like me."

I was sorely out of practice in this game but now, the signs were unmistakable. To have sex with a client would be breaking a rule I'd established long ago, not necessarily out of any sense of morality but because of the complications it might lead to. I hadn't even violated it with Liz, although we came close. And I still can't escape the belief that had I not developed feelings for her, she might be alive today.

But whether it was the wine, the setting, or Paige's undeniable charms, I felt myself slipping.

"Move over, big guy," she ordered gently. She draped her legs over mine and ran her knee up my thigh, her hands caressing my chest. "Some rules are made to be broken."

Eleven

"Stone." My voice was barely above a whisper and I hoped that it could be heard over the muffled roar of the ocean as I stood on the Loveladies' balcony. "Did I wake you?"

"Not really. Actually, I guess you did. What time is it?"

"Just before midnight. Sorry. Is Lisa there?"

"No. She flew out to the coast with her producer. Something about an expanded role at the network. She's pretty excited."

"So you're a bachelor for the weekend. Maybe we can take in a game."

"Hey. I'm a bachelor all the time, Riles. No strings, not yet anyway. So let me get this straight. You're calling me at midnight to ask me if I want to go to a baseball game?"

"No. Just to ask a favor."

"Shoot."

"Can you get by my place early to let Bosco out and feed him?"

"Actually, I need to be in Atlantic City early for a charity tournament. Your place is out of the way but I guess if there's no alternative...."

He waited for me to suggest one.

"Where are you anyway?"

60

"Long Beach Island. Long Story. It's okay though. If it's inconvenient, I guess I can get home and take care of things myself."

"Is there a woman involved or are you on a case?"

"Both."

"I see. Hey, I don't mind taking care of the dog if it'll queer you with this chick, whoever she is." Again he waited for me to volunteer some info, but I wasn't biting.

"Naw. It's all right. I can manage. Thanks, anyway."

"Oh, Riles by the way. I almost forgot. You still on Father Salieri as your main suspect?"

"More than ever."

He said, "Well, you might want to hold off on that until we talk."

"What do you mean?"

"Not on the phone. Just talk to me before you start uprooting things with the good padre. You might want to reconsider."

"I wasn't planning to do much today anyway. When are you back from AC?" I said.

"This evening. Wanna grab a bite?"

"Okay. Call me when you get back. Sure you can't tell me anything now?"

"No, it's complicated. And it may be nothing. Just be careful."

"Okay, see you tonight."

I couldn't imagine what Stone had uncovered but his tone sounded ominous. Wearing only my boxers and tee, I shivered as the wind swirled toward me off the Atlantic.

Paige was finally asleep in the bedroom, and I had snuck out to sit on one of the house's many decks to think about what had just happened.

I hadn't slept with a woman in a while and I was having mixed feelings. Part of me felt guilty --- a residue from my father and the Church, no doubt, and something that I'd probably never be able to shake entirely.

And then there was Paige. In addition to her being a client, I knew that she wasn't thinking long term. Most flames that burn so scorching hot at first don't have much staying power. I liked her and certainly found her attractive; especially after she'd doffed the skimpy outfit she'd been wearing, revealing a taut body tanned to bronzed perfection. And she was an enthusiastic performer in bed, perhaps too much so. Paige made me feel like some kind of toy-boy instead of a semi-reluctant lover.

Tired as my body was, my mind just wouldn't shut down. Whatever Paige had taken must have been good stuff, because she didn't stir a bit as I eased the French door open. The steady procession of waves caressing the beach wasn't creating the palliative effect I desired, so I gathered my clothes and decided that a night in my own bed would be best.

I wrote Paige a brief apologetic note, explaining about the dog and how I hadn't planned on this happening and that I'd be back in the morning to take her to breakfast. I taped it to the mirror over the "hers" vanity, a twelve-foot marble-topped structure that could house the contents of a small apothecary's cosmetics department. Her closet door was open behind me and a glance in the mirror as I was affixing the note afforded me a peek in.

Everything was white. White bra, panties, okay. But every outfit --- shorts, tops, linen pants suit, skimpy sundress --- was white. It then dawned on me; this was Paige *White*, a woman on the fringes of show biz where you need a gimmick to make an impression. There are hundreds of good-looking, smart women in the arts, so how does one manage to stand out?

Be the woman who always wears white. That West Coast feminist lawyer, Gloria Allred, always wore red. Paige was merely following her lead, successfully it seemed.

Maybe I should start wearing only Hilfiger stuff with that little crown emblazoned on the breast. You know, Riley *King*. I chuckled at the conceit as I left the mansion.

Twelve

Bosco was acting strangely when I got back and refused to go out on his own, so I hooked up the leash and trotted him around the neighborhood. He seemed skittish, looking back at me every so often on the walk as if he didn't trust that I was still there. He refused a bacon flavored doggie treat, sniffing haughtily and backing away. He'd never done that before. Had he picked up Paige's scent on me and sensed my betrayal?

Regardless of Bosco's ill temper, it felt good to be in my own bed, modest as it was compared to the California King that the sensuous Ms. White now occupied alone. I fell asleep quickly and spent the next few hours in dreamless slumber until the cell phone rang at eight a.m.

"Where are you, Riley?"

"Paige. Hey look, sorry I had to go but you were sleeping like a baby and I didn't want to wake you. You saw my note, I guess."

"Shut up and get your ass down here. I'm not very happy right now."

"Paige, I couldn't leave the dog alone and I tried…"

"Never mind the whining. Just get over here."

"All right. Loveladies is about a half hour,"

"No, not here." There was a rustling noise on the other end, like she was pulling on a shirt. "There's a place on the Boulevard in Harvey Cedars or Surf City. Callahan's. You know it?"

"Sure."

"Meet me there. A half hour." She hung up.

I deserved what was coming. This was clearly payback for breaking my long held rule about sleeping with clients. I compounded that with another lesson that I'd failed to heed in my desire for a warm and willing body.

I don't know what kind of retribution Paige had in mind. I didn't imagine her making much of a scene since she insisted on meeting me in a public place. She might just fire my ass and demand her retainer back. Since I hadn't deposited it yet, I tucked the check into my wallet --- praying its return wouldn't be necessary.

Bosco seemed bewildered by my torment. "See the trouble you got me in," I said to him, awaiting an answer. "I come home to take care of you and now I might lose a client. You could've held it in, right, boy? You wouldn't have peed all over daddy's carpet, would you?"

As my words echoed through the empty house, I realized what a self-deceiving idiot I was being. They say animals have no sense of time, and I bet Bosco snoozes most of the time when I'm away. If I'd returned just after sunrise, let him out and fed him, he wouldn't have known the difference. In truth, I had fled from Loveladies in a half-assed attempt to make up for my own bad judgment.

So I resolved to take my medicine like a man. Paige had every right to pull a Jimmy Cagney and shove a grapefruit into my kisser, or any other form of abuse she chose to visit on me. In the Audi, I rehearsed my apology and hoped that my overactive glands would not cost the agency too much. Making payroll would be tighter without her retainer.

Paige was in a rear booth, New York Times in hand, working on a bagel and black coffee when I arrived. In the harsh morning light without her city makeup, her years showed but she looked fine nonetheless. I was now thinking mid-fifties. She was clad all in white, (what else) --- this time a man-tailored shirt and baggy tennis shorts.

"Hey." I flashed a reluctant smile, hoping that a penitent look would spare me some grief.

Angry eyes looked right through me. "Hey, yourself. Sure your dog's gonna be all right for a few minutes? I'm surprised you didn't bring him, or is he out in the car?"

A waitress approached but when she overheard the belligerent tone of Paige's words, she discretely veered off and refilled another customer's cup several booths away.

"Look, I've already apologized about that. It's just that I didn't expect things to happen the way they did last night and I didn't make arrangements. He's not a young dog and I didn't think it was right to leave him alone all that time."

"Forget about it, King."

So I was *King* now.

"I didn't bring you down here to rag on you although you *do* deserve it. Nobody pulls *a wham bam, thank you ma'am* with me, sweetie. But let's forget it for now and move on to why I called you. My offices in Fort Lee were broken into last night and I need to go back there this morning. I want you to come. If your dog will let you, that is."

I love it when women say 'forget it' and then spend the next few hours reminding you of it. She now realized that I was the ace detective my ads in the yellow pages proclaimed. Despite my bruised masculinity, she hadn't booted me off the case and that superseded my other concerns for now. But the way she switched effortlessly from aggrieved party to asking a favor reinforced my initial impression of her as a hardnosed pragmatist with no feelings for me, other than how I could be of service.

"What happened? Anything valuable stolen?"

"Apparently not. Jaime came in to do some paperwork this morning and noticed the door was unlocked. Said she couldn't find anything missing, it's not like we keep money or anything of value there."

She acted as though I knew who this Jaime was. I didn't, but that wasn't important now. "Could just be druggies on a Friday night. Amateur hour. When they found there was no cash, they bolted. Did your guy call the cops?"

"Girl. Jaime is a girl. Not yet. Called me first. I wanted your input before I did that. Should we call them now?"

"You're going to need their report for insurance purposes if nothing else. Small town force isn't likely to spend a lot of time on this. Just in case something *is* missing we should bring them in. But let me look things over first, then we'll call."

"I guess. Jaime said whoever it was just rummaged through our storage closet."

"Looking for a safe probably. What do you keep in there?"

"Extra copies of books by our authors. And manuscripts. A signed first draft from John Peterson might have some value I suppose, but other than that, there wasn't much in there you couldn't find at Barnes and Noble at off price."

"I'll get the check. Let's ride."

Thirteen

We didn't talk much on the ninety-minute drive north. Paige kept her BMW's cruise control at 75 most of the way. I love my old Audi, but this newer whip has it beat in spades.

The first third of our journey was over the Garden State Parkway, scenic at this time of year, edged with stately pines and expansive fields of gold. We reached the Driscoll Bridge over the Raritan River in less than an hour and then branched off onto the New Jersey Turnpike, which was every bit as ugly as the Parkway was picturesque. The turnpike was the lasting impression of the state that most casual visitors carried. *"You're from Jersey, what exit?"* LOL! I've long since given up extolling the virtues of my adopted state to mean spirited out of towners.

The borough of Fort Lee overlooks the Hudson, but has lost any charm it may have held ages ago. It's main claim to fame now is the historic traffic jam that got Governor Christie in trouble. Tall overpriced co-ops mostly hide the river from view, and squat glass encased office complexes line the cross streets haphazardly. The downtown area, quaint at one time, is now comprised of grimy three-story brick storefronts hawking cheap services. Many of the signs in the window were Chinese and Korean, an acknowledgement to the influx of Asians over the last quarter century. There were a few strip malls with the requisite *Staples*, *Dunkin Donuts* and *McDonalds*. Paige nimbly wound her way through the congestion to a bland office building near the bridge plaza. Probably built within the last ten years, it bore no signs and could have housed anything from a brothel to police headquarters.

Paige read my thoughts. "The place used to have a Citizen's Bank on the main floor. They were bought out by Fleet then Wells Fargo and now there's an ambulance chaser law office in its place."

"Any security?"

"Not much. We all have key cards to get into the building after hours, but the main lobby doesn't have a guard or even a sign-in sheet. Door's propped open half the time anyway. There's only eight tenants. Not much walk-in traffic."

She parked the Beemer in a private outdoor lot enclosed by a tall chain link fence, a stark line of demarcation separating it from the adjacent public lot maintained by the Port Authority. A small elevator took us to her offices on the third floor. From the hallway's windows you could see the GW Bridge's grand superstructure. Festooned with lights, it must be an impressive sight from here at night.

Jaime Johansen was sipping a latte from a Starbucks cup as we arrived, looking shaken and apprehensive. Paige immediately hugged the younger woman and gently smoothed her short reddish hair. "It must have been scary for you this morning, hon. They might have still been there, baby."

Jaime was tall, slender and cute. At first glance, she looked to be in her early thirties, but little crinkles around her expressive green eyes made me suspect she was a bit older. The butch hairstyle gave her a harder look than I favored, until it dawned on me that maybe Jaime wasn't all that keen on attracting men. There was something in the way that she and Paige looked at each other that made me think these two were closer than just boss-employee. Given Paige's libidinous outlook on life, I could only imagine the possibilities.

"Jaime, this is Riley King. Riley, Jaime Johansen."

We nodded at each other. Jaime seemed to be sizing me up as one of Paige's boyfriends (competition?) since Ms. White had not mentioned that she'd engaged me to find Paul Geist.

"What time did you get here, Jaime?" I asked. "I'm a private detective and Ms. White asked me to help her look into this for her."

I figured that would alleviate any tension or suspicion arising from my relationship with Paige, but Johansen did not appear satisfied.

"Around seven thirty," was her toneless reply.

"Is that unusual? I mean, coming in on a Saturday?"

Her voice was thin and nervous. "I was planning to head out to the Hamptons with some girlfriends this weekend. But I forgot a manuscript that I wanted to read while I was out there so I stopped by here to pick it up."

"Did this ruin your weekend, honey?" Paige said. "I'm sorry; did the other girls leave without you?" Again she

71

caressed the younger woman's hand showing no condescension, just genuine tenderness. Paige might be a tough cookie, but she treated her employees like family. Or was this one a special case?

"I'm driving out on my own. I was hoping to get an earlier start, that's all."

"Well, unless you need to ask her anything Riley, can't Jaime be off now? And take Monday too, dear. You'll need a couple of days to unwind after this I'm sure."

"Thanks. I'll call you tomorrow night."

"Riley? Anything you need to know from Jaime?"

"Only if she touched or moved anything. Or is everything as you found it?"

"I watch NCIS, DiNozzo. I know enough not to disturb anything at a crime scene. I didn't even use the phone when I called. I used my cell."

DiNozzo? Was she equating me with the feckless womanizer played by Michael Weatherly on television? She was being overly bitchy towards me, which only served to reinforce my suspicions about their relationship. *None of your business, Riley.*

"I'm sure Paige has your cell number if we need to ask you anything. Have a good weekend."

They embraced, kissed and made their goodbyes. Paige saw her acolyte to the corridor and then turned to me. "Great kid. English major at Sarah Lawrence. Good commercial sense. She's got the right stuff to run her own business someday."

As far as I could see, an army dispatched by Martha Stewart couldn't find anything out of place. As realtors say in their ads for maintenance-free homes, "Mrs. Clean lives here." The warm décor of these rooms was in stark contrast with the austere modernity of the building's exterior. The outer office was paneled in light cherry beneath a colonial chair rail, topped by grasspaper. There were four desks neatly arranged in the antechamber, which led to a perpendicular hall culminating in a more private section that housed Paige's office. Everything seemed organized for maximum efficiency, not a stray item marred the orderliness of the scene. Each desk was polished to a high gleam, every seating surface comfortably inviting and well kept. While the work area itself was not large, there was a generous conference room off to one side, enclosed in glass and offering a peek at the Palisades. There was a spotless kitchen closeted off the meeting room, outfitted with a Bunn coffeemaker near a small stainless bar sink.

"Everything looks pristine here and no signs that anyone forced their way in. Inside job?"

"I can't imagine that. The storage room is where the damage was done, according to Jaime. That's down the hall, the door opposite my office." We walked slowly down the corridor, past the modern prints on the wall --- decent stuff, but selected more to blend in with the décor than to call any great attention to itself. The door to the storage room was open wide, and the place was as tidy as my living room after a Bosco play date with a puppy friend.

Paper was torn and shredded all over the floor. Bookcases had been overturned. Broken china coffee mugs littered the tile. Paige turned pale under the weak florescent illumination as she took in the devastation. The disorder seemed to upset her more than any potential financial loss.

"Wow, they did a number," I said. "Did you have any sort of catalogue of what was in here?"

"No. We plan to computerize everything, but we haven't gotten around to it yet. We kept things in alphabetical order. Manuscripts on the left, hard cover volumes of our already published stuff on the right."

The right side seemed barely touched, but the chaos created on the left was enough for the entire room. "Paige, anything about those manuscripts valuable?"

"Nothing really. Unpublished stuff mostly. Every so often we clear out the junk and we were about due for that now."

"Let's not paw through this stuff until the cops arrive. In fact, now would be a good time to call them."

She made the call and we inspected the rest of the mess as we waited for them to arrive. "I can't tell if anything's missing," she said.

"That's what's strange about this. Some of these covers look like they've been slashed by a knife. This looks more like vandalism than theft. If someone just wanted to take a specific item, they could have done it without tearing all these other things to shreds. It's almost as if they didn't find what they wanted and tore things apart in anger."

Paige looked shaken but struggled to maintain her composure. "Why would somebody do this?"

"I don't know --- some former client? An author who was pissed at you? Some aspiring writer you dissed?"

"I don't know Riley, that seems like a stretch. When I encourage an aspiring writer, maybe I'll have lunch with them, give them some pointers. But usually no more than that."

"But you never met Paul Geist? Even over lunch?"

"I only talked to Paul on the phone like I told you last night. Mostly we were in contact through email. Honestly Riley, he was a little too pushy for me. I thought his writing showed potential, but he was already talking film rights and paperback releases when I just wanted to encourage him to keep working at it. I deliberately avoided face-to-face meetings with him. I kind of wanted to temper his enthusiasm but not discourage him, if you know what I mean. It wasn't until this last work that I wanted to meet with him."

"Would his manuscript be in here?"

"Normally, it would be here. I got it from this room as I was getting ready for spring cleaning. Like I said. You think *Julie and James* was what somebody was after?"

"I have no idea. But whoever was here made a beeline for your storage room. They didn't try to steal anything of value. So I'd guess someone was looking for a specific manuscript. Geist's is the only one I know about. Was there another that someone would want?"

"Not that I can think of, but why would anyone even want that one?" Paige extended her palms outward in disbelief.

"Someone didn't want it to see the light of day."

She blurted out what we were both thinking. "You think Paul is dead, don't you?"

"No, but unfortunately John and George are."

I said, "Seriously, Paige, I don't know anything. But I'm thinking you may have had it right all along--- that there are people who *don't* want to see this published. Maybe they got to Geist, made him disappear and now want to clean up any trace of his book."

The second I said it I regretted it. It wasn't right to scare Paige. But I had done just that.

She stiffened. "Made him disappear? You mean kill him, don't you?"

"Look, let's say whoever saw this book and didn't want it published, simply paid him off and then destroyed every known copy. Yours would be the only manuscript unaccounted for. It's possible that they weren't even aware that it existed until I started asking questions."

"Why would anyone break into my office and risk getting caught when it would have been much simpler just to get Paul to request it back if they had only just paid him off? Unless Paul isn't alive to do that."

"Don't go there. Paul probably didn't let on that you had a copy to begin with. Maybe he'd forgotten that he'd sent it out. It was almost a year ago, no?"

"Paul was constantly pushing me to read it and critique it, and left some angry sounding messages when I stopped taking his calls. So I can't imagine he forgot that he sent it. But who else actually knew what was in the book? You say that the wife didn't seem to know and the priest claimed ignorance too."

By two p.m., we were finished with the local police and on the road. The first part of the drive was quiet again, giving me space to examine my emotions, as I stole glances at her handsome profile every so often from the passenger's seat.

After a few minutes, she broke the silence. "Riley, look. I hate to admit it, but this whole thing has me a bit rattled. Can you check out the house in Loveladies, just to be sure it's safe?"

"Sure. I can do that."

"I'd really appreciate it. It's funny, all the genre fiction I read has me feeling like there's some vast conspiracy underlying this whole deal. But I can't imagine anyone other than Jaime knows I'm in Loveladies for the weekend."

I did have a kernel of concern that the Loveladies house *was* a potential target. If the break-in upstate was in any way related to Paul Geist's steamy little manuscript, whoever was after it might not stop at Northern Jersey to find it.

RICHARD NEER

Fourteen

It was just past eight and the sun was down. The blue-haired-early-bird-specials crowd had left hours ago, and the few locals affluent enough to spring forty five bucks for a perfectly aged steak now populated the place. Many had come by boat, mooring their craft at a long dock that extended a couple hundred feet into the bay. Stone and I sat facing the water, but neither of us was moved to appreciate the view.

We were talking about Paige and I was explaining why I was having dinner with him instead of staying in Loveladies with her. "She's a client and on top of that, she's too loose for my taste. She likes to do it whenever with whoever's available. I don't want to get involved with someone who I can't trust once they're out of my sight."

"You could have at least hung out and made sure she'd be all right."

"I went back to the house with her and secured the place. I activated the alarm system. I checked all the entry points. Then we talked about it and decided that our fears were groundless. Aside from this personal assistant Jaime, nobody else knew that Paige was staying down here. But then, she disappears to use the loo and a minute later comes out stark naked."

"You could have at least told her to get dressed and stayed around if you still had doubts that she really is in danger. You didn't have to give it up, you wus."

I rolled my eyes and he went on.

He said, "Okay, you want to turn into a mule, fine with me."

I was eager to move on. "Why are you so insistent that I stay with her? Something you're not telling me? Like the little hint you dropped last night? You said you had some cautions about Salieri."

"So you're still on the case? She didn't fire you?"

"Not yet."

"Well, she might be doing you a favor if she does."

"Why? What has little Ricky been up to?"

"Okay, I admit it. I did a little digging for you. I made a couple of calls. Like I said, Lisa took off for the coast with her producer. I had some time on my hands so I called a couple of people I know on the board at Sacred Cross."

"Hey man, I always value the input, you know that. I just wish you wouldn't do anything without checking with me first. I think you know why, right? But now that it's done, what did you find?"

"You're not gonna like what you hear. As I told you the other day, Salieri's a straight shooter. Not like he's some *Excitable Boy*. Vietnam vet. Impeccable credentials. No allegations about young boys, *or* girls for that matter. Buys the Vatican line --- celibacy and the like. Good fundraiser, good administrator."

79

"But?"

"But I couldn't leave it at that. Just knowing what I do about high school sports, you don't build a basketball program like Sacred Cross without getting your hands dirty. You don't recruit kids from all over the state without some inducements."

"Duhhh, Ricky, when I was at Georgetown, we knew there were kids at other schools who got paid under the table. Recruiting runs all the way down to grammar school, with shoe companies doing a lot of the legwork. I'm not really concerned about Salieri giving some eighteen year old a car. This isn't the NCAA."

Stone took a sip of wine. "Salieri's a smart guy. I mean, he's got to know that God isn't just sending him these elite athletes from heaven."

"That's what boosters are for. But we're talking about something a lot more serious than recruiting kids to play basketball. And although I haven't thought about it that much, I don't imagine he needs to offer many incentives to kids to go there. The school's got a great rep with kids advancing to top colleges on scholarship. ACC and Big East recruiters are always looking there."

"I suppose. But what if something threatened the program? A scandal like Penn State? Six thousand empty seats all season, if there even was a season."

"So you're thinking Salieri wanted Paul Geist to go bye-bye because the book could be embarrassing to the school and hurt the basketball team? When you start cutting corners out of self interest and you're a priest and an educator charged with following the rules, where does it stop?"

Stone continued to play devil's advocate. "That's a pretty big leap. Salieri does draw pretty tight lines on a lot of things. He never lets academically ineligible kids play. He's suspended some of his best players when their grades are down. He insists they study and take full advantage of the curriculum. That makes the case for him being pretty conscientious, not some wanton law breaker."

The lights dimmed slowly as the restaurant shifted from early evening mode to prime time. My eyes don't adjust to the darkness as quickly as they used to, and I knew I might have trouble making out the fine print on the menu. No problem. I always order prime rib, medium rare with garlic smashed potatoes every time I'm here anyway.

"You're a piece of work, Rick. You throw down all this shit about Salieri and then get all indignant when I take it to its logical conclusion. Why did you tell me all this stuff about him if you're so convinced he's innocent? Come on, what do you really think?"

He shrugged, caught in the act. On the radio it was to his advantage to straddle the issues. That way, he could twist his words around to appear right no matter what the outcome. But this wasn't a game.

"I believe he is an innocent man." He sang the last words like Billy Joel. "I'm just afraid that some of his friends may not be."

"Friends? Are you going to tell me or do I have to guess."

He took a sip of his wine and looked me straight in the eye.

"Does the name Anthony Gazza ring a bell?"

"The man formerly known as Tony the Ram?"

"Actually, that was his father. This is the son----proprietor of Ocean County's largest environmental cleanup firm. And reputedly head of one of the biggest organized crime families in the state."

Fifteen

Nine o'clock. On a Saturday night. Billy Joel nowhere to be found. I'd devoured my roast beef, passing on dessert (my new resolve to get beautiful again won out). Stone was tired from his day in the sun and wanted to turn in so we called it an early night and made plans to talk in the morning. Maybe I'd make up for missing my evening jog when I got home.

So why was the nose of the A5 pointed south and headed for Long Beach Island?

I'd stopped by the house briefly to take care of the dog, but Stone's words were haunting me. A Mafioso like Tony Gazza --- it would be just his style to dispatch soldiers to Northern Jersey to break into an agent's office and make it look like random vandalism. Someone had acted quickly upon learning that *Julie and James* was a hot manuscript and given his ties to Salieri, Gazza might have as much motive as anyone.

Stone had filled me in on how Gazza had been the driving force behind the Sacred Cross arena, a fact acknowledged by a tiny brass plaque inconspicuously placed near a side entrance. The man had cajoled his fellow contractors to donate labor and materials, enough to cut building costs to less than half of what they'd be if the school was paying retail. Gazza was a Sacred Cross booster; he'd sent his now older daughter there and his boy was a key member of one of their state championship teams a few years back.

I hadn't worked organized crime with the Bureau, but I'd talked to enough colleagues over beers to know that the new breed of felon wasn't nearly as formidable as the old *Moustache Petes*. These fellows were businessmen first, thugs second. They tried to do things above board whenever possible for practical reasons --- to limit exposure to the legal system which could retard the growth of their interests. Only when reason and hard persuasion failed did they resort to threats. Of course, if their subject still balked, the use of force was the final option. They see violence much the same as CEOs of multi-national corporations view bribes to foreign officials--- part of the necessary but regrettable cost of doing business.

Fear is the most important factor they dispatch, so something along the lines of an afternoon's kidnapping of a beloved child usually brings even the staunchest adversary around. Brutalities in the form of beatings are less common but prove useful on occasion. Out and out murder is mostly a tool used *within* the family itself; to weed out potential traitors or territorial encroachers. Strict codes are applied and approval from higher authorities must be obtained before such sanctions can be declared. There are probably more homicides in one season of *The Sopranos* than in a decade in today's mob.

This doesn't make them solid citizens. In my eyes, they are vermin who cross all of civilization's lines when they don't get their way. For all their pious talk about family and protecting their loved ones, to me, it amounts to expedient bullshit that is used to justify the destruction they wreak. They are killers at heart. They can do all the charitable work they want, it takes a warped sense of ethics to forgive their trespasses.

Regardless, if Gazza had declared war on this manuscript, his minions would likely take intermediate steps before hurting Paige. But despite all my rationalizations as to why she was under no immediate threat, I tried calling her cell twice to tell her I was coming down. I'd gotten her voicemail. She was probably in a bar somewhere in Holden Beach hitting on a twenty year old, but I needed to be *sure* she was safe. I had mentioned to Salieri that an agent had hired me. Could he or Gazza have figured out that the agent was Paige? Thus, my late night ride to Loveladies.

With the Berretta on the front seat, I felt I could deal with whatever minor force Gazza might initially send. I weighed calling a couple of my guys for backup but decided against it until I was sure where this was headed. I knew that they'd be there at a moment's notice if we were truly in danger.

All the lights inside and outside the house were blazing as I pulled into Peterson's driveway in Loveladies. I was glad Paige had followed my advice and kept them burning even after bedtime, although if she was in bed this early it was doubtful she lacked company. I rang the doorbell and then knocked several times but no one answered. Trying the latch, I found it was unlocked and the big door swung open easily.

85

"Paige. Paige. It's Riley."

I flashed on asking if she was decent but what was the point?

"Paige? Hello."

Silence. I pulled the gun and defaulted to my FBI training, hugging the walls and creeping through doors sideways, slamming them into their opposite walls in case anyone lurked behind them. With the lights full on, there were no shadows in the main living area where anyone could hide.

A surge tingled through my stomach. My years away from daily peril had made me soft. I told myself that Paige had probably gone out cattin' around and messed up setting the security system. She'd gone out the back and not secured the front door. Maybe she'd come home with someone and in a sexual frenzy neglected to lock up. I could only hope.

I eased my way up the stairs toward the master sleeping quarters.

The door was open and a lamp on one of the nightstands dimly illuminated the king sized bed. Someone was lying on the side farthest from the light, seemingly asleep. The place reeked of pot. Paige had probably gotten high and nodded off.

I reached for the covers and felt something damp as I jostled the inert body.

It was Paige. The front of her white tee shirt was soaked with blood. In horror, I picked up the bedside phone, dialed 911 and then everything went dark.

Sixteen

"Mr. King? Can you hear me?"

The face staring down at mine was craggily handsome in its angular planes. Close cropped tight curled hair, hard brown eyes. High cheekbones hinting Native American somewhere in his genes. The voice was deep and unaccented.

"Mr. King, I'm Flint McCullough, Ocean County detective first grade. Are you able to speak?"

McCullough was dressed in a gray windbreaker, white shirt, jeans. I'd make him at about my size, but at least ten years younger and in the kind of shape I was in ten years ago, in a word --- cut.

As my eyes gradually returned to focus, I began to realize where I was. I was lying on a gurney in some boxy EMS vehicle, the rear door open revealing a panoply of colored lights outside. Crime scene.

I struggled to sit up. "Riley King." It took a moment to sink in. "But you already know that."

"Your wallet. Ran your ID through the computer. You've led an interesting life. This makes two women who you were involved with dead in just over a year. Quite a coincidence, even in your line of work."

Images were flashing back at me now. Paige in the bloody sheets. Someone behind me. Pain throbbing through the back of my skull.

"What time is it? How did you guys get here?"

"It's 2 a.m. Sunday morning. Someone dialed 911."

"That was me." Again I was slow to pick up the obvious. All 911 calls are immediately traced and since this one came from a pricey neighborhood, they assumed it wasn't a prank and sent a car out. McCullough must have been called in after the grisly discovery.

"Do you remember what happened? I wouldn't try to move too quickly. The EMS guy said you may have suffered a concussion."

"I'm okay. But the woman in the house is dead?"

"I'm afraid so."

The cold confirmation was something I'd experienced from McCullough's position many times in the past "I take it you know about my law enforcement background in DC?"

He nodded.

I had to assume that McCullough considered me a suspect, so I needed to be careful about leading him further in that direction. And although I knew I was innocent, that didn't mean that I couldn't have my PI license pulled and while they sorted this out if I became an obstruction. And I needed my freedom to find Paige's killer.

"What was the nature of your relationship with the victim? You don't mind if I record this, do you? Just want to get the details right."

"Sure." I needed to give myself an out, just in case. "Just understand, things may take some time to come back to me."

He clicked on a palm-sized device. "Go ahead."

"Paige was a client. She'd hired me to find a missing person. I first met her Thursday in my office."

"Was that the last time you saw her? Before tonight? And why were you here tonight?"

"Actually, I saw her again Friday night. I had done some work earlier in the day and she suggested we meet and go over what I found."

"What was the nature of that work?"

The interrogation and the blow on the head had distorted my priorities. Paige had been murdered. A woman that I'd spent the day with, had slept with the night before, was dead. The horror was sinking in.

He said, "All right. So you met with her Friday night. Where did you meet?"

"Here actually. Paige was staying in the house and it was more convenient for me to come to her."

"Do you know who owns the house? Is it a rental? We have the owner listed as a Peter Johansen."

John Peterson's real name, no doubt. At least he didn't change it to Poindexter, my jumbled brain free associated. "It belongs to one of Paige's authors. She was a literary agent, a pretty successful one. This guy owns a bunch of houses and Paige told me that she occasionally uses them when he's away."

"She have a relationship with this guy other than professional?"

"Not that she told me, but I'd only known her for two days. There was a lot I didn't know about her."

So far, my discussion about Paige White had been clinical. I tried not to let the shock of her death overwhelm me into admitting more than I needed to. I wanted to get rid of this guy. "Look, detective, I want to help. Paige called me this morning. Her offices in Fort Lee had been vandalized, so I agreed to ride up there with her and check it out."

"Did she file a police report?"

"On the office? Yes. Paige was a bit rattled and decided to stay back here instead of up north. She thought she'd be safer."

"I'm a little puzzled. If the victim was afraid, and you're a private dick, why didn't you offer her some protection?"

"I didn't think that she was in any physical danger and she assured me she'd be okay. I mean, the house has a state of the art security system. I figured I'd just come back and check up just to be sure."

"So you were just coming back to check on her when you discovered the body. The crime scene guys found traces of a substance they believe to be semen present. Know anything about that?"

If I denied sleeping with her, it wouldn't take long for a competent DNA lab to expose the lie. Once I'd completely lost his trust, McCullough might then manufacture a scenario that I'd killed her after raping her.

My decision to talk to him in the first place was stupid --- I realized that now. I should have claimed temporary amnesia, talked to a lawyer and then agreed to make a statement when the fog lifted. But it was too late to turn back now so I tried to talk cop-to-cop with him, not having much confidence it would work.

"Detective, I'm a man: she was an attractive woman. We slept together Friday night. It wasn't planned --- it just sort of happened."

I should just shut up instead of digging a deeper hole for myself.

McCullough nodded, feigning sympathy. I'd used that trick before, too. "I'll be straight with you, King. There were multiple stab wounds in areas of the body that would indicate someone punishing her sexually, a crime of passion. You were right about the security system so we're pretty sure that there was no break-in. Whoever was there, she let him in willingly. Where is this guy Johansen? You know?"

He paused, having thrown a bit of misdirection my way; no doubt trying to get me to lower my guard. He was good at what he did, but I could see through his moves and we were inevitably headed toward stalemate. I had no choice but to play it out.

"She said he was on the West Coast at one of his other houses."

"And were you aware of anyone else she knew on the island? Male or female?"

"I don't know if she had friends here or not."

"So all we *do* know definitely is that you two had been intimate and that you were in the bedroom with the body when we got there."

"And I called 911 before I took a nasty shot to the head. I know where you're going, McCullough. You tell me, are these the actions of a guilty man?"

"Normally, I'd say no but A) We have no proof that *you* called 911, only your word. Even though the calls are recorded, no voice was heard. The call was traced, we sent a car to check. B) Perps have been known to fake injuries to themselves to appear innocent. C) In many cases, perps also are the ones who discover the body. With your background as a fed, you know how that works, including how to manipulate a crime scene."

He'd put together a nice circumstantial case. People have been convicted on less. Hell, I'd convicted them on less. There were little things like motive and the murder weapon unaccounted for and the fact Stone would provide a solid alibi. But as I said, people have been sent away on less.

"So are you charging me? Am I under arrest?"

"I'd like you to come to the station house with me. There're lots of other questions."

Seventeen

"Let's see how I can put this delicately." Stone said. "Okay. I got it." He paused for effect. "King, you look like shit."

Stone and I were at the Starlight, early afternoon, post-Sunday brunch crowd.

"Got home at five a.m. Couldn't sleep so I took a run. Finally got down around nine. Woke up at noon and called you and here we are."

"So you refused to go in for more questioning and they just let you walk? They must not think their case against you is very strong."

"I wouldn't say that necessarily. Wouldn't be surprised if they weren't going for a search warrant on my place even as we speak."

"Looking for…"

"Anything they can find. Blood, prints. Maybe they think I'd be stupid enough to rinse off the murder weapon and stick it back in my cutlery drawer, I don't know."

"So what you gave me to put in my trunk out in the parking lot wasn't evidence? They won't come after me as accessory after the fact?"

Good old Rick. When I handed him the envelope and asked him to hold it for me, he just did it. That was a tangible sign of his unconditional faith in me. But he did have a right to know what he was getting into.

"The manuscript. On an SD card."

"You mean the dirty book that Geist wrote? Why, you think the cops are interested in your kinky reading habits?" He was half joking again, but there was an undercurrent of curiosity.

As bad as I must have looked, that's how good Stone appeared. His face was remarkably unlined and he was clean-shaven and smelled good. Not quite movie star handsome, but close enough not to want for company. Rick was wearing an old gray Syracuse athletic department sweatshirt over faded jeans, a Mets cap perched jauntily over his dirty blond hair.

I said, "Bottom line is that I still think that book is the key to all of this. I need to protect it."

"What do you think is going on here?"

The waitress brought our food. I was envious of Stone's pancakes but I'd settled for a toasted bran muffin, no butter. I could consume an entire buffet table out of nervous energy not hunger, so it was best not to have temptation in front of me.

He didn't even look up from his pancakes. "These are terrific. Sure you don't want any?" he said, his mouth stuffed.

I resisted, though strongly tempted. "Okay, this is how I see it. Like we talked about last night, this book is dynamite to Sacred Cross. If it sees the light of day and the right people seize on it, it becomes scandal material. So Salieri tells his benefactor in the mob of the threat and he sends his boys to make Geist disappear quietly. Guy lived alone, few friends, no woman in his life. Who'd miss him? Plus, he was eccentric anyway. Vanished up to Vermont for months on end."

He shrugged, old news. He took a sip of coffee and I continued.

"So they think the problem is erased until my big mouth enters the picture. I tell Salieri that the manuscript might be published. He tells Gazza and voila! Paige's business is ransacked looking for it. Can't find it. So they go after her directly."

He finally looked up from his food. "Damn, if you can't trust a priest, who can you trust?"

"I guess you didn't read *The DaVinci Code*."

"Fiction and I *did* read it, by the way. And before you start in, yeah, I know that the Church has an unsavory past. But to think they'd sanction killing someone in this day and age is ridiculous."

"Look how they tried to cover up the pedophile priest deal."

"Did they kill anybody over that? And that was over real events, not some book of fiction by an obscure high school teacher. Under your scenario, the Pope should've put a hit out on Dan Brown."

I said, "Come on, this is a local priest protecting his ass. Think about it. If I told you a priest in some bayou parish in Louisiana abused an altar boy, buried the kid in a swamp and got away with it, would you be shocked? Boy gets eaten by an alligator and those redneck cops would just write it off as a missing person, especially if the kid was of color. You telling me you're sure that never could have happened?"

"Listen to yourself, King. You make up a *Theme from an Imaginary Western* and ask me if it's possible. Well damn man, anything's possible. But what's coming through to me is that you hate the church for what they did to you as a kid. And you feel guilty for Paige's death and need to blame somebody other than yourself. I'm telling you, there's nothing you could have done to save her. This isn't on you."

"Bullshit."

He said, "Hear me out. Let's say for a minute I buy your mob related scenario. If a pro crew aced Paige, I doubt that one guy, even a stud like you could have stopped them. Chances are you'd be pushing up daisies too. If they were determined to kill her, the minute you're gone, they do the deed."

"I've already told myself everything you just said. But before any of this happened, you were all over me for not staying with her and making sure she was safe. At the restaurant, remember. And the first thing McCullough says is that two women who were my clients are dead, barely a year apart. I know I didn't kill them, but my actions or maybe inactions were responsible."

"We've talked about Liz a lot over the last months. You just can't get no *Satisfaction*. I thought you'd come to realize that what happened was beyond your control."

The song quotations were starting to get on my nerves. "And you're right, I was almost there. But now, here we are again. I broke my rule. I slept with a client. Maybe if

I hadn't done it in the first place, I wouldn't have run away when she came on to me last night. I was so determined not to let it happen again that I left her unprotected. It clouded my judgment."

"Maybe I'm to blame then. Maybe my poking around set this all in motion."

"So you agree? This has to do with Sacred Cross and that god damned book."

"King, you're formulating theories and then bending the facts to fit them. I'm almost sorry I told you that Salieri knows Tony Gazza. That's an awfully thin thread to base all this speculation on. You're so caught up in your disdain for the Church that you're looking for demons where they don't exist. *Here we go again.*"

"I was raised Catholic as a kid, okay. But when you get older, they tell you that half the stuff they teach you is mythical, because your little mind was incapable of grasping any more. But the brainwashing has already taken. If you read history, you see how corrupt and venal the Church was hundreds of years ago. They admit they've murdered in the past, crusaded to wipe out infidels --- all in God's name. But now, well *now*, things are different. So they admit lying to you in the past, but ask for your trust now. But they still lie, don't they? Talk to all those parents whose kids were molested."

Stone shook his head. "Is this really the time you want to talk the history of Christianity?"

"Ricky, I've thought about it a lot lately. Was it Marx who said that religion is the opiate of the masses?

Keep the peasants in line. Or maybe the whole thing is just a function of coming to grips with your own mortality. We're looking for what's next. We just can't accept that this might be all there is."

"Hey, champ, look what you've been through in the last year. Two women you worked with are gone. But Riles, you told me Paige slept around. Who's to say that this isn't Mr. Goodbar --- that she didn't just pick up the wrong guy at some club last night after told her you weren't up for it? She was stabbed repeatedly. That's emotional, punishment for something, maybe a guy who couldn't deal with being used for sex and then dismissed like she did with you. Multiple stab wounds? Hardly the way a pro would do it. They'd cap her with a twenty-two to the head. Besides, how could they know that there weren't dozens of copies of that book floating out there with publishers and such?"

"I imagine they found that out from Paige. They promise to let her live if she tells them about the manuscript --- how many copies were out there, who'd seen it, et cetera. Then when they find out she was the only one who'd read it, kill her and make it look like a crime of passion."

"But at least one other person had seen it. You."

"Thanks, that makes me feel better. She gave up her life to protect me and I couldn't be bothered enough to skip dinner with you to protect her?"

"Riley my boy, you may have shaken off some of your early training. But that Catholic guilt? It runs deep, doesn't it?"

Eighteen

We were headed toward my place, along Route 9 south in Stone's Mustang, which I not so jokingly refer to as the "Tillmanmobile". Supporting my case was the fact that he acquired the candy apple red babe-magnet shortly after meeting Lisa. The fact that it boasted a top speed of 135 mph was wasted as we crawled along the congested highway, nudging forward from light to light.

"I think you're going overboard with this," I said, as Stone exhaled impatiently after barely missing another yellow.

"Look, I know you're a big boy, but why take chances? If they're coming after you next, what's the harm in staying at my pad for a couple of days? You're feeling responsible for what happened to Paige? Imagine how I'd feel if someone capped you and I could have prevented it."

"But what about you and Lisa for starters. Why expose you guys to this? Besides, my place has a golden retriever who goes nuts if anyone comes with a quarter mile of it."

"Yeah, and if anything happened to that dog, you'd really be toast. My house is hard wired for perimeter cameras, I just haven't gotten around to installing them. Be a nice Sunday project for you. Lisa's not due in until after midnight and she's just going to be here until tomorrow

99

morning. She needs to pick up some clothes and then she plans to spend the rest of the week in Manhattan. So, it'll just be you and me and the dog, and I'll take my chances with that versus Gazza's imaginary goons."

I said, "So you're buying the fact that it *is* Gazza now?"

"No, but why take chances on a *Simple Twist of Fate*?"

What scared me was that I was picking up on all of his music references now. How long would it be before I started getting into the habit myself? We pulled into my driveway. I released the security system with my Homelink transmitter and we came in through the garage. Bosco was poised and waiting.

"Whoa, boy, it's nice to see you too," Stone said as the exuberant animal rammed him in the groin with his snout. This had become such a ritual that Stone instinctively turned and covered up the family jewels with his right hand, while deflecting the dog's nose with his left. Bosco generally greeted me by poking the other end, the deeper meaning of which I never want to decipher.

Stone tossed me an Amstel Lite from my refrigerator. "We're over-thinking this, man. There's always the chance that your biggest worry is going to come from the cops. Whoever did this already had the chance to kill you but they conked you on the head instead."

"Maybe they didn't know who I was then."

"Possible. I'm just worried that they set it up to make it look like you killed Paige."

Bosco began to growl and then bark with growing intensity. In a kitchen filled with hard surfaces, the decibel level was almost painful. My doorbell has become a mere formality and sure enough, there was a nondescript Chevy Impala parked out front and a casually dressed man was standing on my front porch.

"Can I help you," I said, opening the door to a familiar shape.

"Riley King. Flint McCullough, Ocean County police."

"Detective." I nodded. "Don't we know each other?"

He didn't see the humor of it. In the full light of day, I could see that his skin was weathered from too much sun, and that he already sported a deeper tan than one would expect this early in the season. He had the kind of a tough guy face that reminded me of the actor Scott Glenn.

"We've met." I couldn't tell if his reaction was an overly dry wit, or just a concession to my possible concussion. "I just need to ask you some more questions. You know the drill."

McCullough was trying to put me at ease, cop to cop. I had tried that tactic with him --- it didn't work then and I was determined not to let it work now. A call to an attorney would have only heightened his suspicions, so I chose to tread the tightrope again. After introductions, he asked Stone about the exact time of our dinner and Rick answered honestly. He then decided to take Bosco for a walk rather than play third wheel. McCullough seemed relieved that he didn't have to order Stone to get lost, probably knowing him from the radio.

My detective friend started by covering the same ground he had the previous night. Most witnesses get impatient --- repeatedly answering the same questions, but cops are looking for inconsistencies and minor variations in the story and timelines. Even innocent civilians get rattled when these flaws are pointed out to them, but the truth is, our memories of trauma aren't as reliable as most of us like to think. In fact, if a story is too accurately reproduced, using the same phrases and bullet points, a seasoned cop will suspect that it's been rehearsed, always a no-no. I tried to wheedle a time of death from him, but he wasn't biting.

"So, Mr. King, my report says that you and the victim had been intimate last night."

"No, I said we had sex Friday night."

"Oh, that's right. Sorry. There was a discarded prophylactic found in the bathroom trash."

"As I said, I didn't know Ms. White very well. Safe sex and all."

"Even though you stated the act was spontaneous."

"Ever the optimist."

"I see. There might have been traces of ligature marks on the vic's wrists. I don't suppose you know how they got there."

"Nothing that kinky Friday night."

"Bruises on the neck and face."

"They weren't there when I left her Saturday."

He was taking notes only occasionally. I tried to detect a pattern to his scribbles, but they seemed almost at random.

"That's something I wanted to ask again. If you were hired to protect Ms. White, why would you leave her behind, go out to dinner with a friend and then come back two hours later?"

"First off, I wasn't hired to protect her, just to find someone for her. She asked me to drive up north with her when she heard that her offices had been broken into."

"And you went as part of your professional duties?"

"I'm not sure."

"What do you mean, not sure? Weren't you going to bill her for the hours?"

"I don't know."

"Is that how you normally run your business? You don't keep track of billable hours?"

"I knew how many hours I'd put in. I just wasn't sure how to charge that morning. After all, I'd slept with the woman the night before. She asked for a favor. I'm not sure that I was comfortable billing her for something that might be unrelated to why she hired me."

"And was it? Unrelated, I mean."

"I don't know."

"You never did tell us who you were hired to find. Why is that?"

"It has nothing to do with your case. Paige wanted me to find an author of hers she'd lost touch with, that's all.

She thought he might be due some royalties and he wasn't at his last known address which was in Toms River."

"Must have been a big check to pay a detective to find him. Pretty generous of her, don't you think?"

"I have no idea what the amount was. But honestly, finding a forwarding address in this day and age isn't all that time consuming. It shouldn't have come to much."

"So why didn't she have someone on her staff do it? Why go outside to you?"

"She exhausted all the methods available to her first."

"Did you two have an argument on Saturday?"

Old Flint was trying to nail me all along. He struck me as a pretty bright guy, not flashy but persistent.

His hard brown eyes were steady on me now --- like flint. The name fit.

"We did have a disagreement."

"We canvassed the immediate area, restaurants, bars and such to see if the vic had any contact with anyone other than you. We turned up a waitress who remembers you with her. And it looked like you were having words. Care to elaborate?"

"The lady was angry with me for not staying the entire night with her Friday. As you saw, I have a dog and I left at midnight to go home and take care of him. Paige didn't like waking up alone after what we'd done."

"So why did she call you that morning?"

"She had just gotten the call that her office had been turned over and she didn't think the local cops would be much help when she got there, so she wanted another set of eyes on the scene."

"But before you said you weren't sure you were going to charge her because you were doing a favor for a friend. Seems like she wanted your professional opinion."

I shrugged and tried to change the subject, asking Flint how he'd come by the unusual name. I was surprised he answered.

"At the time I was born in the mid sixties, one of the most popular TV shows was *Wagon Train*, starred Ward Bond. The scout for the party was called Flint McCullough, played by Robert Horton. My parents thought it sounded cool."

But my attempt at friendly distraction didn't throw him off his game. "So why, after the break-in, did you leave her to have dinner and then come back?"

"We both didn't think she was in any danger. She was ninety miles away from where she lived and worked. She said that nobody except her secretary even knew where she was."

"So if you believed she was so safe, why did you go back to Loveladies?"

"After dinner I just wanted to make sure she was all right, so I called her cell phone and got her voice mail. She had said she planned to stay in for the night so I was a little worried. I drove down to check up."

"We have your message. You say that you're sorry for before and you're on your way down. What were you sorry for?"

I knew that if I were on the other end, my explanations would be straining credibility about now.

"After we got back from Fort Lee, Paige wanted to, well, do what we had done the night before. I wasn't into it so told her I had plans that I couldn't change."

"But you didn't?"

"I *did* have tentative plans to meet my friend Rick for dinner. We just needed to firm them up."

"Oh. So since they weren't firm, you could have easily gotten out of them, had you wished."

"Had I wished."

"So I take it you'd prefer dinner with your friend Rick over an attractive woman who you had sex with the night before."

"Incredible, but true."

"Incredible, indeed. Not a choice most men in your position would make. I would think, a bachelor, Saturday night. No steady girl. Seems like it's an offer you couldn't refuse. Come on, we're both guys here."

"Believe it or not, I don't think it's a good idea to mix business with pleasure. As for Friday night, well, you make choices that you regret in the cold light of day. I decided to keep things strictly business with Paige; she wanted more."

"She insult your masculinity when you turned her down? Paige White say something that got under your skin?"

"I carry a gun. If I was going to kill Paige in a fit of anger, why use a knife?"

"A knife is much more satisfying, isn't it. Every stab hurts going in. Much better punishment for some bitch who insults your manhood."

He was awkwardly ramping up the incendiary talk. But I had logic on my side and most importantly, I was innocent.

"And I suppose I hit myself over the head and knocked myself out."

"Or the victim did it defending herself and you faked being unconscious. But back to the house --- you say it had an elaborate security system, which you checked carefully?"

"Yep."

"And it was on when you left?"

"I set the code myself."

"You see my problem? There was no forced entry. Other than Paige and Peterson, who was on the other side of the country --- we checked --- we think no one else knew that code. So either Paige let her attacker in, which means she knew and trusted him, or it was someone else who had the code. In both cases, Mr. Riley King, you qualify."

Nineteen

"**M**y main question is why didn't he slap the cuffs on you right then?"

Stone and Bosco had returned from a bracing forty minute power walk a few minutes after McCullough had left. Rick looked as if he'd barely broken a sweat, and Bosco could trot all day.

"Sounds as if he really likes you for this, pal."

I was moving around the kitchen, tossing things into a small cardboard box. If I was going to stay with Stone for even a couple of days, Bosco needed his stuff. I poured several portions of kibble into a Ziploc bag, which excited the hound until I made it clear that dinnertime was still a couple of hours off. I gathered up his chew bones, a few fleece squeaky toys and two of his solid rubber balls. For good measure, I added three different varieties of biscuits, in case he was bored with the standard Milk Bones, (although I can't recall him ever turning one down).

"Simplest solution is usually the correct one. The cops should have that motto emblazoned on their stationary. The stabbings made it look like a lover's spat. I was her most recent lover, far as they know."

Stone was nosing through my refrigerator again, looking for another beer. "Sure does look that way. Problem with a pro job and a cover up is that it's too ingenious on one level and too messy on another. Blood all over, no doubt spattering on the killer. DNA sampling and all. Sounds too clumsy for a real pro."

"Don't be surprised if Flint contacts you. He was pretty skeptical about why I'd honor a loose dinner plan with you than resample Paige's charms."

"Pretty odd of him not to ask me more than just the timing of our dinner when he had the chance. Before you and I had a chance to sync our stories."

"Unless he figured we already had. I'm all set. Let me just get Bosco on the leash and we're off."

Stone drove me back to my car in the Starlight Diner's parking lot with Bosco uncomfortably perched on my lap the whole way. I followed him to Mantoloking in the Audi. It was a gray day, cool and threatening rain. We took the causeway from Toms River to the barrier island, then up 35 north toward Stone's house. Bosco had opted to stay in the Mustang after I got out, since Stone had taken the roof down and the dog loved the rush of air up his snout.

Normally, the fifteen-minute trip was a pleasant one but today no bikini-topped girls were strolling near the boardwalk in Seaside Park and if there were, I was too depressed to notice. It was too early in the season to be very congested, but the townies were at work on the rental properties that Sandy had spared, sprucing them up for the summer. The place still looked like a war zone, but progress was being made by those who either had great insurance or were wealthy enough not to care. Under better circumstances, this renewal would be uplifting but now all I could think about was Paige.

I was confused as to my next move. I run a small shop and I have nowhere near the resources to take on Anthony Gazza and his minions. All I might succeed in doing is getting myself killed and what would that accomplish? The local cops would much rather pin the murder on a private detective who had a recent history with two murdered women. Cops don't believe in coincidence. My suspicions about Gazza would be dismissed as a guilty man trying to cast uncertainty unto a simple scenario.

We got to Rick's place late in the afternoon, and I busied myself with installing the security cameras he'd pre-wired. Since he'd obtained the system through our agency, I was familiar with its workings and had no problems hooking it up, other than trying to keep Stone's rickety wooden ladder upright in the soft sand. The house possessed nowhere near the magnificence of John Peterson's manse. Nowhere near the price tag either.

I'd helped Rick find it five years ago when he'd picked up the dilapidated old Cape Cod at the bargain price of half a mil. A lot of his friends thought he was crazy --- buying a shack that needed so much work.

He and I spent three weekends wielding sledgehammers to demolish the warren of unnecessary interior walls that made the place seem so claustrophobic. We gutted the kitchen, removing old white steel cabinets to clear the space for their sleek maple replacements. We spackled and sanded walls, enlisted a friend with electrical skills to rewire the place, busted out old iron tubs and outmoded fixtures, and stripped the rotting cedar shakes off the exterior.

We hired out the job of beefing the exterior up to a contractor who reconstructed the old roof before covering it with composite slate-like shingles. Although we didn't know it at the time, his work was the only reason Stone's house still existed.

Sandy hit the peninsula hard. But all the high tech storm amelioration measures his contractor took during construction paid off. Metal strapping, laminated windows, deeper and heavier pilings, all contributed to the small house's survival. Stone's house was relatively untouched, alongside more grand and substantial homes that were totally swept away.

Days after Sandy, we returned expecting the worst. Our pessimism was exceeded exponentially by reality. Vast deserts of brown beach sand covered decades old familiar streets that no longer existed. Sturdy concrete and stone bridges were strewn akimbo as if constructed from cardboard. Centuries old pines were now splintered driftwood---- a layer of brown sludge covered yards, roadways and the occasional remains of a car or boat that had been cast aside like toys by the ocean's relentless fury.

Other than some minor cosmetic damage, Stone's house looked as it had the week before Sandy hit. The bank of tempered windows facing the sea was unbroken, and the roof only lost a few random shingles that were easily replaced. The effort spent underpinning the foundation was

111

costly but worth many times the expenditure since despite the devastation surrounding it, this one house stood proud and strong.

He prepared my room in the upper level while I toiled on the security system. When we had completed our chores, he ordered out for pizza and flipped on the Sunday night ESPN game. Rick was struggling to stay awake until Lisa was due in after midnight. He'd offered to pick her up at the airport but she said the network was providing a car.

Sometime during the sixth inning of a tedious pitcher's duel my cell phone vibrated, waking me from a similar slumber.

"Mr. King?"

The deep voice was familiar but I feigned ignorance.

"Yes. Who's calling?"

"We need to talk. Can you meet me tonight?"

"What's this about? Who is this?"

"It's Father Salieri. I have a confession to make."

Twenty

The air had turned chilly and I could see my breath. I don't fancy cemeteries at midnight (who does?) but Salieri had insisted on meeting at an old graveyard several hundred yards from the rectory where he kept modest quarters. A short scrollwork iron fence surrounded a few dozen weathered granite tombstones, the most recent laid in 1866. In the pocket of my black fleece, I clutched the worn grip of a snub nosed thirty-eight, which provided a moment of cold reassurance.

I'd thought about bringing Stone along to cover my backside, but I didn't want to expose him to whatever lay ahead so I snuck out while he dozed. I settled for leaving a detailed recording on his cell—where, when, who and why. I suppose I could have refused to meet with the padre until daylight in a public place, but he convinced me that his message was urgent.

Had my childhood indoctrination made it inconceivable that a man of the cloth would lead me into mortal peril? Although I was anticipating a trap, something in me couldn't avoid the temptation to check this out. I parked the Audi just off the road a quarter mile away and trudged on foot to the cemetery. I hadn't been followed leaving Stone's place --- of that I was sure. To be safe, I jogged a slow loop around the appointed spot, seeking hidden sniper vantages but finding none.

I lifted the latch of the heavy black gate whose only purpose could be to discourage small animals from destroying the flowers. Although, who would be placing flowers on the grave of someone who had bought the farm a century and a half ago?

"Over here, King." The crescent moon didn't provide enough illumination to make out a face; all I saw was the glow emanating from the tip of a cigarette. "I'm sorry we had to meet like this but I think you'll understand when you hear what I have to say."

I edged closer to him, my eyes adjusting enough to distinguish his features. "Why couldn't we have talked in your office the other day?"

"There are some things I need to tell you first. And you're free to walk away if you don't want to get involved."

"I *am* involved. I wish to God I wasn't, but I am. Midnight in a graveyard? I'd expect that from a vampire, not a priest."

He chuckled at the notion, followed by a throaty cough.

"The Church has come under a lot of fire lately. We live in a secularist society, with a lot of opinion makers who believe that religion is a destructive force. I've never seen you at Mass, and you've resisted my attempts to get involved with our basketball program. Are you one of those disaffected Catholics who consider religion an enemy?"

He was feeling me out --- he'd called the meeting, he controlled the agenda. He could just be a humble priest, trying to do the right thing. I had no hard evidence to the

114

contrary. Or he could be an agent of Tony Gazza, setting me up for the kill. It was hard to fathom what this discussion of religion had to do with Gazza, Paul Geist or Paige.

"I *want* to believe in the church but to be honest, I can't buy most of what I learned in catechism."

He lit another cigarette, his craggy face illuminated briefly by the lighter. He offered the pack in my direction and I shook my head.

"King, it's no secret that there is a lot of strife within the church. But she's endured for over two thousand years and I have faith she'll survive this crisis and emerge stronger than ever. I just pray that I can be a positive force and not another sinner."

I waited for him to explain, which he did after taking a deep drag.

"I wasn't completely honest with you the other day. I was afraid that you knew something I didn't about Paul Geist's disappearance. And I was afraid of what my role in this might be."

"Might be? You don't *know* what your own part in this is? "

"You need to hear this from the beginning to understand."

"Why tell me this now and not the other day? What's changed?"

"I learned from a parishioner of ours on the county police force that you discovered the body of that poor woman who was killed on Long Beach Island. When I found out that she was a literary agent, a lot of things started coming together in my mind."

Too much coincidence here. Do churchgoing cops generally share their cases with their clergy? Could Salieri be wearing a wire at McCullough's behest? The vise tightened.

"Did they tell you they think I killed her?"

"Not in so many words, but they do consider you a prime suspect. But I choose to believe in your innocence, and I think you'll understand why if you'll let me tell my story."

"Please."

Again he coughed, harder this time and his voice emerged a painful sounding rasp.

"Some of this you might already know about me, that I served in 'Nam; afterwards I helped found this school. We've been fortunate along the way to find success through basketball to the point where the program not only supports the local parish but is a major revenue stream for the archdiocese."

"I'm not sure I've ever heard a priest use the expression *revenue stream.*"

He found that amusing. "The world we live in, I'm afraid. But the crux of my problem is simply that: money. When so many are depending on you, there's constant pressure to continue to provide and when something threatens that, you naturally look to protect it."

My hands were in my pockets, and I tightened the grip on the .38. Without being obvious, I glanced around casually, in an effort to detect movement behind me. All was quiet.

Salieri went on. "I did see Paul Geist's manuscript. It casts the school and me personally in a very harsh light and I was quite taken aback that Paul saw me that way. He always seemed to consider me his mentor, father confessor, and maybe most importantly to him, a fellow writer. You see, Paul always wanted to be a published author and when he first came to Sacred Cross, he cited the book I'd written about my experiences in Vietnam as a great inspiration to him. Paul respected that since he'd had so much trouble getting his efforts published."

His cough became harsher and more persistent as the damp cold permeated. "At any rate, I talked to Paul about how disturbed I was that he saw me as such a villain and he got a good laugh out of that. He said that Michael Jackson was the main inspiration for the character and that he just imagined what would happen if he were placed in charge of a school for boys. He said the character bore no resemblance to me other than the physical manifestation of a high school principal. I expressed the opinion that people reading this would believe otherwise and the result might bring disgrace to the school."

"Why worry about a failed writer? You said yourself he never had gotten anything published."

"On a strictly literary level, this was clearly his best work. As repulsed as I was by the subject matter, my instincts told me that this one actually had a chance to see the light of day."

"So you were afraid that folks would think twice about sending their kids to Sacred Cross if they believed that any part of this book was based on reality. It'd be like chauffeuring their children to Neverland. The archdiocese might even see too many similarities to think that there wasn't something to it. Why not just change the names and location? I'm sure writers do that all the time."

"That might help a little but still, the author worked at our school for the past twenty years. A reader would naturally infer that he was writing from experience. But the main reason I wanted to speak with you is about what happened on Long Beach Island last night."

He was fishing but Paige was beyond harm now. "Yeah. The late Paige White had an informal arrangement with Geist. Is that what you're after?"

"And she hired you to locate Geist."

"Yep."

He shuddered and began to cough again.

There was no cover for anyone to approach unseen, but I still glanced around while his hacking provided me with a respite. The graveyard was in the middle of a meadow, a hundred yards or so off a double yellow line county road. There were pinewoods surrounding the field, and the incessant Parkway hum was barely audible two miles away. I could see the warm twinkle of the rectory lights across the way. A skilled sniper would find me an easy target.

"When I asked you to come tonight I told you I had a confession to make. I'm the one responsible for Paul's disappearance."

I was really hoping Salieri was going to be one of the good guys, that Stone's faith would prevail over my cynicism. And even now, the priest seemed to be a man struggling to make things right, after stumbling down a path of unintended consequences.

"I really didn't want that manuscript in print," he said, after wiping his mouth with a white handkerchief. "It could only do harm. Even if it wouldn't disgrace Sacred Cross specifically, the prurient nature of the material --- the sexual debasement of students under the care of those trusted to educate them --- would be damaging to many fine parochial schools. It would give further ammunition to enemies of the Holy See. So I tried to think of a way I could control the damage, while not depriving Paul of his lifelong dream. He'd given Sacred Cross twenty years of loyal service and I felt like I owed him that."

"How could you suppress his best work and still advance his career?"

"Let me explain my thinking. Years ago, I tried to raise the money on my own when I wanted to start this school. The book sales helped some, but not enough. One of the men I'd gotten to know in Vietnam was the son of a businessman from here in Toms River. We often talked about what we wanted to do when we got back to Jersey. I shared my dream of an elite academy for children from disadvantaged circumstances, where they could receive a top-notch education and an opportunity to rise out of poverty. His grandparents were immigrants who had attained wealth in this country, so he sympathized. He told me that if I ever needed help, he'd be there for me. So when my money raising efforts fell short, I took him up on his offer. Long story short, he was an enormous help. He not only gave us money, but organized fundraisers with his rich friends, and we were able to take over an old abandoned school building near the Parkway that the town was about to raze and Sacred Cross was born. My friend got us great rates with contractors who put the building right again. And years later, when our reputation was established, he helped us take the next step and built the field house."

"So you decided to ignore Tony Gazza's family business?"

"I was afraid you'd make the connection to Tony on your own and draw the wrong conclusions. I'm here to tell you that you're heading in the wrong direction, and that you might be endangering yourself."

He puffed on the cigarette, coughed again. I could see where this was headed but he needed to tell me the whole story, probably to rationalize his own role in Paige's death. I tried to hasten the process.

I said, "I didn't know the story of how you two met and how you started the school. I guess I fell asleep during the encomiums at your fundraisers. But I did know that Gazza was a big Sacred Cross booster. You weren't worried that the church would frown on an association with the mob? I guess Godfather III did make some sense after all."

His coughing spasm lasted longer and was more violent. "See what I mean about fiction influencing people's view of reality? His business is cleaning and disposing of environmental waste. With New Jersey restrictions getting tighter each year, there's a lot of money to be made without circumventing the law. Look, King, you don't know me well, but trust me, if I thought that the help we got from Tony Gazza was in any way tainted, we wouldn't have accepted it."

"Yeah right. How seriously did you look into it?"

"I told you I know high ranking law enforcement officials. They have nothing on Tony. I know him very well and I trust him."

"So you haven't told me about your scheme to squelch the novel and yet give Paul Geist his due. We seem to have gotten sidetracked on Tony Gazza."

He lit another cigarette. "It's all of a piece. As a friend, I shared my concerns about the book with Tony and came up with an idea. He'd approach Paul through intermediaries and offer him a nice advance for its rights. Then tell him a few months later that upon further consideration this book was not quite good enough but to consider the advance our investment toward his later work."

"And to you this sounds like a legitimate businessman?"

He turned away. "I won't kid you, what we were doing was underhanded. But not illegal and I submit, not immoral. We were suppressing pornographic literature, while not punishing the writer."

"And Geist went for this?"

"He did."

"And Geist never spoke to you about it after?"

"Nothing unusual there. I got a letter of resignation from Sacred Cross signed by Paul in July and it seemed we'd achieved a win-win situation."

"And you didn't consider the possibility that Tony just decided to save the dough and dispatch Geist?"

"The money was inconsequential to Tony. He said Paul was happy just to disappear and devote himself completely to his art."

I walked a tight circle to stretch my legs. I had the sense that Salieri believed this tale, but I scanned the area, just in case.

"So what do you want from me, Father?"

"After I talked to you the other day, I spoke with Tony and I told him that someone had seen the manuscript and was interested in publishing it. He said not to worry, he had a signed contract with Paul that he could enforce legally."

"But now you're having doubts after what happened to Paige?"

"No. Some men on my board alerted me to the fact that a friend of yours was asking questions on your behalf and Tony's name came up. You see, if you start nosing about in Tony's affairs, that's one area that he guards very zealously."

"If he has nothing to hide and is completely legit, why worry?"

He sighed and barked a short cough. "Call it paranoid, but those of us of Italian descent have been raised to believe that the fewer people who know about our personal business, the better. People can use information to harm you so why make it easy to obtain? The concept of omerta didn't originate with the mafia, it sprang from the culture."

"So if Tony thought Paige was messing around in his affairs, he might decide to eliminate her?"

"Have you heard what I've been saying? That is not the way Tony operates and if you still can't accept that, try applying some basic logic. You didn't tell me who you were working for when I asked. So if your premise is correct, Tony would have to systematically start killing every literary agent in the directory. Paul was paid and he took that money and went off somewhere to write his masterpiece. Please --- I'm begging you, if you have any respect at all for me and what this school has meant to the community, leave Tony Gazza alone."

Twenty one

On the ride back from the graveyard, my mind turned over many possibilities. My initial notion was that Salieri had just delivered a warning on behalf of Gazza --- and also was trying to find out if I already knew too much. In that case, his forays were intended to determine if *I* needed to be eliminated.

The only way I could believe that the priest was deliberately involved in this insidious plot was that he was so hopelessly corrupt that he had sanctioned murder in a desperate attempt to save his own reputation. And an intelligent man like Salieri had to know that the carnage might not stop there. What if Paige had shown the book to her staff or sent it out to publishers? The genie might be so far out of the lamp that a series of deaths might not suppress it.

It was also possible that Gazza had saved himself a few bob by feeding Paul Geist to the fishes, rather than paying him off to squelch the novel. And no one was the wiser until I started asking questions about Geist three days ago. Now in addition to the murder being exposed, it was possible that the book would find its way into print even without the late author's complicity.

So Gazza sent his goons to Paige's office to destroy any remaining copies of Geist's book. Upon finding none, they confronted her.

Gazza's men might promise not to harm her if she told them about anyone else who has seen the book. These people don't like to leave loose ends, so she must have figured they were going to kill her no matter what. They tried to make it look like a crime of passion by stabbing her repeatedly.

But why hadn't they just offed me when they had the chance after I stumbled onto the scene if Paige had given me up?

All of this would depend on Gazza. I've been operating on the assumption that he is just a brutal thug who would tell his henchmen to get the book and destroy anyone who has knowledge of its existence. It's possible that he is a *little* more human than that, and might have tasked his geeks just to frighten Paige off, killing her only if absolutely necessary. And since they weren't authorized to spill anyone else's blood, they may have needed their boss's go-ahead before cleaning up the loose end that was Riley King.

If that was the case, they would have reported back to Gazza by now. If Salieri was part of the conspiracy, I would have been cleanly dispatched at the graveyard and taken to wherever Gazza disposes of bodies. Maybe even conveniently popped into an already existing plot right there. My disappearance could be construed by the authorities as an admission of guilt. That set-up would present the local cops with a gift-wrapped conclusion they'd swallow whole.

I hadn't been killed in the cemetery, which led me to believe that if the priest *was* involved, he was an innocent dupe, thinking that he was doing me a favor by delivering Gazza's warning. Or he might have been acting totally on his own, trying to protect me from a man he feared to be dangerous.

I had motive galore but the one thing I had no answer for was how Gazza had linked Geist to Paige. How he so quickly broke into her office seeking the manuscript and then discovered where she was spending the weekend. I would think even a ruthless killer would need more time to ferret out all that information and act upon it. The priest had raised a good point.

In any case, this would be the last night I spend at Stone's. I couldn't expose Lisa and him to a gangland vendetta. I'd check into a motel, in fact, move around to several motels --- paying cash, in case Gazza's men were able to hack into my credit card receipts. I'd have to rent a car since the bad guys no doubt had already marked the Audi. I would avoid the office, linking up to the mainframe by remote. I couldn't lug a seventy pound dog around so Bosco would stay at the kennel or with Stone.

I'd get in touch with Logan and see if he could get me some help with the feds. Publicly, they'd want to avoid the perception of covering up for one of their own in a high profile murder investigation.

But time wasn't on my side. If Gazza had committed his considerable resources toward finding me, I couldn't stay hidden for long.

A dark blue Chevy Impala was inauspiciously parked a few doors down from Stone's. It would have been a common sight in mid-July, perched as it was in a crushed stone driveway a hundred yards north of my friend's house. But on a cold Sunday night in May, parking at the shore is not at such a premium that anyone would leave their car so close to a heavily traveled thoroughfare like Route 35. Unless of course, it contained men who were waiting to kill me.

Sadly, there were only a couple other Mantoloking houses along the beach that still qualified for a certificate of occupancy, so it was hardly a challenge to quietly deposit myself north of my target after circling the block. I pocketed the gun and stole up behind the vehicle under cover of darkness.

In the driver's seat, a dark, clean-cut fellow in his mid-twenties was slouched down, sipping coffee from a Styrofoam *Dunkin Donuts* cup. He had airline-style headphones draped over a Yankees baseball cap. The kid never sensed my presence until I rapped hard at his window.

"Excuse me, can I help you?"

He shot to attention, bolting upright in his seat, brushing the headphones off with his right hand while lowering the window with the other. A faint waft of some indistinguishable rap music floated up from the detached earpieces.

"Uh, yes, I uh, I'm here on police business."

It took him a moment to recognize me, but he tried to disguise the fact. "Do you live here, sir?"

127

He knew damn well I didn't, but didn't want to admit his cover was blown.

"No, just nearby. We have a neighborhood watch and I'm supposed to be on the lookout for suspicious activity. Mind showing me a badge?"

McCullough had obviously sent a junior grade officer to track my movements. Apparently, it had taken the force a while to establish I was staying at Stone's place; otherwise they would have followed me to the meeting with Salieri. Either that or the kid had missed my leaving. Surveillance of this type was cold, boring work, but couldn't be properly done strapped to an I-Pod, boogying to hip-hop.

The badge he flashed was authentic, and for that I was grateful. Even if this clown was incompetent, an extra set of eyes couldn't hurt if Gazza made a move. Maybe my little wakeup call would increase this dude's vigilance.

At first, I tried to hide my sarcasm. "I'm sorry for disturbing you officer. Glad to see you're keeping an eye on the neighborhood. Always good to see our diligent police force at work. On guard in case Sandy comes back, no doubt."

Twenty two

Stone was awake, drinking scotch at his kitchen table when I walked in. The pile of golden fur at his feet was Bosco, obviously too groggy to greet me at the door. In acknowledgment of the arrival of his main source of food and shelter, he raised his head, beat his tail on the floor for ten seconds and then went back to sleep.

"Ten more minutes and I was calling out the National Guard. You frigging idiot, why didn't you bring me for back up?"

"Told you why on that message I left."

"Like you and I haven't been in tight spots before."

"This is different." I explained the Gazza connection, the county cruiser parked down the block and the details of my meeting with Salieri.

"See," he said, when I was finished. "I told you that a priest wouldn't get involved in something like that. Sounds like he was trying to do the right thing."

The scotch looked good but I needed to sleep, although as hyper as I felt, I doubted it would come easily.

"It could be he's leveling with me. But he's still naïve about his pal. He must have mentioned my name to Gazza when he wanted to know who was asking questions about Geist. Or maybe a well meaning friend of mine inadvertently tipped them off."

"Shit. I guess that's possible. Sorry. I was just trying to help. Now what?"

"I lay low. I can't stay here after tonight. If you'd take care of Bosco for me, that'd help a lot."

"Why can't you stay here? Bring in a couple of your guys to keep watch in shifts. Gazza doesn't know you're here, does he?"

I poured myself a scotch, the hell with it. "How hard would it be for him to find out? The guy probably listens to that lame-ass radio show of yours. How many times have you mentioned on the air that we hang together? The man is connected in town. It wouldn't take him long to check this place out and in case you hadn't noticed, it ain't exactly a fortress. Although Sandy made it easy for us to see if anyone is coming, since the whole area looks like a scene from *Lawrence of Arabia* now. Look, Rick, I figured I was okay for one night. But even the Ocean County cops traced me here within hours so how long will it take Gazza? I still can't figure how he tied Paige into this but if he did, he has resources that run pretty deep."

"You're sure he's behind it?"

"Who else has motive? And opportunity?"

"Don't kill me on this, but what about coincidence? What if Gazza was telling the truth about just paying Geist off and he really is somewhere in East Jabib working on his next masterpiece? And what if Paige just picked up the wrong guy at a bar like we discussed yesterday? You told me she could be pretty tough on men who fall short of satisfying her. What if she pushed the wrong button and some dude freaked out?"

"All possible. Willing to bet your life on it? Or mine?"

He had no snappy comeback for that one.

I said, "Look, you've helped enough. Just take care of my dog. You're a radio talk show guy. This isn't your area of expertise."

"Leave it to the pros, eh? Think I'm not up to the task?"

"Nobody I'd rather have with me in a foxhole, buddy." We made eye contact, which we rarely did being guys and all, but that moment told us both all we needed to know. "Damn, I didn't even ask. Is Lisa back from the coast? Everything go okay out there?"

"Uh, yeah. Looks like she might even get her own talk show. Some kind of variation on *The View*, I guess. Just gave me the headline version and then sacked out. The flight took a lot out of her."

"You don't seem overjoyed by the prospect, Ricky."

"The show would be based in L.A. and she'd have to move out there."

That was the bitch about two career show biz couples. Long periods on opposite coasts. Long periods in the company of attractive members of the opposite sex. Long periods of time with others who share *artistic* moral values, (read: non-existent). Lisa was as down to earth as anyone could be in television, which is to say she always had both feet within a day's drive of terra firma. But it never seemed to me that she'd give up her career and six (soon to be seven) figure income to live on the beach with Rick. And he was doing too well to shuck it all and retire as a kept man. His domestic problems briefly took my mind off my own troubles.

"So what will you do? Los Angeles isn't exactly New York when it comes to sports."

"You know as well as I do, radio is local. No one's ever heard of me outside of this area. And even if I could get a job out there, television talk shows get cancelled and moved all the time. I can't follow her around the country. I guess we'll have to be bi-coastal for a while and see how it works out."

"That's why they invented planes."

"I've got an early meeting at the station. Lisa doesn't have to be in the city until the afternoon so if you wake up late, I'll probably be gone."

He started for the master bedroom, which was down the hall off the kitchen on the first floor.

"Don't tell her I told you about her show unless she brings it up," he said over his shoulder. "A lot of media people like to keep word of things like this from getting out until everything's *Signed, Sealed, Delivered, I'm Yours.* Paranoid, but in this business, you have to be."

Paranoid? I can relate. At least he didn't quote Black Sabbath.

Twenty three

I'd have slept later but Bosco was having none of it. Normally, he was up by seven, whimpering to go out or be fed, not necessarily in that order. In deference to my late night and the fact I'd taken him out before retiring, he let me sleep until nine. It was still misty over the Atlantic as I tugged on jeans and a sweatshirt to take him for a walk on the beach.

Stone had already split for work, leaving behind a quick note and a full pot of coffee. I checked to see if the county cruiser was still there (it was) before stepping off the rear deck onto the soft wet sand. Feeling relatively safe with the thirty-eight tucked into a pocket, I cautiously lit out, keeping a wary eye on the dunes. Bosco was on a leash, although he would have been perfectly happy to dance around the waves that slowly surged in at low tide.

I thought about the dangers that awaited me and my initial inclination was taking the battle to my turf and on my terms. As I've gotten older, I've become more selective on which wars I need to take on.

Paige White was a stranger to me a week ago. I'd probably spent no more than twelve hours with her since we met, and at least half of those were kept in simmering silence. There were a few moments of what passed for passion. So I'd slept with a stranger than I was ambivalent about. At worst, her mission was to publish a novel that would disgrace a community --- my community; at best, it would make a few bucks for a struggling writer who might not even be around to enjoy them.

In order to bring her killer(s) to justice, I'd have to take on a crime family that the FBI hadn't been able to crack. It might further involve destroying a school that had given hundreds of children the opportunity to better themselves. As I tried to total up the ledger for the greater good, it was hard to justify further involvement with avenging Paige White.

Something in me nagged that I would be taking an unmanly course of cowardice if I gave in to the simple rationality of the situation. Chivalrous notions were counterproductive when challenging big battalions, but somehow I still clung to them. I tried to imagine a limited role, where I could quietly work toward a solution traveling under Gazza's radar, but I doubted that airspace existed.

Could I enlist McCullough as an ally? With his cop mentality, he'd focus in on one suspect--- me, and rebuff any attempts to divert his attention elsewhere. There was a chance that I could get help from Logan, perhaps unofficially marshalling some assistance from the few friends I still had with the bureau. After breakfast, he'd be my first call.

I needed to pick up a few things at my house before finding a cheap motel where I could hunker down for a couple of days. Luckily, there were a string of them on Route 9 on the mainland, and most of them were pretty vacant during the week this early in the season. I needed to get some cash at an ATM, and stay away from credit cards after that. It would be a hard habit to break.

When I got back to Stone's, Lisa was up, reading the Asbury Park Press at the granite breakfast bar.

"Hey, Riley, how's it going? Coffee's hot. Help yourself."

She was wearing a pink L.A. Raiders tee shirt. I don't know what would have given the late Al Davis more of a fit, the fact that it said "LA" or that it was pink. Given the size, likely it was one of Stone's that he'd carelessly washed with a red sweatshirt.

I released Bosco and he immediately charged over to Lisa, sticking his snout where he normally did to get acquainted. As she bent over to shoo him away, I noticed a couple of things. First, she wasn't wearing much in the way of underwear and second and that her smooth bottom sported no tan lines. Her trip to the coast hadn't been all business.

"How was California?" I ventured.

"Great, just super. I went out there with my producer, and we stayed in Catalina. The network's head of programming has a great house there. Private beach, pool, tennis courts, the whole deal. Even has a putting green, where I took some serious money off him."

"Sounds nice. Anything come out of it?"

"Sure did." She beamed, her perfect teeth glistening. "You're looking at Fox's answer to Meredith Vieira. My own daytime hour-long talk show with a male host to be determined. I'll still be able to do football on weekends if I chose. My agent has to get with them on money, but from what they were talking about informally, it's not going to be a problem."

"Well, congratulations. And you'll do this from New York?" I hope I wasn't playing dumb too obviously.

"That's the only thing. I will have to move to the coast. Actually, I don't mind. I love the weather there and I'll still keep my apartment here, at least for now. Most of the folks they see as guests for the show live out there. They see this as their counter to Michael and Kelly and they're too established in New York for us to fight them over guests."

She hadn't mentioned Rick in all of this. She broke off a piece of the muffin she was eating and fed it to Bosco. Her shoulder length blonde hair fell over her face as she patted my bad boy on the rump. "Now leave me alone and go see your daddy," she admonished him.

"Fat chance after you've given him food." Sure enough, Bosco sat at attention at her feet, hoping to catch a stray crumb or engender more pity from her with his soft brown eyes. "So you and Rick will be bi-coastal."

She eased off the counter stool with the effortless grace of a dancer. Even in the morning without makeup, Lisa Tillman was a knockout. With her mix of brains and looks, the possibilities were unlimited.

"I suppose we could try that, maybe. I know what you're thinking, Riley. Look, all my life I've wanted to be on television, ever since I was a little girl and did pageants in grade school. Rick knew my priorities going in, I knew his."

"Lisa, I'm not thinking anything. Hey, I wish you luck. This is great for you. We'll just miss you, is all."

"I'll miss you guys, too." She pecked me on the cheek. "I've got to get dressed. My producer is picking me up soon."

"I'm out of here pretty soon myself. Rick's going to take care of Bosco for a few days while I'm on a case. I'll get the door if your guy comes early."

"Thanks, Riley. You're a sweetheart."

She walked toward the bedroom and I was struck with the hollow feeling that I might be seeing her for the last time. I was picking up vibes that she wasn't planning on flying east at every opportunity, and the few conciliatory words that an invitation to visit her in California hadn't been top of mind for her. He'd fly out to see her every chance he got, and it would take a few months of her not reciprocating before he got the message. Lisa Tillman was already outta here, but he'd be the last to know.

Checking messages at home, Logan and Tommy (Yusef) had called, both smart enough not to leave anything pertinent on the machine. Still too early to call the Coast, I rang Logan first on Stone's landline.

After running down what had happened since we last spoke, he was quick to offer help. "I might be able to spring a forensic unit. You know if the security cameras had a timestamp? If things went down like you said, it shouldn't be too hard to prove that you got there after she was already dead. Locals may not have the smarts to figure that out themselves and are just jumping to conclusions. Problem is,

137

I'd have to bigfoot them as well as convince my boss that this is a federal case. Might be a hard sell."

"Dan, the forced entry angle is a tough one --- it would take someone very sophisticated to override that security system and not leave a trace."

"No murder weapon?"

"Not that I know of. With all the water around here --- lagoons, the bay, swamps and the ocean ---- I doubt they'll find anything."

"Unless someone wants them to. Let's say someone pressed your fingers on the knife while you were unconscious."

"Still, they would have found it by now in the house. It's not likely I would have killed Paige, disposed of the weapon in the ocean and then come back and hang out at the scene."

"You've been away from the bureau a while, my friend. These local guys treat our lab folks like they're magicians or something. Seems every other TV show deals with crime scene units. They take evidence invisible to the naked eye and build an airtight case around it."

"They've done some amazing things, even back when I was there. And the technology has advanced tenfold since then."

He said, "True. But my point is, since the locals know you were a fed, they can picture you dispassionately coming back to cover up the crime, and using some imaginative scenario to make it look like you were a victim, too."

"Why even link myself to her? Call 911 and be there when they arrived? If I'm such an artist at covering up, that is."

"Logical, but crimes involving emotion aren't always so well thought out. They'd like this to be a simple case of an attractive woman hiring a PI who develops the hots for her, gets rejected so he rapes and kills her. Simplest solution is usually the correct one."

A motto not just for local cops, it seems. "I suppose."

"Look, buddy, that's where our guys can help. You say they found a condom. Well, even with a condom, we can now pin down within a couple of hours based on sperm degradation the time it first was exposed to the atmosphere. They could back up your story that you had sex with her Friday, and not right before you killed her Saturday."

"I've heard some clinical descriptions of sex before but sperm degradation after being exposed to the atmosphere is as cold as it gets."

"They also might find a way that someone could get in without forcing the security system. Plus, your brother agents won't be looking to pin this on you. Quite the contrary. But hey, I'm sorry for what happened. Even though it sounds like you didn't know this woman very well, it's got to shake you up."

"Thanks, I'm dealing with it. Anything you can do, even off book, is appreciated. By the way, did you have time to check on Geist?"

"He never left the country. Ran a credit check on him. Paid off his cards last summer and hasn't used them since or reapplied for new ones. Sure looks like your boy's a goner or off the grid for some other reason."

"What about Gazza?"

"I was about to bring him up. I'm going to insist on making him part of the deal."

"Meaning, you want me to help you nail him?"

"Just the opposite. I'm willing to help you out of this jam buddy, but in exchange I want you to steer clear of Gazza."

"And why is that?"

"Think about it. Maybe Anthony Gazza really is legit. He's become a pillar of the community, incapable of what you think he may have done. In which case, you're wasting your time chasing him. Or if he's still dirty, he's light years ahead of you and could annihilate Riley King without a trace. So the deal is I'll do everything I can to help but I must insist you stay away from Gazza."

"So we let him get away with killing an innocent woman?"

"I didn't say that. If we develop leads that point to him, we'll follow up. Maybe he's lost his marbles and has slipped up on this one. But one guy, working solo in Central Jersey? No offense pal, but you don't stand a chance and I'd kind of like to see *The Book of Mormon* with you this August. Look, I've got a pretty full plate the next few days. I'll do what I can, but don't panic if you don't hear from me. I'll help you out, but hands off Gazza. Deal?"

I tried to make it sound like I agreed. Logan and I had been in some tight spots together and I knew that he wasn't some chickenshit bureaucrat afraid to take action just because the odds weren't in his favor. I had to give weight to his warning, but it wasn't in my nature to let it pass.

The doorbell sounded, and Bosco's raucous barking occupied all my attention until I could guide the dog by the collar into Stone's office and close the door. Still cautious, I peeked out a side window lest Gazza's men try a direct approach. Outside, a black Lincoln Town car sat in the driveway, a black suited driver behind the wheel. At the door stood slender young man that I could handle in my sleep. He wore baggy shorts, sandals, and a shirt open to the navel, making a concealed weapon unlikely. Since when did gangsters arrive in limos?

"Can I help you?" I said, looking him over.

"I'm Lisa's producer. Ronnie Glickman. She's expecting me."

The kid was handsome, maybe too handsome. Thick, long dark hair and a day's growth gave him a French film star look, and I detected a whiff of marijuana about him. *Smoking a joint in a limo at ten in the morning.* TV people inhabit a different planet.

"She'll be right out."

Lisa, dragging a wheeled valise, came up from behind me. Upon seeing this, the driver sprang from the car to assist her.

"Ronnie, hiii. You're right on time." She didn't bother with introductions.

I felt like the invisible man. She gave Glickman a warm hug and a kiss on the lips that lingered a beat too long;

from which it was clear that producer was not the only role that Ronnie served in Lisa's life. It didn't take an ace detective to know that Rick and I were already in the rear view mirror.

Twenty four

I needed to run by the house to pick up a few things: my laptop, some clothes, and a shaving kit, in preparation for my life on the lam. The cops watching me had either become a lot more clever or had been dispatched to other duty because I didn't catch a glimpse of them as I pulled away in the Audi. If I was being followed, it was by someone of superior skill.

Windows on the Bay was a quarter of a mile from my house, and I parked the car there, walked through the front door and without stopping, proceeded out the back. I could see my house from across the bay and so far, nothing looked out of place. I half jogged past acres of wetlands that had protected my house from Sandy. The egrets, wood ducks and other wildlife that inhabited the marsh fields paid me little mind as I slogged toward home. It felt like I'd been away for a week but a quick look around satisfied me that there had been no intruders since I'd left with Stone a day earlier. Without a clear plan of attack I started to leave for the motel, only to find my next move had already been decided for me. A black Caddy sat in my driveway, complete with two serious looking thugs in dark suits and sunglasses leaning against the hood. These guys were not effete Hollywood TV producer-types.

"I swear, I'm not an alien," I shouted. My *Men in Black* reference did not penetrate.

"Mr. King, we'd like you to come with us." The taller man's voice conveyed the simple direct order, evoking neither amusement nor malice.

"Gee fellas, I'd like to but I have plans. My luncheon companions are waiting for me in that restaurant down the road. Hey, you look like sports fans, you may know them. The New York Giants offensive line? Big guys and they don't like to be kept waiting."

"Very funny. Just hop in the back. We'll call the restaurant and let them know you won't be able to join them today."

My .38 was in the gym bag. One of the men was about my size. The other was shorter and stockier, and seemed to be missing his neck.

"What did you have in mind? A picnic on the beach?"

"I think you'll like the food where we're going. If you think your lunch dates don't like to be kept waiting, well, let's put it this way, our boss places a premium on punctuality, too. And leave that bag on your stoop. You can pick it up later."

"I'm sorry, I must have missed the part where you told me who we were meeting?" The fact they hadn't searched my bag was encouraging, and the idea of me picking it up later rather than someone going through my *effects* could be construed as a positive sign. Of course, if I were going to shoot someone and dump them in a swamp, I'd try to put them at ease with similar assurances.

"He also values the element of surprise. Now, will you get into the car, or do we need to resort to more persuasive tactics?"

The big guy was quite eloquent for a local hood although his smaller friend had yet to speak. I had the feeling that the tactics he referenced had to do with the bulge near his left armpit. The isolation of my house, set on a small peninsula with only three other residents, all of whom were part time, was great most of the year, but a negative today. These guys could pop me right here, stuff me in the trunk and no one would be the wiser. The fact that they hadn't already done so gave me a small ray of hope.

"Okay, fellas, I'll accept your invite. But it might rain later so do you mind if I take my bag with me? Hate to ask your boss to reimburse me for ruining a two thousand dollar computer."

"Take the goddam bag and get in." His patience with my witticisms was running out and his accommodating manner was coarsening. It probably wouldn't be a good idea to push it much further. Bringing the bag with me was a small victory. If the ride was looking like it was one-way, I could try to somehow extract the .38 to make it a more even fight.

I climbed into the back seat as no-neck held the door open, after which he piled in next to me, still silent. He smelled of Jade East, a cologne I hadn't used since high school. Were they still making the stuff, or had he perspicaciously hoarded a thirty-year supply?

145

Both men made no attempt at conversation or tried to mask our destination as we headed up Route 9, then passed through town following 37 out toward Mantoloking. The thought crossed my mind that Logan had hired a couple of actors to scare the shit out of me, in hopes of dissuading me from going after Gazza. But these dudes seemed to be the real deal. Either that, or Lee Strasburg had personally tutored them.

Just before the causeway to the barrier island, the car made an abrupt right and wove past the bridge abutments toward the water. My optimism that I would be returning immediately sagged. I knew of nothing under this bridge other than marinas and jet-ski rentals, most of which would be closed on a mild weekday in May. A perfect place for execution and disposal. With my foot, I tried to ease the zipper of the gym bag open but couldn't get the sole under the clasp.

We pulled into the parking lot of a sleek one-story building that bore no windows facing the street; the tasteful gold script near the entry proclaimed *Malavista*. The low-slung edifice was clad in Tuscan yellow stucco, crowned by a shallow red tile roof. A barrel vaulted burgundy canopy supported by brass stanchions marked the only front entry. There were about a dozen cars parked in front, mostly Mercedes and BMW's. Despite the incessant whine of tires speeding over the bridge, the impression was quite elegant.

My heavyset companion pinched my elbow with his thumb and forefinger, a vise-like grip I probably couldn't break without ripping flesh. He guided me through the front door, three steps behind his partner who cast a perfunctory nod at the maître'd.

They'd been here before.

Unlike the rather bland exterior, the inside of Malavista was bright and airy, a wall of glass framing the view of Barnegat Bay. French doors led out to an expansive slate patio, pocked by dark green umbrellas that sheltered small cast aluminum tables for outdoor dining. None of the two dozen patrons had chosen to lunch alfresco on this breezy afternoon but inside, a large gas fireplace warmed the understated décor.

My captors ushered me toward a mahogany door, which revealed a small dining room designed to host private parties or conferences. A rustic bleached oak table dominated the center of the space surrounded by a dozen upholstered armchairs, which provided luxurious seating. At the far end of the table sat the room's only occupant, his back to us, presumably staring out at the bay. As we entered he arose, and smiled warmly. He was a trim figure of average height, dressed in a flawlessly cut Italian suit. His hair was Caesar-cut; short silver curls ringed his deeply tanned face.

"Mr. King. A pleasure to finally meet you," he said, extending a manicured hand. "I'm Anthony Gazza."

Twenty five

"You kidnap me and then ask me to shake your hand? I'll pass if you don't mind."

"I imagine I'd feel the same way in your place. Please sit down. I'm about to order lunch and I hoped you'd join me."

"I'm not particularly keen on breaking bread with kidnappers either. Federal offense, you know."

"Mr. King. Let's get this out of the way. If I'd sent an engraved invitation to lunch, I doubt you would have responded. I instructed my men to be firm but reasonable and that if you physically resisted, to let you go. But I think you'll find it in both our best interests to discuss this matter like gentlemen."

"Gentlemen don't send thugs to force someone into a car against their will."

Gazza sat and smoothed his hundred dollar silk cravat. There was nothing even remotely thug-like about him, a *bella figura* impeccably tailored, immaculately groomed --- an impressively sinuous build for a man over sixty. His sonorous voice was devoid of *Joisey* or Brooklyn; his blue eyes twinkled with a sense of good humor. He reminded me of an older Gabriel Macht. It was hard to imagine this distinguished looking man commanding an execution. But the same had been observed of the most cold-blooded war criminals at Nuremberg.

"Again, my apologies. I'm actually quite an admirer of yours, even though you cost me some major dollars when I could least afford it."

He had me baffled with that one. To my recollection, this was our first face-to-face meeting, and none of my cases either here or with the bureau had involved any of his interests.

He saw the look of puzzlement on my face and explained. "You see, I'm quite the college basketball fan. And in my younger, more reckless days, I wasn't averse to laying a couple of bills on my alma mater --- Seton Hall. I was referring to that game when you scored five points in the final thirty seconds to beat my Pirates."

I wasn't sure if a couple of bills meant tens, twenties, hundreds or thousands. The game he was talking about was one of my sophomore year highlights. It was ostensibly garbage time at the end of a game but we were doing a good job at frittering away what had been a substantial lead. Coach was *this close* to putting the starters back in but I was determined to send a message to Thompson that I deserved more minutes. A couple of aggressive drives to the hoop, one of which resulted a three point play didn't earn me a starting spot, but it helped me climb into the sixth man role that defined my steady but less than stellar college career.

"In fact, Mr. King, you still look like you could out dunk players half your age."

Gazza was trying to put me at ease with flattery, and it was working up until that point. He'd correctly gleaned that my college basketball exploits were the one area in which I still hold some vanity. But whoever had fed him his research had blown a detail that gave lie to the whole thing.

"Never could slam it down. Lots of guys can at six two, but my legs were always too heavy."

"My apologies once more. I seem to recall a couple of tomahawks but that was a long time ago. At my age, the memories tend to amplify actual events. You were a hell of a player, smart. You understood what it was like to be part of a team. You weren't flashy, you knew what your role was and you took care of business. Something I wish would get through the heads of some of these players today. The same lessons would benefit my employees, as well."

His nimble mind was capable of improvisation, I had to credit him with that; compliments on my old school approach to the game had found another sweet spot. But despite the genteel small talk, I had to be alert --- this puppy could bare his fangs at any moment. I wasn't keen on my "heavy" legs becoming permanently anchored in the mucky bottom of Barnegat Bay.

"You ever play, Gazza?"

"Tony…. please. I play weekends, mainly to keep in shape. Always had a nice jump shot in high school but I was too short. And slow. A lethal combination, as you know."

If his choice of words was intentional, he was gently reminding me that he was a gangster who had demanded my presence, against my will and under threat of my life. I read it as a signal that it was time to get down to business.

"I'm sure you didn't bring me here to relive my glory days or offer me a job coaching your CYO team."

"Obviously. Let's order and then we'll talk. I know that because of certain things you may have heard about me, there's a bit of trepidation about this meeting. Let me assure you that you're in no danger now, and I think we can come to an agreement to keep it that way."

The underlying message being that if we *didn't* come to an "agreement", I *would* be in danger. Conversation, negotiation, then ultimatum. From the nuns to my dad to my bosses at the FBI, I dreaded being in this position. But my alternatives were limited at the moment. Was there anything I could say --- any sharp turn of phrase or dazzling logic that could reverse momentum and put me in the advantage? Gazza figuratively had a gun to my head. I could stall for time, but he was in control. The only consolation was that if he had already decided to kill me, we wouldn't be having any conversation at all; it would already have been accomplished.

It was clear that I was being given the courtesy of another warning, which I could ignore at my own risk. Was Salieri's admonition last night part of a coordinated effort, or had these two old friends arrived at the same conclusion independently?

"Why don't you order for me, Gazza? I'm not hard to please."

"Give me a moment then. You enjoy seafood? I'm sure you'll appreciate what I chose for you." He walked over to an extension on the outer wall, murmured brief instructions and returned to his seat, beaming. He'd been blessed with a naturally perfect smile, or thousands to spend on undetectable caps.

"I'm sampling a new Chianti for possible inclusion on our wine list. Would you like to try it?"

"A little early for me. And something tells me I should keep a clear head."

"As you wish." He swirled the wine expertly in his glass, inhaled its bouquet and sipped, after which he raised his glass. "You're missing a real treat. Welcome to Malavista."

"Doesn't Malavista mean 'bad view' in Italian?"

"Our little joke. We named it in the nineties. You know, when in street idiom, bad meant good. Now it just means bad again but we're stuck with it."

I had no answer for that and I responded inanely, "So this is your place?"

"I have a small interest. I guess it's become what you'd call a mob hangout."

For a guy who had gone to great cosmetic lengths to deny his heritage, he dropped this tidbit in passing.

"Mr. King, let's lay our cards on the table here and now. My father was involved in organized crime. That's a fact. Gambling, prostitution, drugs. And although he never spoke about it directly, he probably arranged more than a few one-way trips to the Pine Barrens for his enemies. But after my mother passed, he became a truly religious man. I don't think he was ever proud of what he did for a living. He was second generation, carrying on his father's work. I suppose he felt he had little choice. But it didn't really suit him. He was constantly looking for ways to expand into legitimate enterprises, in the hopes that I, his only son, would be the man he always wanted to be. He brought me up to love this country. When the draft came and Vietnam beckoned, he could have used his influence to get me out of it. I'm sure he pulled strings to keep me off the front line; I was a chef at the officer's club in Saigon most of my tour. But I saw firsthand what armed conflict does to men, and any taste I might have had for violence evaporated in the fog of war. I can't even watch violence on television these days after what I saw in 'Nam. That's where I met Greg Salieri, who also had a profound influence on my life. You know what they say about converts having stronger faith than those merely born into it? When I got back to the states, I was into all the causes --- feminism, the environment, the civil rights movement. The only time I've ever been arrested was demonstrating to free Hurricane Carter."

"Congratulations. I'm sure they'll nominate you for *Honorary Soul Brother #1* at the next NAACP meeting."

I let him drone on about helping found Sacred Cross with Salieri. How it had helped kids rise up from their disadvantaged lives and live the American dream, like Italian immigrants had some generations prior. Almost with lawyerly precision, he was building a case for his good works outweighing the occasional misdeed he'd been forced to commit. I was waiting for him to explain how Paul Geist and Paige White became unwitting casualties of this Holy War. When he paused to enjoy his Chianti, I couldn't resist pointing out the hypocrisy.

"Given your background, I can see how *you* might believe what you're saying. But how does patron saint Salieri sleep at night, knowing it's all financed by blood money?"

The blue eyes flashed a hint of anger that receded as quickly as it had come. "I'm sure the good father sleeps like a baby with a clear conscience, thank you. I believe you'll understand as well if you'll allow me to finish my story." His politesse silenced me for the moment.

"Back in the seventies, my father allowed his illegal activities to be taken over by others. Good businessman that he was, he foresaw stricter environmental regulations coming. Of course knowing him, he probably greased a few state politicians to help move the legislation along. But it was money spent for a good cause. Now we're the largest asbestos removal company in the state. We manage toxic waste. We have multi-million dollar contracts with the local and federal governments. And for almost thirty years, our activities have been completely legitimate."

"And if some competitor decides to challenge you? Do they become part of that toxic waste?"

"There are dozens of small companies that do what we do. If they're well run, we might try to buy them out, just like any conglomerate would. Some national company undercuts our price, we throw loss leaders, get leaner, and outlast them."

"And if that fails, there's always the Pine Barrens Special."

"No. Look, I won't lie, there have been times when rumors about what happens to those who cross us get whispered, but we never act on them. Usually, the folklore of what the mighty Gazza family was like in the fifties scares off interlopers. But honestly, our tactics are what any American business employs to expand its reach. I've become fabulously wealthy as a result to the point where I don't even draw a salary anymore. Our company is involved in charities throughout the state. As hard as it may be for a former fed like you to accept, we're the good guys now."

"You're right. It *is* hard for me to accept. Funny, Bill Gates never sent two muscle heads in dark suits to kidnap me for a luncheon date, however entertaining the host's delusional ravings are."

It would have been interesting to see what his reaction to that would have been in had a waiter not arrived at that very moment, bearing steaming plates of food. As they were set before us, Gazza nodded his approval with the presentation and dismissed the man wordlessly.

"I must insist you try the Chianti. The perfect complement to this meal," he said, pouring a healthy measure into my wine glass. It seemed a perfect metaphor for our discussion. Gazza would politely ask me to do his bidding several times, but if I continued to refuse, he'd force the issue.

"All right, if you insist. After all, from the minute I got into that car, it seems I've had no choice about anything."

"Mr. King, Mr. King. May I call you Riley?"

"Why not?" Why bother to protest?

"Good. What I've been trying to tell you today is that we're on the same side. I can't be much plainer. The only thing that troubles me and the reason I summoned you here was that I'm told that you're making inquiries into my private affairs and I'm afraid that's where I have to draw the line. There are very legitimate reasons for this, but unfortunately I'm not in a position to reveal them to you. But I want you to know the truth about the item you're investigating in the hopes that you'll accept it and move on."

"Let me get this straight. You want me to trust you that your story about Paul Geist is gospel. Boy, if I lived by that philosophy, I'd be a hell of a detective, wouldn't I?"

I was amazed at the man's impulse control. As tempted as he might have been to overturn his plate over my head, he delicately speared a small shrimp from the seafood pasta dish he'd ordered for us both, savoring the experience before responding.

"The truth is the truth, no matter how it's arrived at. The hard way or the easy way. Here's the easy way. For the next ten minutes, you can ask me anything you like on the narrow subject of this man and his little dirty book. I promise to tell you the absolute truth as long as it doesn't intrude into my other affairs. After that, I will consider the matter closed. As I've told you, I'm not a violent man. But if you can't leave it alone and your inquiries compromise my privacy, well….."

He shrugged, letting the "well" hang as the most ominous threat I'd ever heard.

"Your privacy, huh? Here, take my cell phone. Call someone who cares."

Ignoring my remark, he took another bite of the pungent seafood dish, followed by another sip of Chianti. "Don't let your *Zuppe del Mare Malavista* get cold, Riley. I do have other business today so if you want to ask me questions, I'd advise that we begin soon."

"Why don't you just give me your version of what happened with Geist and we can both attend to our other business."

"That's all I ever wanted. In a nutshell, Father Salieri approached me last spring. He was troubled by this book that one of his teachers had written, very afraid that it would bring shame on the school. He wasn't asking me to do anything about it necessarily; he was just seeking my counsel.

"He gave me the *Cliff Notes* version of the manuscript as much as a priest can, given its nature. That's when I suggested that we purchase the rights to the book, and essentially squelch it. With me so far?"

The story gibed with what Salieri had told me, so I merely said, "Go on."

"So that's what we did. I got one of my associates to pose as an editor. We trumped up a story about how Father Salieri through his publishing contacts had recommended we take a look at his book. He was only too happy to provide a manuscript, and after a reasonable interval, we contacted him again and told him of our interest. *We thought we were making him an offer he couldn't refuse.*"

He chuckled at his own Brando as Don Corleone impression.

"But to our surprise, he did. My man spent all sorts of time, sweetening the deal, promising the moon, but none of it worked.

"So I took the easy way out. We took the teacher for a ride and not to a nice restaurant in the middle of the day, but to an old warehouse we were working on in Perth Amboy. Blindfolded in the middle of the night. I played the capo role to the hilt. I told him that we'd gotten wind of his work and that we were prepared to be gentlemen and offer him a fair price to forget that it ever existed. Otherwise, he'd never return to his bed that night."

"Classy. Clearly the work of a *reformed* gangster."

"Amateur theatrics. I told you earlier we weren't averse at times to using our unsavory reputation to scare people. We figured after logic and friendly persuasion failed, we'd scare him. He signed over a document, which I'm prepared to show you, stating that Andolini publishing, which of course doesn't exist, owned all rights to his book in exchange for a substantial sum. Cash, untraceable. We scoured his house for extra copies, paper or electronic, wiped his computer's hard drive and so on. We told him if the book ever came to light, he'd be sleeping with the fishes. Laid it on a bit thick, but he bought it hook, line and sinker."

Back to the seafood, pleased with his cinematic and Piscean references. He shoved a densely worded page my way, which I skimmed down to the signature line, which was signed 'Paul Geist'.

"Anything else you need to know, Riley?"

"Where is Paige White's name on this contract?"

"Who?"

"Paige White. His agent. The one who was killed?"

"Oh yes, the one you're accused of killing. We weren't even aware of her until we heard she'd been murdered. We knew he had an agent, but his attitude was that she'd never done anything for him in the past so why should she be paid? She could hardly be expected to share his, well, how else can I say it, *hush money.*"

My turn to appear blasé. I finally tasted the wine, which lived up to its hype. "And of course you didn't know she had a copy of the manuscript?"

For the first time, he appeared mildly surprised. "She had a copy of the manuscript?" He turned over this newfound fact in his mind for a moment. "And do you know where it is now?"

"I assume the guys you sent 'to make her an offer she can't refuse' disposed of it. Don't tell me they're withholding it to blackmail you?"

"I'm a patient man, King, but this little game you seem to favor --- tossing out unfounded accusations --- has to stop. I never sent anyone to harm this Paige White. I had no idea that we hadn't destroyed every trace of that manuscript. We would have attempted to resolve it legally, even if she had demanded a commission. We do own the rights, as you can see."

I was getting to him now. On one hand, anger might cause him to let something slip that his otherwise cool demeanor might conceal. He'd already admitted he knew that Geist had an agent, and I couldn't be sure that the "she" was uttered post facto or the he had known about Paige all along. That could explain how quickly he'd dealt with her.

The downside of riling him was that he might decide that he was wasting his time talking with me, and bring in no-neck to close the deal.

But as quickly as his annoyance surfaced, he went back to his meal as if nothing had happened. After a minute's uneasy silence, he looked up at me. "Let me share a little guilty secret with you, King. I kept a copy of the manuscript and read it before I tossed it into my fireplace. I'll be honest with you. If it was merely the most disgusting filth I've ever read, I wouldn't have a major problem with it. Trash like that gets published all the time, and nobody takes it seriously. But I have to admit, this was really well written and therefore dangerous. Reminded me of Strelnikov, you know that Russian genius who was famous for fifteen minutes in the seventies. Can't tell you how many times I got laid quoting some of his juicier passages."

Somehow in my jock days, I'd missed this guy Strelnikov that everyone was comparing *Julia and James* to.

"I thought you'd become a liberal way back when. Freedom of expression, first amendment rights?"

160

"Pornography, in the hands of adults," he shrugged. "I say live and let live. I told you my dad ran hookers once upon a time. I'm no prude. But the content is so thinly veiled and reads so realistically that most people will believe it's true, which in turn might bring down a school I've devoted my life and fortune to? No, I cannot allow that to stand."

"And you'd be willing to kill to prevent that."

His blue eyes narrowed to slits. "King, you never served in the military, right?"

This seemed a complete non sequitur, but Gazza was a man of many parables. "College deferment. I played basketball. By the time I graduated, the shooting wars were over."

"What if you hadn't had that deferment and the war was still going strong? What would you have done? Gone to Canada? Or shipped out to basic training?"

"I'm not sure. I'm glad I never had to make the choice."

"Precisely. That's how I feel about that book. Would I have killed to prevent it from being published? I'm grateful it never reached that point. I've never ordered a man killed. Never. If you want to say that the blood on a father's hands passes to his son, that's your prerogative. But I've always found another way to accomplish my goals. And I've learned to accept defeat once in a while. I don't make a habit of it, but sometimes, a strategic retreat is the wisest course." He raised his eyebrows and winked. "I don't advertise that fact though. I suppose it's stupid of me to tell you this, given what I'm asking you to do voluntarily."

161

"Don't worry. I'm not sure I believe you anyway."

To this, he responded with a hearty laugh. "Oh sweet Jesus, image is everything, Agassi had it right." He downed the remainder of his glass and poured himself another, but only after topping mine off first. Always the considerate host.

He said, "I don't suppose you and I could ever be friends, Riley, but damn it, that's a shame. I think we'd enjoy each other's company. I really do."

I wouldn't give him the satisfaction of telling him so but I had to admit, for a Mafia chieftain, he was a pretty engaging fellow.

"So, that's it, Mr. King. I paid the little man off, he disappeared with the money and not a word was said until last week when I was told you'd been hired to look into his disappearance."

"From Salieri, of course."

"Ummm."

"And why exactly did you wait until three days later to put the fear of God into me?"

"We've tried all along to handle this matter like gentlemen once we were aware of your interest. The good father spoke to you last night. He wasn't convinced you believed him. So I hoped that hearing the story directly from me might convince you."

I took another sip of Chianti but I hadn't touched the meal. I was not about to let him believe that kidnapping can be a civilized experience.

"So bottom line, Tony. What's the deal you're offering me now? I back off and you let me live?"

"You present me with a dilemma. I can't have someone snooping into my affairs. I wish I could be completely open with you as to why; you'll just have to trust that my reasons aren't nefarious."

He leaned forward and spoke even more quietly. "We're on the same side. Don't be a fool, King. Play ball with me. You know, I have a little influence with the county cops. I don't think you killed that girl. I can help make this go away. But I can also make it worse for you. Your choice. Work with me, man."

I was tempted to make a deal with the devil. If I could trust him, he was offering me a clean way out. But wiseass that I am, I had to make a statement.

I stood up, pushed my chair aside and said, "Check, please."

Gazza shook his head sadly but offered no resistance as I walked out.

Twenty six

I had no ride waiting for me outside, other than the free taxi service Gazza had generously provided with no-neck and friend. Even though hoods simpatico to Gazza populated the joint, I doubted that he'd sanction any violence in front of the paying customers. I didn't need George Armstrong Custer to tell me my best exit strategy was to call a cab and hustle into it before Gazza's muscle could act. I'd worry about the gun and laptop in the back of the limo later.

I was forced into a sudden change of plans. At the bar, cradling what appeared to be a club soda with lime was none other than Flint McCullough. Gazza's boast of influence with the county's law enforcement officials was no idle claim. Dirty cop or no, it gave me an opening.

"Detective, fancy meeting you here. Casual luncheon by the water or here on business?"

"And I might ask how it came to be that you're just coming out of a reputed mobster's private room," he said, his voice a harsh rasp.

I shook off the solicitous barkeep. "I thought you guys were keeping an eye on me. You didn't notice a couple of thugs abducting me to bring me here?"

"I just happened to be driving by your place and noticed you getting into a big black car. Thought you might be headed somewhere exotic, like the Lakewood airfield and then to parts unknown. Didn't expect a meeting with the boss."

"As I said, I was brought here against my will."

"Funny, when you got into that car, I didn't see any signs of a struggle. Sure makes connecting the dots easier for me, when a murder suspect meets with a known underworld figure. In for a final payment, King? What's the going rate these days?"

"The way you connect dots, you must've been left back in second grade. So now you think Tony Gazza hired me to kill Paige? The first time I laid eyes on the man was a half hour ago."

"Really? These things are done through intermediaries. I'd think even a former fed would know that. Actually, I am a little surprised meeting with him in person today."

"Ah, glad to see the county only employs the best and the brightest. Riddle me this, Batman. You know I was aware that you guys were watching my every move. Do you really think I'd be stupid enough to meet with Gazza at his place in broad daylight? And even if your opinion of *me* is that low, you think Gazza's that much of an idiot?"

His bland expression conceded my point.

I said, "Look, detective. It might be good for both our interests to share some information. I assume your car is outside. Why don't we take a ride?"

Figuring he had nothing to lose, he extended his palm toward the door. The only complication was my gym bag, still in the back of the Caddy, where my gun would improve the odds if No-neck Inc. followed us. The sun was breaking the clouds as I reached the parking lot where Gazza's henchmen were leaning against the side of the car, striking the exact pose they had at my house.

"I'm sure that you two know Detective McCullough of the Ocean County Police. Would you mind fetching my bag from the back seat? After that, I won't trouble you anymore."

"Mr. Gazza said that we were to take you back to where we picked you up." No-neck's pal still did all the talking. I'd never heard the squat man speak, even when directly addressed. Although his face suggested Mediterranean roots, he bore more than a passing resemblance to Harold Sakata's *Odd-Job*, right down to the bulging suit he'd outgrown in junior high. I wasn't kidding myself that any of the two-fifty he packed onto that 5-9 frame wasn't muscle.

"That was very considerate of him. Be sure to thank him for me but I'm afraid this nice police officer has asked I come with him. I'm sure you guys are familiar with that type of request."

I wasn't sure why I was wasting my wit on a couple of goons who wouldn't appreciate it, but it might subliminally suggest to Flint that I wasn't part of Gazza's posse. No-neck's consort was uncertain whether to follow his boss's direct order or yield to the situation. While he lingered, I walked over to the car, opened the back door and pulled out my bag. I didn't figure the goons would act out in front of a cop, but I wasn't going to wait around any longer than I needed to. Paralyzed by indecision, they watched helplessly as I piled into McCullough's gray Chevy.

"Anything in that bag I should be worried about?" he asked.

"Laptop and a .38. Registered, concealed carry permit."

"Hmmn. Your ride, King. Where to?" His demeanor wasn't exactly radiating the warm and fuzzies.

I didn't want to talk to him anyplace where he could assert his authority. I had enough of that at Gazza's restaurant. I needed a neutral site. "There's a taco joint on 37 about a mile up on the right. I doubt anybody from your force goes there. So you won't be embarrassed being seen with me."

"Not into that Mexican dung they serve there. Gives me agita. But if they have coffee, it's as good a place as any."

Enduring withering looks from the counter help for only ordering coffee, Flint and I found a quiet table at the fast food joint and settled in. Someone had used a greasy rag to clean the Formica, leaving a nasty smear that killed any appetite I may have had. McCullough was probably used to eating on the run so the e-coli wouldn't faze him much. His narrow eyes darted about the room like any observant cop scoping out potential trouble, and finding none, he drew his gaze toward me.

"So King, what have you got to say?"

Any lawyer will tell you that cooperating with the law is a dangerous game if you bear any culpability: look

---

what happened to old Martha Stewart when she talked to the feds without her attorney present. Having been on the other side for so long, I know that we tend to promise anything as long as we don't have to commit it to writing or transcription. Any offer of immunity for cooperation had better be witnessed and documented; otherwise a cop can deny ever making it.

I've been burned on the other side as well. A potential witness can recant testimony, either because the suspect intimidates them or they just have a change of heart. Informal conversations are dangerous for both sides. But both sides keep having them for obvious reasons. Rather than piece a case together from the outset, a snitch can help an investigator skip a number of steps in drawing a conclusion. It's far easier to reverse engineer a scenario when you already know the ending, as opposed to flying blind. From the semi-culpable suspect's side, small fish do get tossed back occasionally in if they lead to bigger ones.

My little trip to Malavista convinced me that Gazza had the power to snuff out my life on a whim, and I'd be kidding myself to think that even if the bureau devoted their entire energy toward busting him, he wouldn't get me first. From the grave, I could leave a trail of evidence that would eventually lead to the man. That would be revenge served cold indeed, and keeping my body temperature as close to 98.6 as possible was a priority.

So against all advice I'd give to others, I spelled things out to McCullough--- right from the beginning. I didn't tell him that I still had copies of the manuscript stashed with Stone. Other than that omission, I let it all hang out --- even the unflattering parts regarding my sexual prowess. I figured that if Flint was dirty, by swearing that I'd bow out and let the police handle it, he'd clue Gazza in that I no longer posed a threat. And if McCullough was just an honest cop, having him as an ally would be useful.

"Interesting, King," he said, when I finished. "So you think that Tony Gazza killed this writer to squelch his book and knocked off the agent when he thought she had a copy of the manuscript. So why are you still alive and talking to me now?"

"I told you, he threatened me just now. Plus, he thinks he has me framed for the murder. He's letting you take care of me. Keeps his hands clean."

"So far, what you've given me is a list a suppositions, suspicions and nothing I can use. Of course, you've gone out of your way to maintain your innocence in all of this."

"Detective, I'm giving you a roadmap. You've got a murder and a disappearance --- which I'll bet dollars to doughnuts, is another murder. Who else had motive for these two?"

He ran his long fingers across his brow. "That's *if* the two are related. And we have no proof that this guy Guest or whatever his name is, is dead. I can make an equally strong case that the guy took Gazza's money and split, just like he said. And that you had a spat with Paige White and killed her."

169

Point taken. *I* knew I hadn't killed Paige, but Flint's scenario played just as well as mine to an objective audience.

"I don't know what more I can say," I said. "By the way, did your guys check the timestamp on the security camera? Compare when I got there versus time of death."

He sighed deeply. "The system was a few years old, and the disc was conveniently missing. Something an old fed would think of. I may come off as a hardass to you, King but I can't totally discount what you've told me. So let me give you a little nugget in return. I've been trying to nail Tony Gazza for years. When I was growing up, my dad --- who was a cop too --- told me stories about Tony's dad. But this guy's got someone so high up in county law enforcement in his pocket that anytime I get within a mile of him, I get backed off. I'm told to focus on something else. Another more pressing case surfaces, or maybe I just get reassigned at random. I get stonewalled at headquarters. Believe me, I'd like nothing better than to put this guy away for good."

The corners of his mouth turned in a disdainful smirk. "Frigging Dapper Don shit. I've done this dance before with old Tony and all you've done just now is weave a little tale that it's my job to prove. That's the hard part."

He took a sip of the rancid coffee that'd been left over from the lunch hour and said, "By the way, don't think that because we've had this little chat that you're still not on the hook."

He had to bust balls until the end; it was in his DNA. "Thanks for caring. Look, just so you know, I made a call and maybe the feds will help. They could go through Paige's office. Maybe one of Gazza's guys was careless and they can come up with trace evidence at the break-ins."

"Right. I didn't tell you about the time I thought I had an extortion case going against Gazza and the feds big-footed me off that one, did I? No offense, but your boys in Virginia are too busy chasing terrorists and covering their asses as to why they didn't get them before 9/11 to help on a small fish like Tony Gazza."

I was tired of butting my head into a brick wall. "Okay. I tried. Can you drop me off in Bayville?"

Twenty seven

The house was strangely quiet without Bosco greeting me at the door --- everything had changed and it wasn't just the absence of my faithful companion. It no longer seemed like a sanctuary where I could feel safe and comfortable. The house was cold and uninviting. Even my bedroom felt like it belonged to someone else. I wondered how long it would be this way. Would it pass as soon as my current troubles were over? Or would I never be able to seek refuge in this place again, memories of its violation lingering like the aftermath of a fire?

Gazza knew where I lived. Flint still had me in his sights.

My message machine was blinking. Logan's voice. "Call me on my cell."

No elaboration. I called.

"Remember one down, runaway?" he asked, as soon as he knew it was me.

"Yes."

"Do it in five minutes. Here."

He reeled off a ten-digit number.

One down, runaway was our code when we needed to have a private conversation on non-scrambled phone lines. *Runaway* meant to find a clean phone, and *one down* meant that the number he gave me was one digit higher than the one he wanted me to call. Thus, area code 784 becomes 673, and so forth.

The restaurant down the street still had a rare pay phone, so I gathered up a roll of quarters and lit out on foot. He picked up on the second ring.

"King?"

"Why all the cloak and dagger, Dan?"

"Are you sure this line is safe?"

"Reasonably. No reason for anyone to tap it. I'm down the street, at Windows."

"Nice place. Someday, when this is over, you'll buy me a Porterhouse there."

"What's up?"

"Not in the mood for chit chat, I see."

"I can chit chat with you from home. What's going on?"

"Hey, if you're having a bad day, you don't need to take it out on your friends. I'm at a pay phone, boyo. Just trying to help out."

I told Logan about Gazza.

"Okay, pal, that's what we need to talk about," he said when I was finished. "I've been doing a little digging on your behalf. Here's the long and the short of it. I've been told in no uncertain terms that you're to leave Anthony Gazza alone. That there is no way that he had anything to do with the death of your girlfriend. He's clear on the teacher as well. And if you want any kind of support from your ex-employer, you are to cease and desist any contact with Gazza. Message delivered."

"From whom?"

"Can't say. Look, I have my neck stuck out on this one. That's why the charade with the phones. I went around official channels here. The bureau will do everything it can to help clear you, but off the books. In exchange, you back off Gazza."

"Why?"

"Don't bite the hand that feeds you. You know me, I wouldn't ask you to look the other way if the man was guilty. But whatever Gazza has or hasn't done, he hasn't done anything in regards to what you're looking into. Leave him alone and he'll leave you alone."

Dan Logan had always been a better company man than I. He might raise a murmur in protest at a direct order he didn't like, but he knew when to back down. I didn't and that's why I'm no longer a fed.

"Dan, how can you promise that? The guy threatened that if I didn't stay out of his affairs he'd regretfully end my time on the planet. He said it with class, I'll give him that. But does that sound like an innocent man to you?"

"I have it on the best authority that he had nothing to do with Paige White's death. And that he's telling you the truth about the writer."

"And your source is someone who you can guarantee Gazza doesn't have his tentacles around?"

"Yes. I have no doubt. And Gazza told you himself that if you back off, he'd leave you alone. Why can't you just accept that?"

"Maybe because I promised myself that I'd do everything I could to find out the truth about a woman I was responsible for."

"Riles, we've known each other a long time. You need to trust me on this. The locals are on the verge of arresting you. We might be able to hold them off for now but if you keep going after Gazza, well, I'm afraid we can only protect you so far."

"Logan, why is this mobster more important than an honest taxpayer who used to work for the government?"

"That's not what's going on here. All right, since you're being so stubborn, I'll kick it upstairs one more time and see if they'll allow me to fill you in on the details. Maybe I can convince them to trust you since you were once one of them. Give me some time. Promise you won't do anything until you hear back from me. Maybe when you get the whole story, you'll understand."

I could wait a short time. Hell, it might even be what I needed to start thinking clearly again without emotion clouding the issue. I could take Bosco and get lost somewhere down at Cape May, and sort things out without looking over my shoulder every time the wind blew a twig behind me.

"All right, Dan, you got it. I'll disappear until Wednesday afternoon. Call me on my cell then."

"You got it. Go get lost at Bali Hai or your own special island. I'll do what I can for you. Rossano Brazzi, signing out."

175

Musical comedy references, at a time like this? Between Stone with his classic rock and Logan with Broadway, I wonder if either of them had ever constructed a sentence that wasn't inspired by their hobby.

As soon as I hung up the phone, paranoia began seeping in. Any lead-time at all would give Gazza time to find and kill me. Was Logan's source at the FBI in Gazza's pocket, waiting definitive word if Riley King was a problem that wasn't going to go away on its own? Was I being stupid to give a message of surrender to bring back to Gazza?

It was three o'clock now; pleasantly cool, so maybe a nice slow run would be the ticket. Might work off some stress.

My cell phone, laptop and gun were still in the gym bag. I'd take the gun and phone on the run, and hide the SD card somewhere in the house, just in case. As I unzipped the bag, two unanswered messages beeped on the cell. They were both from Stone.

"Riles, get here as soon as you can. I need to talk to you."

He sounded awful. The timestamp said two twenty.

"Riley, where are you, man? I'm home. I..." Quarter to three.

I'd never heard him sound so morose. I stuffed the computer, gun and phone back in the bag, locked the house, and pointed the Audi toward Mantoloking. While driving, I called WJOK and got Stone's boss, Ted McCarver. He told me that Rick had seemed fine when he left after his show.

Nothing had happened on the air to upset him and as far as he knew, everything was kosher.

I called Rick's beach house and got no answer. I tried his cell.

Voice mail.

What the hell was going on? I made record time to his place. His Mustang was parked in the crushed stone driveway but the front entry to the house was wide open, only the flimsy screen door standing guard between intruders and the home's contents. And it didn't have a lock. Pretty careless of him considering my warnings.

"Rick?"

No reply.

"Rick. Bosco?"

Nothing. My best friend and my dog were missing. And if anything had happened to them, I wouldn't be able to live with myself.

Twenty eight

I carried the portable phone around the house while on hold, looking for any clue that might help me find Stone. Knowing Rick, he would have tried to leave something behind, something only I would notice. But there was no sign of any struggle, nothing out of place. The only thing that seemed askew in his garage was his golf bag, tossed carelessly on the floor near a lally column. He'd always been very fastidious about cleaning and storing his clubs.

His driver was missing. Rick had recently switched to a Titleist, a pricey little item that had set him back a grand. The large titanium head was the maximum size allowed by the USGA, and would make a formidable weapon against anything short of a gun. The head cover lay on the floor next to the bag, suggesting that it had been removed and discarded in haste. Not like Rick at all.

The only landscaping in the back was ornamental grass, spouting from the dunes at random intervals. The area in front of the house was covered with the orange gravel that Stone had refreshed after the storm. It was pretty hard to distinguish footprints amongst the small pebbles, and again, there was no indication of anything unusual.

On the ocean side, paw prints, which might have been Bosco's, left a trail up the nearest dune toward the water. Had Stone's assailants come by boat? And if they had taken the dog, why were the tracks so regular? Bosco would have screeched down on all fours if he were being dragged somewhere he didn't want to go. I learned this the hard way whenever I mention the word "vet" in his presence.

I climbed the dune, hoping that the firmer sand near the breakers would yield better evidence. I spotted them: two familiar figures that made me dizzy with relief.

"Stone. You bastard. You had me worried sick with your calls."

He didn't look up, although Bosco's tail began to whisk away the sand beneath him as he rose and rushed to greet me. Stone had carried out a bucket of range balls and was systematically thumping them into the Atlantic, swinging harder than I'd ever seen him do on the links.

"Richard. What's going on?"

He turned to face me, his eyes red. "It's Lisa. She's gone."

"Gone. As in kidnapped?"

"No. She left a note." He placed another long tee in the sand and sent another blast to a watery finale.

"Hey, don't let any of your neighbors see you doing that. They'll call the EPA and put you up on pollution charges." My attempt at distraction drew no reaction.

I tried again. "I don't know about you, but I need a drink. And it's near Bosco's dinnertime. What do you say we pack it in?"

He took another mighty swing, then flung the driver into the sea. Leaving the bucket and remaining balls behind, he trudged toward the house. Bosco followed him for a

179

moment, then realized I wasn't coming, so he stopped halfway between us, casting furtive looks back and forth.

"Back to the house, pal." I gestured toward it. "I'll be along."

Throwing an expensive golf club into the ocean wasn't going to bring Lisa Tillman back. I waited a minute until a large wave swept the driver back ashore, retrieved it and went back in.

Rick was sitting in his kitchen. He'd already poured two neat scotches, and was making great headway on his while glaring at mine across the table.

"Thought you might be needing this sometime," I said, holding up the club.

"Hooking everything with the frigging piece of shit anyway."

"As hard as you were swinging out there, I'm surprised you were hitting it at all. Did the dog eat yet?"

"No. I've had other things on my mind."

"Sure you have. Me, too." I poured some kibble into Bosco's dish and he noisily wolfed every morsel down before I got back to my chair. "So… what happened?"

"Nothing. That's just it. Nothing happened." He pulled his fingers down across his eyes. "No argument. No ultimatum. Just a note and she's gone."

"What did the note say?"

"Not much, just that she decided to leave. She said she'd been thinking about it for a while now. She thought it was best for both of us to end it clean. Same bullshit lines people have used on each other since the beginning of time."

"And you didn't see this coming?"

He poured himself another scotch. I shook him off when he tried to top off my glass.

"Go easy on that, my friend," I said. "We've got other problems coming and you need a clear head. But talk to me about Lisa. This came out of the blue?"

"Pretty much. I mean, she got in late last night. Didn't want to make love. Said she was too tired. I tried again this morning but she wouldn't wake up."

I tried an appeal to his rational side. "So, you never talked about the future, long term? With this new job offer, I thought you guys might have talked about where you two were headed."

"We never got into it too deeply. We talked about it a little, but kind of left it hanging. I figured she'd be back east a couple weekends a month. With the summer coming, I'd go out there for a few days on vacation. She was realistic about the show. She said that the success rate on new shows is not good, so it'd be foolish to make permanent decisions on things when she could be cancelled after thirteen weeks."

"Maybe the network gave her a longer commitment this weekend?"

"Whatever. I would have thought she'd have told me that. Even if it was just in her note. Come on, Riles. I know you're trying to go easy on me but we've both been around the block a few times. Shit like this happens, there's usually another man involved."

I thought of the young producer and the kiss they'd exchanged when he came to pick her up.

181

I said, "Maybe. So what are you going to do?"

"She said she'd send for her things, although it seems she took most of her stuff with her." He put his head in his hands. "God, it hurts. I thought she was *the one*. Everything was so perfect. She loved sports as much as I do. She was smart. Great looking."

Lisa had a rare talent for agreeing with everybody without appearing to pander. You'd say the earth was flat and she'd rattle off all the brilliant minds that believed that prior to Copernicus. Never ridiculing even your most outrageous your beliefs, she could make you believe she was sympathetic. A dazzling smile and legs like Cindy Crawford's will do that for you. Of course, if you analyzed what this sexy TV star actually had said, you would understand how skillfully she was playing you. Since her charms were off-limits to me, I was able to make this observation objectively without getting caught up in her charisma. I could have relayed my fears to Rick, but I learned long ago that you don't knock your best friend's girl unless you want to lose them both.

"You going to try to talk to her?" I said.

"I have to. I need more than just a half page note to let this go. And if I find the guy, I'll bash his frigging skull with that club." His anger was rising to the surface, replacing his grief.

"No, you won't. *If* there is another man, it ain't his fault. It takes two, buddy, I don't have to tell you that. This one's on her. I never said anything when you guys were together but I always thought that Lisa was only showing us what she wanted to."

"Women have secrets. Some more than others." He patted his hair back over his forehead. "Hey, I questioned this from day one. I'm going on forty-nine. She's twenty-eight. She's on TV and she's a knockout. I'm no fool, I know I'm starting to sag a bit. I make respectable bread but I'm not really rich. I kept thinking, why me? Why does this gorgeous creature think I'm something special? In the end, I guess maybe she didn't."

I eased into what I had always feared was the real reason she hung with Stone. "Ricky, she loved sports and God knows you're a walking encyclopedia. You can name my teammates at Georgetown better than I can. You know the first hitter Tom Seaver struck out. A girl who wanted a career in sports couldn't have had a better soul-mate. And a better teacher."

"So you're saying she was using me to further her education? Tuition was sleeping with me?"

"That's a tough way to put it but if that was the case, that's her bad, not yours. Who knows what she was thinking all along. Maybe she doesn't either. Look, maybe you gave your heart to someone who didn't deserve it. I know it's hard man, but you should just let her walk. If she's the person you thought you fell in love with, she'll be in contact. If not, the hell with her. You're well rid of her."

I was dispensing good advice. Advice of course, I would never take if the roles were reversed. My belief was that Lisa Tillman had shown her true colors by blowing

Stone off for a TV producer who could help her career more. Rick taught her everything he knew and therefore had exhausted his usefulness. If she *were* such a cold-blooded manipulator, there'd be a string of broken hearts on her way up the ladder. The only consolation to those left in her wake was that someday when her tits started to sag, her smile faded and a new and improved model came along, she'd encounter those same people on the way down and they'd exact their revenge. In fifteen years, she might be the subject of derision; behind-the-back snickers speculating on how much plastic surgery it had taken to keep the old girl tight. Her facile mind might be relegated to radio where the wrinkles don't show. She'd be back at Rick's level, but by then he'd be so over her that it wouldn't matter to him.

I was being hard on her to make Rick feel better, but there were other explanations. People *do* fall out of love, or fall out of infatuation. We're a consumerist nation --- always seeking a bigger house, a better job, a nicer car. We're never completely satisfied where we are in life; if we were, there would be no dreams, nothing to strive for.

In just about every relationship I've ended, I've learned that my partner's shortcomings are rarely the problem. You may tire of the same old face, however attractive you initially thought it was. The same body, whatever heights of pleasure you attain with it. There's always something different and intriguing out there. But after a time, they all become old and comfortable and the wandering spirit seeks new conquests. The search for perfection is never ending and never attainable. One can only find modest upgrades in some areas, balanced by trade-offs in others. A great body is countermanded by a shallow mind. A lively intellect might be emotionally insensitive. A selfless humanitarian may be physically unattractive. The whole package is never there and even if it was, you'd feel hopelessly inadequate trying to live up to that standard. A twenty eight year old rarely is self aware enough to grasp the concept.

At the end of the day, you compromise --- settling for a partner that won't make every night a freshly minted page from the Kama Sutra but will be steadfast when you need them. Someone who will see you at your worst --- fuming and farting and vomiting and cursing--- and still love you. Someone you'll want to take care of when they need to take more than give. Someone you respect too much to dishonor by seeking transitory gratification elsewhere. *Real* satisfaction comes from within yourself and not from someone else's appraisal of the trophy mate you've snagged.

Lisa Tillman would undoubtedly find someone handsomer than Rick, someone wealthier, someone smarter, but never someone better. She'd realize that someday. But I wasn't about to tell my friend to wait around for that day to come.

I felt a twinge of guilt at welcoming this crisis in Stone's life, because for a few minutes, it took my mind off my own problems. As awful as he felt now, he'd have felt a whole lot worse if he still had Lisa in his life but Gazza had him in his grasp. Though in his present state, he'd probably sign on for that.

185

I just feel like such a fool," he said. "I was thinking about marrying this woman. I was thinking that I might quit WJOK and move out west with her, see if I could find a job out there. I was willing to turn my whole life upside down for her and what I get in return is a note scribbled on loose leaf."

"But see, you've already found your place in the world. I imagine you'd be satisfied doing mid-days at your station for the next twenty years. You've found something you like and you're sticking with it. She's not there yet. She wants to be Julia Roberts or Meredith Vieira or something. You've accepted that you're never going to be Howard Cosell. But Lisa wants to be a star. I don't know that you can have a normal life, a family, at least not on the way up in the business you've chosen. Who knows, when she's fifty herself Lisa may look back and regret that she never settled down with you."

We sat in silence for a moment as we both reflected on the clichés for what might have been. I broke the silence, trying to console him but knowing that the sting wouldn't go away any time soon, no matter what I said. "I'm sorry it worked out this way, but for now, you've got to let go."

"Easier said than done."

"I hear you. But you're telling me you're not a kid anymore. If you want to start a family, it seems that Lisa was holding you back from finding someone who'll share that life willingly with you. And no offense pal, your chances are better at finding that sooner than later. Before the rest of your hair falls out."

"Thanks."

"Kidding. Hey, Kojak did okay with a shaved pate, no reason you can't too."

"Screw you."

Ah, my old friend Stone was taking his first baby steps on the road back.

Twenty nine

It wasn't my idea. Stone, who at the time was lubricated in the extreme, courtesy of a potent dose of Scotland's biggest export, had broached the subject. Deep in his cups over Lisa, it had dawned on him that much like his travails had taken me away from my own burden for a time, my troubles might put his into perspective.

After listening to my story of the day's events, he tersely said, "I don't see where you have any choice. You've got to kill the bastard before he kills you."

Stone had laid out all the reasons why I should assassinate Tony Gazza. I'd be doing the world a favor, saving many lives in addition to my own. I was uniquely qualified for the job: as a former fed, I knew how to avoid detection. I could create a rock solid alibi and leave no evidence. Set it up like a typical gangland slaying that no righteous cop would waste much time investigating.

He had set up a monitor in the great room of his house that cycled through the perimeter cameras every few seconds, and my eyes were nervously flitting back and forth from my distressed pal to the flickering screen. Did I want to live the rest of my life like that? Stone asked.

Everything my inebriated friend said made sense if I accepted the worldview of *get them before they get you*. It was out of character for him to even advocate what he was suggesting, and as such, it underlined how seriously he was taking the threat. But I still was hesitant to make that leap. Isn't that what separates the good guys from the bad guys?

"I'm done," Stone said after making his case, rising unsteadily for bed. "Think about it. I'm behind you whatever you decide. You know that."

Bosco stirred from his sleep at the movement and started after Rick, turning to me at the threshold of the bedroom. I nodded. *Go on, pal, he needs you more than I do tonight.* Somehow my dog read my thoughts and continued on through the open door.

I sat in the darkness alone for a while, the windows open and the peaceful sound of the surf at odds with my inner turmoil. I needed another viewpoint, one that also might provide the added advantage of beneficent mediation with my adversary. I called Salieri and he agreed to meet me at the school. Even if I had totally misread the man, it wouldn't give him time to set up an ambush. I was there in twenty minutes.

Pacing across the empty gymnasium at Sacred Cross, I vacillated on what I hoped to accomplish. This wasn't the first time I'd been alone in an empty field house at night. Back at Georgetown, I'd wheedled a key from a janitor --- I thought without Coach Thompson's knowledge. The solitude of the gym was comforting back then --- the only sounds were my labored breathing and the echo of leather hitting hardwood, steel, Plexiglas and less often than I liked, twine.

189

As I waited for Salieri, I looked around for a stray practice ball and found a rack of them in a far corner. After a couple of embarrassing bricks, I slowly found my range and started hitting jumpers, from close in at first, then working out to the high school three point line. The old form was still there.

"A shame a sweet touch like that never made it to the NBA."

The sound of his voice broke the zone.

"Thanks, but I wasn't even good enough to start in college. There was no shot at the pros."

Salieri coughed. "Ah, but so many who never excelled in school go on to have productive pro careers. A different game for money, you know. And you were a money player, Riley King."

"Yeah, well. Up until now, things have worked out okay for me."

"And now?"

I told him about my meeting with his friend. He listened, nodding and coughing every so often, his face chiseled from granite for all the reaction I could read.

When I was finished, he spoke slowly in that deep rumble of his. "So, now that you've actually met Tony, what is there to fear? It sounds like he just wanted to reassure you of what I've been telling you all along."

"There's a quiet sense of danger about him, something of the night. Like everything he says, you have to read between the lines. Call it professional instinct honed by years dealing with bad guys."

"But you don't believe you have enough to go to the police, do you?"

"No, and I doubt I ever will. He's too smart. Father, I know this will be hard for you to hear, but maybe the only way to take care of this is to act pre-emptively."

"Meaning?"

"I think you know."

"And what do you want from me? Approval from the Vatican to commit murder, based on your 'professional instinct'? That's not going to happen. Listen to yourself, man. I'm not sure why you wanted to meet with me unless you're hoping I'll talk you out of it."

I picked up a ball and hoisted a long-range jumper that hit nothing but net. "I guess I was thinking you might come up with a third way."

I heard a noise from the upper reaches of the building. Metallic. I looked up to where I thought it originated, but saw nothing in the darkness.

Salieri had a glint of amusement at my jumpiness. "Ghosts. That was the reason I was a little late meeting you. A student reported seeing someone moving in the shadows at the field house and the security guard reported back just now. He couldn't find anything. Not you working on your game, was it?"

"Tonight's the first time I've picked up a ball in months. Got here five minutes before you."

"But back to the matter at hand. It's one thing if Tony comes at you directly, then you have every right to defend yourself. But if you merely *think* that he has bad intentions toward you, morally you can't take action. You'd be culpable, in every way. What if you're wrong?"

"Somebody should have told Bush that about Iraq."

Another noise, this time a click. It sounded like a gun being cocked, at least that's what my paranoia told me. Salieri and I were sitting ducks, chatting in the middle of the court. *Is this the way you want to live the rest of your life?* Stone's words replayed in my head.

"Father, my old legs are tired. Let's go sit down, if you don't mind. Over here." I guided him to a corner sheltered by a concession stand, which would afford a sniper no clear shot. Mimicking an itch to divert Salieri's gaze, I reached under my jacket and unbuckled the holster housing my Smith and Wesson.

More coughing. He said, "Obviously you're aware that even in the confessional, if I know of a crime about to be committed, I'm obliged to report it. By the Church and by the state."

"I know the law but I didn't say I was about to commit a crime."

"Riley, I think I need to tell you something. You've been too polite to mention it, but my constant cough has to be annoying."

"I didn't want to say anything but you should have that checked."

"Thing is, I have. And although almost no one knows this, it is cancer. Terminal. They can't say whether it was the stuff I breathed in 'Nam or the smoking, but my time is short. I'll never see another basketball season."

I've been surrounded by stoic men all my life, from my dad, to my teammates, to the bureau, but I doubted that any of them could face death so matter of factly. There wasn't a hint of a tear in his eye or catch in his voice. It was just as if he was saying that it might rain tomorrow.

I almost said that I'd pray for him and I almost meant it. "I'm sorry, Father. I really am."

"Promise me this then. Let me talk to Tony. He knows I've been ill but he doesn't know I'm dying. I'm absolutely certain, no doubt at all, that he'll tell me the truth once he knows. He'd never dishonor me like that. If he tells me that he sees you as a threat that must be dealt with, I'll go straight to the police with you. I have to say that I believe he's been truthful all along, but if this old priest is wrong about a friend, I'll do what's necessary. I swear on my vows. Give me another day. Just twenty four hours."

I agreed to hold off, how could I not? Despite my shaky relationship with Catholicism, lying to a dying priest had to be a sure ticket to hell.

Thirty

T hat night I lay in my own bed, eyes wide open, contemplating what I might have to do. I had left Bosco at Stone's place, along with some more dog food and toys. I figured if I didn't make it out of this that Stone would make a good master.

Premeditated murder. That's what we're talking about here. I was planning to kill a man in cold blood and trying to justify it and I was having a hard time with it.

In addition to the morality issue, it just seemed so un-American. Didn't the cowboy heroes of my youth always allow the bad guy to draw first? Some even waited for the first shot to sail harmlessly over their head, or deflect off their metal badge before retaliating. Even when the old lawmen of the West like Matt Dillon from Gunsmoke went proactive, they offered their antagonists the opportunity to turn themselves in peaceably before reluctantly resorting to the ultimate solution.

I want to believe that it wasn't all the conceit of Hollywood scriptwriters, cosseted comfortably in their Beverly Hills cottages, immune from real world criminals. Didn't America stand for honor? Even in time of war, we didn't sanction in sneak attacks; we preferred to face our enemies front and center, exposing ourselves to the same peril.

Maybe my naive inner child was emerging to tell me that what I was planning was wrong. But my adult experiences told a different tale. How many times had I seen cops prod a suspect into defiance, their only goal being a flimsy excuse for violent retribution, ostensibly saving the public the expense and anguish of a trial? Even the most priggish of FBI agents weren't beneath a little "constructive provocation" as they put it, then chalking it up to *suicide by cop*?

Perhaps it was always thus. I'm no great authority on world affairs, but I watch the History Channel enough to know that when our country had an interest in joining a war, that folks like McKinley, Wilson, Roosevelt and even the sainted Lincoln weren't above trumping up imaginary transgressions to justify their reactions. In our eternal quest to be seen as the guys in white hats, the public is shielded from this knowledge contemporaneously. Even decades later, history texts are sanitized to rule out any possibility that little incidents like the *Lusitania*, the *Maine*, and *Pearl Harbor* and even *9/11* weren't really just excuses for acting the way we wanted to all along.

Tony Gazza wished me harm. The man had kidnapped me. Circumstantial evidence pointed towards his involvement in two murders: a school teacher I'd never met and an innocent woman with whom I'd become intimate. While neither would qualify as Medal of Honor recipients, neither deserved to die for wanting to publish a novel.

Was this self-defense or revenge? After turning over my own motivations for the last couple of days, I decided that it didn't really matter. Whether I was just protecting my own skin or acting as judge, jury and executioner, the act qualified on all counts as murder one.

It would be lovely for my conscience if Gazza would throw off his goons and say, "Fellas, this one's for me and me alone. You stay out of it." Like a movie villain, he'd appear in my doorway and launch into a full confession before pulling the trigger. But Bosco would bark on my silent signal to distract him, then I could try to wrestle the gun away and in the struggle, it would go off. He'd flinch, flash a sickly smirk, and drop to the floor. Hollywood.

How I could make something akin to that happen? Could I isolate him from his henchmen, get in his face enough to make him strike out in anger and then blow him away? There would have to be a trial, or at least an investigation, but I was confident I would be exonerated, even celebrated. There would even be a little Western honor in that approach because it could be seen as giving the bastard a fighting chance.

I could just commit a wanton act of murder --- scout out Gazza's movements, catch him in an unguarded moment, and put a slug in his ear. I'd toss the gun, cover my tracks, literally and figuratively, making it look like a gangland hit. I then would lie to everyone who asked, including Stone.

I was in a very lonely place.

Thirty one

Dan Logan calling.

"My phone's safe. How sure are you about yours?"

I said, "Not very."

"Okay, I'll make this quick. I can't tell you any more than I did yesterday. Despite my sterling character reference, they don't trust you. Nothing personal, but you're a civilian now. But I was told to repeat what I've been telling you all along. Stay away. There's more going on than meets the eye and you could be viewed as an impediment to something way bigger."

I knew better than to ask what he meant by that. Daniel Logan was a cautious man, and he was out on a limb. But although I consider him a friend, I also realize that he's a man who gave up his wife and kids for the job. I wasn't sure what his game was. He could be just a longtime buddy looking out for me, or he could be a conduit that someone in the bureau was using --- someone oblivious to my well being versus their own career goals.

"I hear you. Message received." I added a few more reassurances that I'd seen the light and he clicked off, seemingly satisfied. I chose my words carefully so that it sounds like I was heeding Logan's plea to stay away from

Gazza if ever a record of this conversation did surface. It could protect us both someday.

I was sitting in a back booth at the Starlight Diner, sipping a cup of their excellent coffee while waiting for Stone. I'd half a mind to order a hearty breakfast; a condemned man's last meal. I needed something to do as I absently scanned the Times. It wasn't like Rick to be late --- his years in radio had made punctuality an inviolate rule.

I tried to make use of the time by plotting the day ahead. I had to find out where Gazza lived, the route he took to work, in short, his daily routines. I gave myself a deadline of seventy-two hours. I'd packed some essentials into a small duffel and figured I'd do the multiple motel shuffle for a few nights until I could draw a bead on my target. Hopefully, I'd get him before his guys could find me. I was thinking like a criminal now, but my mindset was that of a righteous assassin, doing a dirty job that polite society would rather not know the gory details of, but would applaud the end result. Like making sausage.

But why had Logan warned me off in such strong terms? His not-so-subtle hints led me to figure that the feds had compiled a case against Gazza themselves and were waiting for an opportune moment to spring their trap. Or maybe Gazza himself had turned confidential informant --- after bigger families, perhaps even stretching across state lines into New York. I could be compromising an operation they'd worked years to set up. This all may be true, but I could also be his final victim while waiting for them to spring their trap. I hadn't decided for sure if I would or could pull the trigger, but I needed to prepare for the eventuality.

"Hey, Riles." It was Stone, eyes ringed dark from lack of sleep with a defeated slump to his carriage that I'd never seen in the decade and a half that we'd known each other.

"You look awful, man. And you're twenty minutes late. What's going on with you?"

"Had to feed and walk your damn dog, that's what. Frigging thing wouldn't go and I didn't want to come home to a roomful of shit."

There was no trace of humor in his voice, and the fact that I knew he loved Bosco almost as much as I do was the only thing keeping me from responding in kind. Stone was hurting bad, so I backed off. At least the rock lyric references were gone. There was that.

"Sorry, man. I just figured he'd be safer with you. Bosco'd never go in the house. He'd wait till you got home, no matter what."

He didn't apologize. He just sat slowly and to avoid looking at me, opened the menu. We've eaten at the Starlight enough to know their simple cuisine by heart and could probably even prepare most of it.

"Don't suppose you heard from you-know-who." I said.

"You don't suppose right."

I wasn't sure whether to go there or not.

"Who's on your show today?"

"Don't care. Took the day off."

"Oh. How come?"

He didn't answer right away, perusing the menu as if seeing it for the first time. "I'm not really hungry. How's the coffee today? Crappy as usual?"

"It's pretty good actually, I'm sure they have a fresh pot up. Not like that stuff leftover from the lobster trick."

He beckoned loudly for the waitress. "If you're not too busy bullshitting, a light coffee here. Like today sometime."

"Hey Ricky, cool off man. No need to treat the girl like that."

"Sorry, Miss Manners. Since when are you giving etiquette lessons?"

He was spoiling for a fight, and given the tension in my own situation, it would have been easy to accommodate him. My more pressing troubles had given me a modicum of restraint when it came to his so I could deal with being a punching bag if it made him feel better.

"Okay, so you're pissed at the world. But you don't need to spread your misery around. Dump it on me if you want, but don't go screwing up your life because some chick didn't have the smarts to know what she had in you. Come on man, you know how bad I was last year when Liz died. I thought the world was over. You helped me get through it. I owe you."

"It's not the same. Liz didn't walk out on you. I don't suppose you saw this."

He reached into the saddlebag he always carried and pushed a copy of the *New York Post* across the table, opened to Page Six, their gossip section. On it was a picture of a thong-clad Lisa Tillman, sun tan oil being applied to her naked back by the young producer who'd come to pick her up the other day. His lithe, hairless physique gleamed in the sun. Below the photo was a blurb on how Lisa had scored her own syndicated talk show, with her studly paramour at the helm.

"Wow" was all I could muster.

"I feel like such a fool. This didn't just start this weekend. She must have been doing this guy all along. How was I supposed to compete with young Brad Pitt here?"

The photo in the paper left little to the imagination as to how Lisa and he would look coupling --- the way she arched her back to receive his touch while his hips thrust slightly forward was as about graphic as a tabloid newspaper could get. I grimaced at the pain Stone must have felt. Loss of love was bad enough, but public humiliation added to the misery.

The waitress laid his coffee on the table, not pausing to ask if we wanted anything else. Stone's surly treatment of her would be repaid in kind. I hoped she hadn't spit in it.

I tried to refocus on Stone's problem.

I said, "Look, I don't know what the future holds, but I do know that as shitty as you feel now, you'll get over it. It may take a while but it gets better."

My words were ringing hollow even as I dispensed my unoriginal advice. Her television syndicator would doubtless mount a big campaign to promote Lisa's show, and Stone would probably see her picture in every magazine and paper he read. Each sighting would be another reminder of what once was his --- someone who now slept with another man.

His problems were trivial compared to mine; his life wasn't at stake. But to him, the pain was just as intense.

"Come on Rick, you know I'm right. Not like it's our first rodeo."

He drummed his fingers on the table.

"Yeah," was all he said.

Thirty two

I needed a run to clear my head, so after checking into a low rent motel off Route 9 in Forked River, paying cash for two nights, I did a slow three miles. The unfamiliar terrain wasn't as scenic as the bayside trots around my neck of the woods, but I barely noticed. Back at the motel, I took a rinse-off shower and headed out for the library.

Thankfully, the Internet ports at the Ocean County branch don't require any identification. I was thinking like a fed now; if I suspected Riley King of offing a mafia chieftain, I'd first check his web trail for any research done on the potential vic.

Gazza's address was a snap. County tax records showed him to live at 676 Bayview Ave, Toms River. I expected some dummy corporate ownership but the property was listed in his wife's name ---assessed at .9 mil, probably 35% less than it was actually worth, more than that if he used connections at the appraisal office. An acre and a half near the water, which made me think the house itself might not be so grand, given that the land alone would be bumping up against the assessment. Checked out Zillow. Four bedrooms, four and a half baths. Either built or renovated recently, given the modern trend toward separate baths for each suite, as they now referred to what used to be known as bedrooms.

A search of some private sites revealed that Gazza had two kids, a grown boy in his mid twenties and a girl a few years older who had moved somewhere out West with her husband. Tony had been married to the same woman for over thirty years. A three-year-old magazine photo of her revealed a handsome if somewhat mature woman, who'd aged benevolently.

The Internet yielded some nuggets that needed fleshing out to be useful. One headline in particular reminded me of another source. Jay Caruso was a former employee of mine who'd done a book on the evolution of the mob a couple of years back. Maybe he could flesh in some personal stuff about Gazza that hadn't made the book, details that might reveal vulnerabilities.

I rang his home number and after exchanging pleasantries, I asked, "Jay, what do you know about Tony Gazza?"

"Why do you ask?"

"Long story short, I'm on a case where he might be involved in eliminating a witness. I didn't deal with much organized crime when I was in the bureau, so I have a hard time separating fact from fiction."

I could imagine him smoothing back his jet-black hair, adjusting his collar and proceeding. "I see. Well, Gazza is a real enigma. Everybody clams up when you ask about him. Cops just shake their heads. My best source was a chap from another family and he said that Gazza wasn't even a player anymore. Had cleaned up his act. Sanitation stuff was legit. He'd inherited a small container service at Port

Newark from some cousin. Couple of dilapidated piers and a few trucks. Minor league. I mean, knowing how crooked the docks are in Jersey, I wouldn't be surprised if a few DVD players disappear now and then but hardly anything to write home about."

"What about Tony himself? What I'm getting at is, would he think twice about having somebody killed who got in his way?"

"Somebody doesn't get to where Tony Gazza is without breaking a few eggs. But the impression I got from my sources was that he doesn't crack heads to get what he wants. The other families don't consider him an expansionary force. He's even given away some territory to keep the peace, which is unheard of in the mob. But they all seem to respect him. Does that help?"

It didn't, except to confirm what Gazza had told me himself. Caruso was a good reporter, not easily fooled. "Yeah Jay, good stuff. One more thing. Did you find out about any weaknesses the man might have? Women, gambling, drink…anything?"

"Hmmn. Nothing that jumps out. Seems to be a faithful husband. Actually goes to Mass instead of letting the little woman do the praying for them both. Pretty devout. Dotes on his grown up kids. Sorry I couldn't be more help. Let's grab a beer soon, huh?"

"Sure. Give my regards to Eva. Later."

Thirty three

S alieri was my next call. I wanted to trick him into revealing the details of his upcoming meeting with Gazza, but it turned out to be unnecessary. He volunteered the information between coughs without me even asking. He divulged the time and place of the meet in small talk. I'll admit part of me felt rotten about using a priest this way and how easy it was. Maybe the cancer had spread to his brain and affected his judgment or maybe he just trusted me.

I wasn't sure I could do it tonight, but it seemed I'd been handed a perfect occasion to catch the mobster at an unguarded moment. In addition to my little arsenal, I would bring a compact parabolic microphone that could amplify speech from a distance. I figured that I could decide for myself if Gazza was being straight rather than trust Salieri's subjective reading. The opportunity might even present itself to shoot the man now if I was convinced beyond a doubt.

The late spring rain was gentle, but cold enough to make me shiver. Perched on an evergreen knoll in the pine needles and wild fescue beneath the new growth trees, I lay on my stomach on wet ground, the dampness penetrating the thin fleece sweatshirt. Salieri and Gazza were a hundred yards below in a dirt and gravel parking area, just under the Toms River causeway, which led to the barrier island. By day, the place was used as a public launch for those unable to afford private dock space. Judging from the condoms that littered the waterfront, teens might favor it as a make out spot by night. I'd scoped it out that afternoon, then driven back to the motel. I changed, showered and armored up before going back to the launch to wait until darkness fell.

Salieri arrived at dusk, alone. Nervously pacing and chain smoking unfiltered cigarettes, he seemed a pitiful and weak old man as he indulged the very behavior that had sentenced him to death. I guess if you've only got a couple of months left, you take pleasure where you can.

Gazza got there about ten minutes later. The two men shook hands, hugged and the conversation began. There was a fresh breeze rustling through the pines --- between that and the waves ---- even with the microphone, I could only catch snippets. The most recognizable sound was Salieri's persistent hack. I thought I heard Geist's name a couple of times. Salieri had his palms upturned as he pleaded his case. Gazza was slowly shaking his head. Gradually, they both became more animated, their words harsher and louder. I distinctly heard Gazza say "King" once, and I didn't care for his body language as he uttered my name. Salieri grew more persistent, Gazza more vehement.

"No guarantees. The bastard will get what's coming to him."

Those words reached my ears as clearly as if spoken to me directly. Providence. Gazza turned his back to the priest, rubbing his palms together as if washing his hands of responsibility. Pontius Pilate couldn't have pantomimed it better. Salieri placed his hand gently on the mobster's shoulder.

But then a shocking thing happened. Before Gazza could turn impatiently to face his comrade, a gun appeared out of nowhere, somehow finding its way into Salieri's hand. He raised it to Gazza's head and fired twice.

A muzzle flash and muted retort, and Gazza was crumpling to the ground.

The wrath of God.

Salieri calmly walked toward the water. I was shocked. His actions were as premeditated as mine would have been, although I doubt I could have executed it as unemotionally as he had. He'd deliberately packed a weapon and lured his colleague into this desolate spot. Their friendship had made the man feel comfortable enough to come alone, without protection. Gazza could never have imagined this act of violence from his priest.

Salieri had skillfully twisted my own game against me. That must have been why he had yielded the time and location of the meet so easily that afternoon. He knew I likely would stake him out. He had anticipated my options. Was he sacrificing his almost extinguished life to save mine?

I couldn't imagine Salieri pulling the trigger if any doubt had remained in his mind about his old colleague's guilt. I'd just seen him do it and I still couldn't believe it. Had Gazza confessed to killing Geist and Paige? Was it evident that I was next on his list?

I needed time to think. Salieri had just betrayed a lifelong friend who never saw it coming. What might he have in store for me? Did he truly act selflessly on my behalf or was this part of a bigger game? It flashed through my brain that maybe I had the roles reversed. That Salieri had killed Geist and Paige and that Gazza was merely an unknowing accomplice.

The surf and the wind were howling in my ears now. I ran to my car and high tailed it out of there.

Thirty four

"I frankly see no purpose in discussing this further," the priest said.

We were back at the Rectory kitchen, a cup of tea at six in the morning. The kitchen had been built in the fifties and precious little had changed about it since. It radiated a musty charm though, and the sturdy pine table where we sat would probably fetch a nice price at an antiques auction.

Salieri wasn't budging."I don't know what you're talking about."

"Father, what I want to know is why. You're supposed to be a man of God, not an executioner. If you thought you were protecting me, you had no right to do that. It's up to me to take care of myself."

"And I'm sure you can and will in the future."

This dude could stonewall with the best of them and I had no leverage. No legal authority. And given my own plans for Gazza, no higher moral ground to stand on. Still, I tried to appeal to his conscience.

"But you've devoted your whole life to your God. You've done nothing but give to others and as far as I can see, you've taken nothing for yourself. And now, nearing the end, you do something that wipes away all your good deeds and damns you for all eternity according to your Faith. Why?"

He steepled his fingers. "Let me speak in the hypothetical. Osama bin Laden murdered three thousand Americans. He had sworn to kill many thousands more. When our special forces found him, were they wrong to do what was necessary to end the evil?"

I couldn't disagree but I had to press my case against his imperfect analogy.

"But if they had him cornered and could have been extracted at no risk to the Seals, shouldn't he be captured and tried? Doesn't a civilized nation have a constitution and a process for dealing with murderers?"

I couldn't believe I was playing Devil's Advocate with a terrorist to make my case, but I needed to understand how this so-called man of God justified his actions.

Salieri said, "So you'd let him spew his venom in a public forum at a trial? Become a martyr to the cause. Or perhaps his forces would take innocent hostages and demand his release under threat of beheading. I'm sorry but a quick execution serves the greater good."

"But a priest as executioner?"

"God might choose whoever was best suited for the job. Let's be honest, Mr. King. Do you believe that He anointed you for this task?"

"Father, I don't pretend to know what God wants us to do, or even if there *is* a God in that sense who controls our actions. If your religion is valid, I'm going to hell anyway. But whatever, *I* was the one who was wronged. *I'm* the one who's justified in protecting himself."

"And I wasn't wronged?"

211

"So you're now telling me that you're convinced Paul Geist is dead on the orders of Tony Gazza?"

He hadn't coughed since I'd knocked on his door at sunrise. He now made up for it, launching into a series of convulsive paroxysms that had made afraid he might expire then and there. After what seemed an eternity, he gulped some tea which soothed him momentarily.

"Sorry. It gets worse the longer I'm up."

"So, Gazza confessed to killing Geist? And Paige?"

"I think you know that I can't answer that."

"It wasn't a formal confession. You're not bound by those rules."

"Suffice to say, your job is over. You have no need to look for Paul Geist. If he's no longer with us, well, the guilty have been punished. If Paul is still alive, so be it. In any case, you can get on with your life."

"Easy for you to say. When Gazza turns up dead or missing, someone's bound to come after me. Tony wasn't working in a vacuum. His soldiers will want revenge. And the Ocean County cops know I had it in for him. I'm sure I'll be one of the first people they talk to."

He coughed again, not as long as the previous time. "Mr. King, let's say that I have a source who will keep me informed. I'm sure the real culprit will come forward, if need be. He has little to lose."

"Begging your pardon, but what about his reputation? His good name and the school he founded? Doesn't that mean anything?"

Again he sipped his tea. "I'm sure it won't come to that."

"And why is that?"

"I can't tell you. You'll just have to take it on faith."

My turn to attend to my teacup. "Faith that a priest will do what's right? The same one who tricked me into witnessing what I saw last night? That kind of faith?"

"I'm sorry you feel deceived. But I never forced you to be where you were last night wherever that was. Free will. It was your choice. Again, trust me. Just try to believe that God is taking care of you, whatever instrument He chooses to protect you, have faith that He will. This chapter is over for you. Let it go. Now please excuse me. I have to say Mass at seven. I need to prepare."

He gestured toward the Dutch door in the kitchen that led outside, and left me sitting at the table, dumbfounded. The phrase *God works in mysterious ways* never seemed so appropriate. He was so convinced that I was no longer in danger that I did gain a certain sense of peace. The nightmare might finally be over.

Thirty five

"Hey, Riles"

Logan's tone was decidedly warmer than the last time we spoke a few days earlier; just his greeting tipped me off to that. He wasn't furtive, didn't instruct me to run to a secure line, it was just "Hey, Riles."

"Hey yourself."

"Look, I'm sorry I couldn't get clearance to fill you in on Gazza. But I'm afraid just my asking has compromised you. I can't talk long but I need to ask you something."

"Why the sudden 180?"

"No 180. I've tried to help you all along and that's why I'm giving you a heads-up. Have you seen Gazza since we last spoke?"

"No, why?"

"Can you account for your time between now and then?"

"Why do you ask?" I knew why. But I needed to play dumb. I also needed to assume that this conversation was either being recorded, listened to by others or both.

"I'll lay it out for you, pal. Gazza hasn't been seen recently. Now his wife hasn't reported him missing or anything, but we have sources. He hasn't been where he was supposed to be, He's either on the lam or…."

"Or dead? Is that what this is about? You think I killed Gazza."

"Who said anything about him being killed? He's missing, that's all I know. But me telling the higher-ups about you before drew their attention and then the guy turns up missing? Well, ain't going to be long before you start catching some heat. Unless I can short circuit it before it starts, you dig?"

"Sorry, nothing I can do about that. I've spent a lot of time by myself lately, mostly to stay away from Gazza's soldiers. So no, I don't have solid alibis for the last forty-eight hours."

"Hey, I believe you but you were in my shoes once upon a time, you know how it works. So help me out here. Give me some ammo to support your word. Do you know anything about what might have happened to Gazza?"

Of course I did, but I wasn't going to help anyone go after Salieri. The priest had probably saved my life. He was going to meet his Maker in a short time anyway. Why drag his life's work down for justice for Gazza, whom the world was better off without.

"Don't. Sorry. Daniel, I can't tell you that I didn't think about how my life would be better without Tony Gazza in it. But I did nothing to make that happen."

"And you wouldn't know if anyone did? Come on Riles, I know your MO. You keep friends close and enemies closer... the old line. You had to be keeping an eye on Gazza."

"You give me too much credit. I went into a defensive shell here. Covered my own ass. Besides, I promised to lay low until I heard from you. I was thinking about mounting an offense, but I never did."

An uneasy silence on the other end.

Maybe I could get some information of my own. Long shot, but it couldn't hurt to try. "So what are they thinking down wherever you're calling from? Do they think Tony's on the wrong side of the grass?"

"We don't know a thing. Just curious, that's all. He's a person of interest to us. We don't like it when they go missing. Makes us think maybe he's up to no good."

"Wish I could help you, man. But I've told you all I know."

"I hope so. You know that I'm on your side; at least I hope you know that. But the next time you hear from the bureau, whoever they send might not feel the same way."

"Gee, Dan, if I didn't know you better, I'd say that was a threat."

"Come on, Riles. We're friends but we're both pros too. We have jobs to do. My neck is out talking to you now. Someone might construe it that I'm giving you a chance to cover your tracks."

"Don't need to, but thanks for the thought."

"Just be smart. Call me if you hear anything. God, Mitzi Gaynor had great legs, didn't she?"

"The best. Later."

How long would it be before Gazza's body washed up somewhere? Salieri had no answer when I asked him how he disposed of the body. But if he had professional help, they'd know how to make it look like Anthony Gazza never existed.

Bing!

A light went on. Logan knew that Gazza was missing because the feds had someone inside the organization. That's why he wanted me to stay away. They were planning a sting, or better yet, were quietly building a case that would tear down not just Tony's empire, but something bigger. Whether Gazza's murder facilitated that or impeded it was a question I couldn't answer. But clearly, it had thrown them a curveball.

Was I being set up? My only protection was a dying priest who'd told me that he'd come forward if the law came after me. But Salieri was a man who'd manipulated me into witnessing the shooting. He tricked his old pal Gazza into walking into a trap. Who's to say that he didn't plant trace evidence from me at the scene? I needed someone to talk to, someone I could trust.

Stone. Sober and clear thinking. Admittedly, a rare state for him lately.

I also needed to see my dog.

Thirty six

It was just after five o'clock and Stone was drunk. In all the years I've known him, I'd never seen him reach the point of slurring his words. He never got sloppy drunk. Happily high on occasion, but never embarrassing, which he now verged on.

I'd come in through the front door and he barely acknowledged me as he sat in the darkened room, watching ESPN with the sound off, which made sense if a game was on but watching Kornheiser and Wilbon argue on *PTI* with the sound off was like listening to a Schwarzenegger action flick without the picture.

"Hey Rick. Where's Bosco?"

"Oh shit. I let him out to go a while ago. I forgot. Oh well, he's probably out there somewhere."

It was like an alien had taken over my friend's body. He loved Bosco, but now he seemed indifferent. "How long ago?"

"I don't know. Around one I guess. What time is it now?"

I was already out the back door, out of control angry at Stone's callousness. My anger turned to relief when I immediately saw Bosco lying on Stone's back deck, blissfully sleeping in the shade.

"Come here, boy. Did Uncle Rick forget about you?"

He ambled over and licked my hand as if nothing had happened. He followed me back into the house and jumped up onto the sofa where Rick was sipping another scotch.

"Hey, you're wet. Off the couch. You're getting sand all over the place."

He raised his hand as if to swat Bosco way, but the dog was quicker, leaping over the corner of the coffee table to escape his wrath.

"Hit that dog and you'll never speak to me again. What the hell's wrong with you?"

His hand was still in the air, and he regarded it as if it were a foreign object. He lowered it slowly and ran it down his face.

"Sorry, man. He was messing up the furniture."

The furniture wouldn't have known the difference. I'd never seen this house in such a state of disarray. Newspapers were strewn about the place; empty cans and glasses were resting haphazardly on any surface that wasn't cluttered with torn wrappers or pizza boxes. Stone had a woman come in once a week to do the heavy cleaning, but usually he kept things orderly between visits.

"Have you fed him yet?"

"This morning I think, or was that last night? I forget."

"You got home from work at one? Aren't you on the air until one?"

"Got off early. For some reason they brought the guy after me in early. Said he had some special guest or some bullshit like that."

I'm not one for giving lectures. One of my college education classes at Georgetown stressed how unproductive such speeches are, versus eliciting the response from the students' own logic. But I couldn't resist now.

"Can you blame them? Would you put a drunk on the air?"

"Who you think you're talking to?"

"You. My tough guy friend, who's letting a hundred and ten pound lightweight destroy his life."

He sat silent, soaking in the abuse,

"You know what? I don't know that I've ever been as disappointed in you as I am now."

"You weren't such hot shit when Liz died." His face was red.

"Attacking me ain't gonna fix your problem. I worked over the last year. If I drank too much and I'll admit that I did, it wasn't on company time. Because I know that no matter what, I'm still alive and whatever happens the rest of my life, Liz can't be part of it. You've got to come to that realization about Lisa pretty soon or nobody will ever want you again."

"Nobody wants me now. Look at me. Losing my hair. Flab around my gut no matter how much I work out. Bags under my eyes that won't go away no matter how much sleep I get. Not like I'm George Clooney or anything.

What woman is going to want me when there are millions of young hard bodies walking around?"

"The type of woman who wouldn't want a hard body, that's who. A grown up. Someone who can look past some of the character lines and see what's important. The kind of woman who'll see you for who you are inside, not the exterior."

"And what is that? A sportscaster. A jock sniffer. A guy who spends three hours a day on the radio pontificating about bullshit games that couldn't matter less in the scheme of things. Expert on trivia that nobody cares about but homebound losers who can't get it up to jerk off without Viagra."

"Whew. I wish I had that on tape so I could play it back for you when you're sober. You're an entertainer. You make that three hours special for those people you seem to have such contempt for. You do a public service. And that's not to mention the stuff we've done together. We've righted some wrongs. Got some justice for the little guy. That's worth something."

He took another pull on the scotch as thrust the bottle out toward me. "Don't make me drink alone, Riles."

I said, "I'll never touch another drop if it makes me stupid like it's made you."

"Why am I stupid? Because I fell for a gorgeous woman who was in my line of work who actually professed to love me for a while? Yeah. I guess that makes me an all time idiot."

"And no one else ever made the same mistake? Look at my man Bubba. Got himself impeached and she wasn't even all that hot. Besides, you're looking at this all wrong. You're looking for reasons she left. How about what attracted her to you in the first place?"

"Right. So she just went for me because I could help her career. Not because she wanted me for me."

"Guy like you is the last guy I'd think would be wallowing like this. You got it made. You got money. A certain amount of fame. And despite what you're saying, you're not entirely bad to look at. And your biggest ace in the hole --- look who your best friend is."

Even he had to laugh at my bravado. "A washed up fed who a two bit gangster has a contract on."

"And who needs your help to stay alive. After that, feel free to drink yourself into oblivion."

He broke into hearty but sad laugh. "Couple of hopeless losers when it comes to women. You've never been married. Me, I'm oh for one and a half. Makes me think we'd be better off if we were gay."

"My cue to take my dog and get out of here, Seriously, though I need to talk to you about some things. If I make some coffee, you think you can get coherent and thinking straight?"

"Got my mind right, Luke?" he said, quoting Strother Martin in *Cool Hand Luke*. "Yeah, I guess. But do me a favor. Turn off that TV. That strobe thing is giving me a splitting headache."

It wasn't the television. A flashing light was playing along the wall, emanating from a window facing the street. Ocean County fuzz, McCullough heading for the front door.

Thirty seven

I didn't wait for the bell to ring. Whatever McCullough wanted would not benefit from Stone's inebriated presence.

"Detective. To what do I owe the pleasure?" The phrase sounded stilted the moment it escaped my lips, but so was my false cheeriness.

"No pleasure. Business."

"And a good day to you too. Was the cherry top really necessary? What can I do for you?"

"I wanted to make an entrance. You had me fooled, King. You really did."

"Okay. Pleasantries dismissed. What are you talking about?"

"I think you know."

"You know, I really don't. But I'm sure you'll get around to telling me eventually."

"Gazza."

"Yeah. What about him?"

"Dead."

So the body had been discovered. Of immediate interest to me was whether McCullough had anything concrete to tie me to the murder, or he was just following up on a hunch.

"You know I'd be lying to you if I said I was sorry to hear that. But if you think I had anything to do with it, you're mistaken."

"Oh it doesn't matter what I think and you know it."

"You're giving me credit for clairvoyance that I don't have. It'd come in handy in my line of work but why don't we stop with the guessing games and cut to the chase. Gazza's dead. Okay. And since you're here, I assume he was killed and I also assume that you think I did it. Right?"

"A twenty two, left side of the temple. Two at close range. Yeah, I'd say he was killed."

"And do I get to know when and where this happened or are you hoping I'll blurt out something incriminating?"

"Like I said, my opinion doesn't matter. And you know why."

Common police technique. Imply something. Get the suspect to volunteer information that he shouldn't be aware of. Done it myself a few dozen times. Rarely works but there are exceptions.

"Look, it's obvious that you think I had something to do with this. I'd think the same thing in your place. Gazza's a threat to King. Gazza's offed. King's happy. Pretty elemental. But I didn't do it. If you're here to arrest me, I'll call a lawyer and we can shut down this dialogue right now. But if you'd care to informally share some information, maybe we can talk."

"Awfully big of you. All right, I'll lay it out for you. Body washed up on Money Island this afternoon. Looked

225

like it had been in the water a couple of days. Dressed expensively. Unfortunately for us, marine life had done a number on the face, so we couldn't identify the body right away. But as luck would have it, the stiff still had his wallet and the water hadn't destroyed one of our new laminated New Jersey photo ID drivers' licenses. It was Gazza."

"First class detective work."

"Smirk all you want. We're about to process the body when the feds swoop in and take over. Claim jurisdiction on RICO statutes or some such bullshit. Whisk the corpse away, thank you very much."

"And you think they were tipped off? To what end?"

"Like I say, don't matter what I think. It's their case. But if you're curious, yeah, I think that whoever did this had ties to the feds. Maybe even had their approval. So you're in the clear. I'm sure your buddies in Washington will cover this up for you. I'm sure my bosses will be glad to be rid of one less gangster and won't ask too many questions. And everyone will live happily ever after. I guess I should be grateful to you in a way for removing a stone from my shoe."

We were standing on Stone's front porch, a small ornamental nod to the Cape Cod style of his house. Who would sit on a porch facing what had until recently been a major thoroughfare when the Atlantic Ocean was around back?

"I know you won't believe this, but as much as I'm relieved that Gazza isn't stalking me now, I had nothing to do with any of this. So throw your *Magnum Force* theory out the window, detective. If I were you, I'd think in terms of a rival family or maybe an up-and-coming soldier who was impatient with how slowly he was getting ahead. Twenty two to the left temple sounds like a pro to me. Someone he knew and trusted."

"A pro like *you*, King. Hey, I'm off the case. I'm just here out of curiosity. I wanted to know how you managed it and I thought since we had such a pleasant chat the other day that you'd level with me off the record. You know. Cop to cop."

"Boy, if I ever get back into law enforcement I'll have to remember that one. That's original, I'll give you that. Create a phony story about the FBI. Tell a suspect you're off the case, encourage him to brag about his work and then bam, you got him. Very clever. And if I was guilty, who knows, I may have fallen for it. But like I said, I had nothing to do with it."

He said, "You give me too much credit. Or not enough --- I'm not sure with you. But I'm telling you the truth. The feds have it now. And if you're leveling with me and this is all above board, they'll be knocking on your door pretty soon. Consider that a heads-up."

"Why thanks, Flint, I will. But I have nothing to hide. I don't know what we're looking at with time of death but I might even be able to account for that time."

"Oh. I'm sure of it. Well, thanks for nothing. No, that's not right. Thanks for ridding the county of a scum who I've been trying to nail for a while now. Just don't make a habit of it, eh?"

"King, get in here." Stone's shout was barely muffled by the heavy door.

"Something wrong with your friend?" McCullough asked.

"Broke up with his girl. Taking it hard."

"Riley, get in here quick. Hurry up." Stone was screaming.

"Sounds like the man's in trouble. Probable cause, I'm going in."

I couldn't keep him out. Stone did sound like he needed help. Probably a TV promo for Lisa's new show had twisted the knife anew. But barring a policeman's entry would make me look like I had something to hide in the house. And besides, there's nothing illegal about being dead drunk in your own house if you're over 21.

I've never seen a man go from totally in the bag to sober in less time. Stone sat ashen faced in front of his large screen television. ESPN had been replaced by CNN ---an aerial shot of chaotic activity on some waterfront.

A caption read, "*Major human trafficking discovered in New Jersey port. 9/11 terror ring connection broken by Homeland Security and FBI*"

Thirty eight

For the next minutes, we sat transfixed in front of the television. McCullough called in to offer assistance, but his dispatcher told him to stand by; his help was not needed immediately.

Details filtered in. The live helicopter shots were shaky as the television stations used extreme zoom lenses to steal a look at the action. Although I never have worked a crime scene of this magnitude, I knew it would be a matter of minutes until the bureau set up a pool reporter and cameraman to inform the public.

The local anchors were clearly in over their heads, spouting inanities about the Indian Point power plant and such until more facts were revealed. It boiled down to this: girls, as young as twelve, were being smuggled into the country to serve as under-age prostitutes in a Newark neighborhood. It was suspected that the profits were being funneled to terror cells in the area to finance their planned operations.

The governors of New York and New Jersey were on the air now, praising the work of the FBI and assuring us that their administrations had offered the office of Homeland Security any cooperation they might request. Knowing how territorial the bureau still was, I doubted that the states were even aware of the sting until it had been completed. Even in this age of interdepartmental sharing, some operations are best kept on a "need to know" basis, and this surely qualified.

McCullough's dispatcher squawked in and he left hastily, not bothering with goodbyes. We barely noticed his departure. All I could think of was Bogie's line in *Casablanca* about how two peoples' problems didn't amount to a hill of beans given events of the world. Gazza, Salieri, Paige White and Geist seemed distant concerns now.

The local anchor with the most gravitas had been dispatched to the scene. In appropriately sober tones, he recapped what we knew so far. He was standing in the late afternoon sun as agents buzzed about in the background, clad in their blue windbreakers with FBI in yellow block letters on the back. The port was a decrepit looking place; piles of undistinguishable refuse scattered about the stained concrete surface. The anchor stood back and surveyed the unsightly scene as the camera panned about the docks. Reacting to a cue from the studio, he turned to an FBI spokesman, who read a statement, basically outlining what the anchor had just said, adding almost nothing. After his communiqué, he answered a few questions, again reassuring the public that Homeland Security had done its job and that several suspected terrorists linked to this operation had been apprehended.

The reporter's queries on civilian involvement and who might have tipped the bureau off went unanswered. Made sense --- why endanger your source when retaliation from the remnants of the cell was a real possibility?

When the tension eased a bit and it became apparent that no new revelations were forthcoming, I began to rummage around Stone's refrigerator for something to eat. Pickings were slim and I began to search through his drawers for some take-out menus of places that delivered.

"Hey, Riles, you know that guy from the bureau you used to hang with? The doughy looking dude who was into Broadway plays and stuff?"

"Yeah, you mean Daniel Logan. You met him a few times. Why?"

"Camera is just scanning the scene now and I think that's him over there. He looks like he's in charge or something. Seems to be directing the whole thing, or at least a good part of it."

"Really? Let me see." I rushed over to the television and sure enough, there was Dan, barking out orders.

"They wouldn't fly in a total outsider to take charge. This Logan dude must have been in on this all along," Stone said.

"Looks that way. I've been talking to him lately about Gazza but we always were on cells or public phones so I had no idea where he was. Last I knew he was in the Midwest."

So much for friendship. But as I thought further on it, if Dan was working on something this big, he was perfectly justified in keeping his whereabouts a secret, even from me. In fact, it was surprising that he even had time to look into Gazza for me, given the importance of his task. I'd wait a couple of days before calling to congratulate him.

But the thought of Logan and Gazza triggered something that started to bother me. It was nothing tangible, but it was like a little virus, spreading through my brain. Something was out of place but I couldn't determine what it was. Somebody had said something that was at odds with reality. What the hell was it?

The only one I'd had any sober dialogue with lately was McCullough. Had he insinuated something that started me thinking this way? I dialed his cell.

"What do you want, King? I been thinking this terrorist thing comes at a good time for you. The feds will be so busy sorting this one out that they won't have time for a little fish like you. That is, if they ever did."

"Let me ask you something. You said that Gazza had two shots to the *left* side of his head? You're sure about that?"

"Yeah, it was the left side. Smart guy like you will try to fabricate some defense from that somehow. But like I say, I'm off the case. Save it for your friends in DC."

He hung up.

Flint was giving me credit for more cunning than I possess. Greater minds than mine had engineered this one.

The picture from a few nights ago was still emblazoned in my memory, despite all that had happened since. The bureau might be busy with terrorists, but someone was covering up something regarding Anthony Gazza. And my first visit would be to a dying man who held the answers. My appetite was gone. The chase continued.

Thirty nine

I didn't sleep very well that night, undoubtedly joining most of New Jersey in my insomnia. Leaving the television on, searching for more details on the foiled trafficking plot, but the pundits were driving me crazy with their ill-informed, jingoistic platitudes. Finally at around midnight, I turned it off, popped an Excedrin PM and dozed off fitfully.

At 6 a.m., something awoke me and I gave up trying to get back to sleep. I gathered Bosco up and ran three miles along the beach with him. I put on some coffee, fed the dog and scanned the Asbury Park Press I found on the doorstep. It barely made mention of Gazza; there were a lot of words about the terror connection but little additional reporting to fill in the gaps left by television.

Leaving a note for the still sleeping Stone, I lit out for the rectory, which I figured would be up and running this early. I bought the New York Times and the Star Ledger to keep me company if I had to kill time while Salieri said Mass.

Traffic was light and I was at Sacred Cross within minutes. I made my way to the rear kitchen door of the rectory, where a somber looking woman was going about her morning ritual, the *Today* show flickering in the background.

"I'm here to see Father Salieri. Is he in?"

"Oh my heavens, you haven't heard? I thought I'd notified all his morning appointments. I'm sorry, your name sir?"

"Riley King, ma'am. Actually I didn't have an appointment. Is there a problem?"

"I'm afraid Father Salieri has taken ill. We checked him into the Toms River Medical Center yesterday. We expect he might be there for some time. Can any other the other priests be of assistance?"

So it was beginning --- the long death throes of his cancer. I'd experienced it with my grandfather and it wasn't pleasant. Every so often when pondering my own mortality, I reflect back on when he went through and pray that the end for me comes swiftly.

"No, thank you. I'm sorry to have bothered you. Please convey my best to Father Salieri."

"I will."

The drive to the hospital left me with an hour on my hands before they would allow me to see him. I read all the papers, practically cover to cover, looking up only when my own troubles caused me to lose concentration. At around nine, the nurse at the front desk nodded at me and pointed toward the elevator leading to Salieri's room.

He looked frail, a far cry from the man I'd interviewed in his office barely a week earlier. His short hair was matted and thin. Breathing tubes were taped to his nostrils and his eyes looked rheumy and unfocused. He tried to sit more erectly upon seeing me, but the effort was more pitiful than anything else. He'd obviously taken a bad turn.

"Please Father, don't try to sit up. Am I coming at a bad time?"

He coughed out an ironic snort. "I'm afraid they're all going to be bad times from here on in. The doctors told me this would happen. One day everything would seem pretty normal, the next I wouldn't be able to get out of bed. Some days will be better than others but I may have said my last Mass. I only wish I had known. I might have done a better sermon."

"I'm sure it was fine. Anything I can get you?"

"New lungs would be nice but I fear we're past that point." His attitude was more lighthearted than I imagined mine would be. "No, I've been preparing for this ever since the diagnosis, as much as one can prepare."

"I envy you your Faith."

"Don't. Can I tell you something? Something I don't want disseminated?"

"Why trust me with your secrets at this point?"

"Because you're here. And because you and I already share a pretty big secret."

After all that had gone down, I still didn't know what to make of him. Was he a good man who had rid the earth of a terrible scourge, or a corrupt enabler who had silenced a threat to his spotless legacy? Maybe killing Gazza was in his own interests, eliminating a co-conspirator who might reveal the plot to make Geist vanish.

"I'll abide by your wishes, whatever they are, Father."

"I lost my belief in Catholicism years ago."

"So you're telling me that you don't believe in God?"

"No, that's not what I'm saying. But I do believe that we've corrupted our concept of God to suit our own selfish goals, which generally revolve around what America's real God is ----- money and power. And the rationalization we cloak it in ---*my religion is better than yours. If you don't accept that, we'll kill you.* My economic system is better than yours and on and on. I'm so sick of it that I'm not so sad to be leaving this earth when I am."

"And yet you've remained a priest and a headmaster all these years. How do you square that?"

"Obviously, you haven't bothered to attend Mass lately. If you'd heard my sermons, you'd understand that I'm not fire and brimstone, thumping the bible as all that's sacred. I've spent many a sleepless night contemplating where we would be without religion, if each man were totally free to decide for himself what was right and what was wrong. And my conclusion is that the human race would be worse off. Most of us need a set of rules drilled into us from an early age. Otherwise we'd be adrift with no conscience, no guidelines as to how to act. We need to be led. Need to be told what to do. Whether it's because of a two thousand year old myth or merely logical arguments regarding the greater good, we need rules. In the end, does it matter which mechanism we use to construct them? So I honor my vows by working for righteousness, in my own way."

His monologue left him slightly out of breath. His words took on a power far greater than their weakened delivery.

"It's kind of ironic that I've been having the same discussions with a friend lately, about God. I'm sure you've seen the news out of Newark this morning, Father."

"Islamists, they say. I certainly ran into quite a few Muslim fundamentalists during my recruiting trips in northern Jersey."

"I'd have thought they would have seen you as the enemy."

"You'd be surprised. They have more in common with me than you would think. But King, you didn't come to see me to discuss religion or politics. Or to comfort a dying man, did you? They're going to shoo you out of here soon because I'm scheduled for some more tests this morning. Waste of time really. But while you're here, I can at least listen to what's on your mind. I can't say that I'll be able to give you any answers, but I can listen."

"Okay, fair enough. A body that was identified as Tony Gazza washed up onshore yesterday. But this body had two bullet holes entering his left temple. I clearly saw his assailant shoot him twice from behind --- in the right temple."

He was silent. He wasn't about to volunteer anything that would make connecting the dots easier.

I went on. "So the body they found wasn't Tony Gazza. But he had Tony's wallet and identification. Now being a former fed, I know that they wouldn't issue a positive ID based only on that."

I waited for a response and got none.

"So I'm left with one conclusion. The FBI wants us to *think* that Tony Gazza is dead, to the extent that they'd fake his killing. Why would that be?"

"How would I know what the FBI's motives are if what you say is true? Perhaps your memory is not accurate in terms of what you think you saw."

"No, I know what I saw. What I saw was a staged murder. What I saw was two buddies from 'Nam staging a death so that I'd get off the case of one of them."

"And why would we do that?"

"You set me up to see something. I don't know why. I'm asking you."

"I'm going to say this once and then I'm going to have to ask you to leave. The last time we spoke, I asked you to trust me. That whatever I did, my motives are pure. I'm only a few days from the end, so I have nothing to gain personally by deceiving you. But I need you to let this go."

"I can't."

"You must. I can tell you this much: no good can come of what you may uncover. Please, if you have any shred of trust in me left, let this go."

"Paige White is dead. I think that Paul Geist is dead. I believe that Tony Gazza was behind their deaths. You wanted me to just write them off on your word. When you saw I wasn't buying that, you arranged for me to see you execute Gazza, or should I say fake his execution. I assume you did this to satisfy what you think is my desire for revenge."

"Think it through, King. Under your scenario, Tony Gazza would be a willing collaborator. You think that he'd play dead and give up his whole life just to placate you? If he was the villain you think he was, wouldn't the simpler answer be to just eliminate you? Please --- Tony Gazza is gone. I can state unequivocally that you'll never hear from him again. Why can't you just accept that and move on?"

My head was spinning. Gazza *wouldn't* give up his empire just to get me off his back. That made no sense. But I knew what I knew. And Salieri's defenses were those of a man tiptoeing around the truth, on the basis that I couldn't handle the truth. *Ah, the Jack Nicholson defense.*

"Riley King, I think that you're a very good man. But I'm begging you now, please let this be. No good can come of it. Promise me that you'll do as I ask."

"Rest. All I can promise is that I'll think about it. And that we'll speak again."

I didn't know what to say next. *Get well soon? Try to stay comfortable? Take care?* None of the usual parting chestnuts applied.

"Goodbye, Father."

Forty

M y next stop was Gazza's house. His street was inland and high enough to be spared the storm's floodwaters. The neighborhood looked exactly as it had before that fateful October night in 2012. You would never guess that mere blocks away, bulldozers were still clearing the wreckage of homes where families had resided for decades. I parked directly in front and strode up the driveway as if I'd been invited over for midmorning coffee.

The house had been stripped bare --- nothing but walls and floors. No furniture, area rugs, no cars in the garage, nada. The window treatments had even been removed, so it was easy to look in at what little there was to see. The refrigerator door was propped open and there was no light emanating from within, an indication that it had been disconnected and sanitized. I circled around back, hoping to find something there, but it was a blank canvas.

No one's wife and family vanish so completely a mere day after the body is discovered. I knew that the children had moved out years ago but one would think that their father's death would have brought them home temporarily. I was trying to figure how and why a house that was fully operational a couple of days earlier would be so empty now. Lost in thought, I made my way toward the front again and was startled when I heard another voice.

"Excuse me, are you Mr. Garza?"

Standing on the front porch was a stunning blonde, whose Nordic good looks belonged on a runway somewhere. Dressed elegantly in a long scarlet vest sweater over stylishly cut worsted slacks, her shoulder length hair complimented the clean lines of her lean physique. Ice blue eyes and invisibly applied makeup radiated good health. She was no kid; I made her for mid to late thirties but Stone's TV star ex had nothing on this babe.

"Uh, no. Riley King. Nice to meet you."

"Jenny Lightower, Coldwell Banker Realtors. Are you an agent as well? They informed me they might be speaking with other companies."

"Actually I'm a friend of the family."

"Oh, and they asked you to be around to keep an eye on things. Understandable, I guess. Some realtors have been known to help themselves to some loose change lying on the counters."

I wrinkled my brow and she smiled, pearly whites lighting up the porch. "Come on, I was only kidding. Let's go inside, shall we?"

No reason not to play along. I had contemplated breaking in to see what I could find, but she had a key and maybe she knew some things I didn't.

I cast a line. "So how did the Gazza's find you? They're pretty picky about who they deal with."

"Gazza. Oh, I was calling them Garza. Well, obviously I don't know them or I wouldn't have mistaken you for Mr. Gazza. No, I just got an E-mail yesterday from someone representing them. Asked if I'd be interested in listing the house. I said yes but I'd like to see it first and they replied that the key along with the security code would be taped under the mailbox. A little secretive but sometimes wealthy people are that way. They don't want their neighbors to know their business."

I wouldn't have any trouble getting information from Jenny. Like most realtors I've met, information is their stock and trade. They know all the latest local gossip and aren't shy about sharing it, in hopes of picking up leads. Who might be divorcing, who is suffering from a terminal illness, whose company is about to be sold. All of these items portend a move and a move means a sale and a sale means commission. That's why I was a bit surprised that she hadn't picked up on who Gazza was and why the house was for sale. We entered through the front door and although the place was devoid of decoration, it had impressive bones.

Inside it was much larger than it appeared from the exterior. The entry soared to two stories, and the rather shallow living room featured a wall of windows overlooking the pool. The entire first floor was paved with tumbled marble and like everything else in the house, the floors were immaculate.

"Where's your office, Jenny? I don't recall seeing you around town."

"Oh, I'm not from here. I'm based in Colts Neck. Usually we refer folks from Toms River to our agency down there but this one looks like it might go in the seven figures so I kind of poached in on the territory."

"Really. You think over a million?" I was playing dumb.

"No doubt. The question is how much over. It's got an acre and a half, 5000 square feet, gorgeous landscaping. The finish inside is a bit much. Usually we see wood floors; all this marble tile is more typical of Florida. Mr. Gazza moving down there or is that none of my business?"

"You really don't know much about them do you? I'm afraid that Mr. Gazza passed on."

"I'm sorry to hear that. Were you close?"

"Business mainly."

"When did he die?"

"Well, the authorities think a couple of days ago."

"Authorities?"

"I guess you didn't see it in the news. Tony Gazza was murdered a couple days ago."

She lost color for a moment. "Wait a minute. Tony Gazza. Wasn't he like a mafia guy or something?" Her mind was racing ahead now and she looked fidgety as she jumped to the logical conclusion. "Oh, I'm sorry if you're in the same business."

"No, I'm not. As far as Gazza goes, there were allegations of ties to organized crime, but nothing was ever proven. I'm surprised you didn't research that."

"Call me naïve. I did look up the property on the tax maps. It's nice and all that, but it didn't seem too out of the ordinary. I would figure some kind of crime boss would be living in something a little larger and more ornate."

I guess that men who have watched the first two Godfather movies a hundred times and have read all the books—fiction and non --- about the mob, know that most made guys live rather modestly to hide their money and the source of it. Questions like, "How can you afford a million dollar house on a thirty five thousand dollar a year sanitation man's income" are not welcome. Although I didn't deal much with organized crime with the bureau, I knew guys who did, and they told me that *Casino* and *GoodFellas* were pretty accurate representations of mob life. They may flash wads of cash around and buy their wives and girlfriend expensive baubles, but nothing that couldn't be stuffed away if the feds came knocking.

I shrugged.

She said, "Well, I'm as greedy as the next girl but I'm not so sure I want to get involved with these people."

"I don't think they whack pretty real estate agents who bring in offers under the asking price. Besides, it seems you'd be insulated. The Gazzas didn't call you directly. Your message came through intermediaries. Add that to the fact he's dead and I don't think you'd be in danger."

"Yeah, but how long has this house been empty?"

She walked through to the kitchen, eyeing every detail with the coolness of a veteran appraiser. "This place has been professionally cleaned recently. There's very little dust, maybe a week's worth. You say this man was murdered a couple days ago? I'd say this can't have been done in the last twenty four hours. This place looks like it's been vacant for a while."

I had to improvise. "Actually, the Gazzas moved out of state a while ago. They have a service come in weekly to maintain the grounds and stuff."

"Why wait till now to list it?"

Again I had to vamp. "I don't know for sure, but I'd assume that they wanted to hold the property for a while on the chance they may move back. But Mr. Gazza's death precluded that and I guess his widow decided to liquidate."

"Pretty quickly I'd say. I'm not married but if my husband died, I wouldn't be on the phone with lawyers to sell the house the next day."

"There may have been arrangements made with the legal folks in the event of his untimely passing. Always a risk in his alleged line of work."

She crinkled up her pretty little nose and sniffed. "You know, I'm just not comfortable with this. You may be right that there's no direct connection but I think I'm going to pass anyway. The commission would be nice but I value my life a little more. Trouble is, whoever I refer the property to needs to know about this Gazza character's line of work." She smiled at the private joke. "Although, knowing our business, most agents won't care."

I couldn't really argue with her without divulging my suspicions. "Suit yourself. By the way, who emailed you about the listing? This all happened so suddenly that the family didn't fill me in on the details. Did it come from a law firm?"

"There was no one name on the email, but it came from what I assume was a law firm --- Freeberg, Borkus and

Izzen. I tried looking it up but couldn't find anything. Do you know them?"

I had to stifle a snicker. It was undoubtedly some bored bureaucrat's idea of a little joke. "No, not really. He had some pretty diverse interests. These guys are probably clean as a hound's tooth. But I understand your hesitation. You do what you feel comfortable with."

"I will. Funny, I feel comfortable with you and yet you claim to be an associate of Mr. Gazza's." She looked up at me fetchingly. "If it weren't for that, I'd be comfortable asking you to lunch."

Wrong time and place but it heartened my old bones to know that this gorgeous female found me attractive enough to flirt with. "You know, I'd love to do lunch with you sometime. I've got to sort some things out regarding this Gazza situation, but I can assure you that I'll be able to put your mind at ease in terms of my connections in a few days. If you've got a card, why don't I call you as soon as I can be a bit more forthright."

She pondered that for a moment. "Sure. I'd like that."

I nodded, walked out onto the front porch and waited as she re-entered the security code and locked up. Force of habit, I memorized the four-digit code. I wondered what kind of alarm system Gazza had, and who got called automatically in case of a breach. Local cops? Would that qualify as ironic?

Of course, as I watched Jenny hop into her brown Mercedes C300 and drive away with a jaunty wave, I had ironies of my own to ponder.

Freeburg, Borkus and Izzen. *FBI.* Very cute.

Forty one

Now to Gazza's restaurant. On the way I dialed Logan's cell, not at all confident that he'd pick up.

"Hi, King. Too busy to talk. Try me in a year."

"Hold on, Daniel. I just need a minute and you'll want to hear what I have to say."

"Shoot. Clock's ticking."

"First off, congrats on the bust. Promotion's in order, I presume."

"Thanks. What do you want?"

Either I'd somehow gotten on his shitlist or he was busy tying up loose ends on a bust that would define his career. Maybe a combination of the two. My usually effusive pal was curt and business-like, and it was waste of time to try to warm him up with an opening joke or a song and dance.

"Okay, here's what's up. Gazza isn't dead."

"Oh, really. That's not my case. You want the agent in charge? But before you speak with him, be prepared to be marginalized into permanent crackpot status. You're sounding suspiciously like a wannabe fed who's lost touch with the real world. Come back to us, Riley."

"I thought you knew me better than that, Dan."

"Riley, I'm telling you this for your own good. Leave this to the big boys. I told you a couple days ago that the situation was under control and to leave it alone. All you're going to succeed in doing now is undermining any credibility you once had, and just maybe messing up a case somebody's worked on for a long time. That could mean jail time for Mr. Riley King."

"Now listen. I can't tell you how I know but the body they recovered in the bay yesterday wasn't Gazza's. The FBI supposedly spirited it away from the locals but I'm not so sure it really was the feds. I went by Gazza's house. Clean as a whistle, like no one ever lived there."

"Man's dead, wife's moving on. Sad, but it happens."

"Has the bureau's prints all over it. Or someone trying to make it look that way."

"Great. And you're basing all this on the fact the guy's house is clean. Sounds pretty flimsy to me and I *want* to believe you. Try convincing a skeptic if you can't even convince your friend."

"All right, maybe this will get your attention. Gazza controlled some major docks at Port Newark. Gazza's best bud from 'Nam has ties to Muslims in Jersey City and Newark. Interested now?"

There was a shuffling noise on the other end. "Riles, I'll say this once more then I've gotta go. You don't think we know who works the docks where that container came in? You don't think we're aware that they had help from some citizens, unwitting or not? We're on it, and all you can do is muddy the waters. Drop it, man."

"Look, if Gazza was helping the bad guys and decided to liquidate his holdings and vanish, he must have set this up way in advance. I have an in with his best friend and maybe collaborator. I might be able to help find out where he really is."

"You're way off the reservation on this one. But look, if it'll make you feel better, why don't you give us this guy's name? I'll hand it off to the agent in charge of the Gazza file, and on the off chance that it's relevant and they aren't aware of it, he'll follow up. Happy now?"

It was clear that "following up" meant stuffing it into the back of an already packed file, to be dealt with long after Salieri was in the ground. "Yeah, you're probably right. Forget about it. This is over my head. Sorry to bother you, Loges. Again, congrats on the bust."

"Yeah. Me and Dolly Parton. Take my advice, Riley. I'm a friend. Don't forget that."

"Yeah. Bye."

Two possibilities. The first was that the FBI was very aware of Gazza's treachery, but that he gave them the slip at the last minute and bailed out with whatever the terrorists had given him. So the bureau cleans out his house with a crime scene team, trying to extract prints and trace evidence that might point to the leaders of the cell. Gazza may have even been playing both sides. If that was the case, faking his death might have thrown the feds off for enough time for him to get away.

But why would Gazza risk everything on a gamble like that? The feds or CIA would chase him to the ends of the earth, and he'd be throwing away what seemed like a sweet life. Even his fellow gangsters would hate him for exposing his country to such danger. How much money could you pay an already rich man to make that deal with Satan?

No, if he did that, he had to be a true believer. A man who hated his country so much that he'd be willing to kill untold numbers of his fellow citizens. Had Vietnam warped him so badly? Or was he a Manchurian candidate, a sleeper for three decades who'd been awakened to perform this one task.

Great movie plot but too far out for New Jersey. Gazza had shown no signs of being anything but a patriot. He'd volunteered for Vietnam. He'd been a generous benefactor at a Catholic school. Could Sacred Cross be a training school for terrorists, a madrassa in disguise?

What made more sense was that the terrorists had duped Gazza. They'd posed as drug dealers or counterfeiters who needed to smuggle in a small parcel of contraband. Maybe even a load of hijacked bluray players. But when Gazza found out about the real contents, he dropped a dime to the feds and fled before the shit came down on him.

In any case, Paige White and Paul Geist would be viewed as "collateral damage" by anyone investigating the plot. Depending on Gazza's involvement, the government might cut him a deal, even make him a hero if he led them to others higher in the chain. If they could find him, that is.

I knew how it worked. I'd made deals myself with slime balls, hoping to catch bigger fish. And if push came to shove, were two murders all that consequential when it came to a dirty bomb that would kill hundreds of thousands and cripple the economy? Dan Logan was right. I was out of my league.

Still, I needed to know the truth. I couldn't trust the bureau to do the right thing. I had to make that call myself. It was times like these that I wish I had a god to call on for guidance.

Forty two

I skipped my side trip to the restaurant and spent the afternoon at the Ocean County Hall of Records instead, mostly wasting my time. The Malavista had been sold two months ago to one Salvatore Manuche for a cool two million bucks. The new FEMA flood zone maps might actually render the land worthless for further development, except as a buyout by the government.

The house was owned by Gloria Gazza, accessed by the county for tax purposes at 900 grand. No listing for his sanitation business, probably owned by some shadow holding company. I found nothing in their name in Monmouth County on their dot gov website. I decided to knock off early, pick up Bosco at Stone's place and spend the night at home alone in my own bed.

The alone part, alas, was not to be. Waiting in front of my digs was an inconspicuous black cruiser, with detective Flint McCullough slouched in the front seat.

"Geez, how much of the county's money have you spent, sitting there waiting for me?"

"Ralph Nader, you're not, King. Don't worry about the taxpayers. They get their money's worth with me. We need to talk."

"I thought you were done with me."

"So did I. But you got me to thinking."

"Oh oh, that's dangerous." I meant it, even though my tone was facetious. I didn't want any interference from a ham fisted county dick, even if the truth was ostensibly on my side.

"Funny, King. But my problem was with that little question you asked me. Why did you want to know which side the entry wound was? And you know what I think?"

"No, but I'm sure you'll tell me."

"I think that you knew that it was on the wrong side. And how could you know that unless you were there?"

"Okay, detective. Let me share a little thought with you. Let's just suppose that I'm working with the government, sort of undercover on this. Let's say for a moment that I'm not exactly an *ex-G* man. Maybe I even have someone who looks good for this. But he's a lefty and I can't square that with the forensic evidence."

"Nice try, King. But if you were still with the bureau, you wouldn't be asking me about the side of the wound. You'd know."

"What if I didn't trust the agent in charge on this? What if I thought he had something to do with Gazza's murder?"

McCullough shifted his feet uneasily. My made up scenario had him stumped for a moment. "So you're telling me that you're still a fed working on this case?"

"I'm telling you nothing of the kind. But I advise you not to start pawing around in matters that don't concern you. You were happy that Gazza's out of your hair. Leave it at that. Because I can promise that if you screw this up after you've been warned, some hotshot in DC will dream up some pretty original charges to throw your way."

"That a threat?" he said.

"Advice." I was using the same tactic that Logan was using on me, with similar effect.

"I'm not swallowing your story, King. My guess is that you're knee deep in the hoopla here, and you're trying to talk your way out this with bullshit jargon you learned back when you *were* a fed."

McCullough was smarter than I'd given him credit for. He was like a dog with a stick that wouldn't let go. He wanted to bring me down and nothing short of the truth was going to deter him.

So I told him.

I told the whole story mostly, including the fake shooting. In a way, it was a relief, knowing that someone else knew what I knew. Someone whose only agenda would be finding the truth. A kindred spirit.

When I finished he shook his head slowly. "That's some story."

"Sure is. I don't know where to go next. My ex comrades in Washington are in on this. They'll scream national security and cover-up, all the way to the top. I've got no proof Gazza was involved in the trafficking. But isn't it coincidental that Tony's death is faked, right as this terrorist thing is going down?"

"And what's your stake in this? It seems they're willing to leave you alone, especially if as you say, they faked his death."

255

"*Seems*. But let's say this is a rogue operation. They were willing to let Paige White become collateral damage. Maybe Geist as well. One more wouldn't make them lose a night's sleep."

"I see what you mean. You go public insisting that Gazza's not dead and that he helped the bad guys right under the FBI's nose and they let him get away, well, who knows what shit would come down."

"Right. I don't know why I told you all this. But I think that Gazza's out there somewhere and he got away with killing Paige and Geist and helped some enemies of our country. And he got away with it and is probably laughing at us even as we speak with millions of dollars, ensconced somewhere with no extradition. And honestly, I don't see what a couple of little guys like us can do about it."

"I see your point. If the bureau wants to cover this up and Gazza's in Dubai with a harem, we'll never find out. And they'll never admit to blowing him away when they eventually do. It'll just be another drone strike on a classified target."

Just then it hit me. The cathartic effect of spilling my guts to another cop lifted the fog and all of a sudden ---a eureka moment--- it all became clear.

What an idiot I'd been! I needed to dump McCullough and see the one man who could confirm everything that was rushing through my mind. I only hoped it wouldn't be too late.

Forty three

I almost *was* too late. Father Salieri was slipping pretty fast. When I got to his floor at the Toms River Medical Center, I was stopped by a receptionist who told me that the Archbishop was in the room, performing Last Rites. I waited in the hallway for about ten minutes when a solemn man emerged, looked both ways down the corridor and then motioned back into Salieri's chamber. Another man in a dark suit came out, followed by the Archbishop himself. I lowered my head respectfully as he passed, unable to shunt off the years of catechism.

I slipped into the room, hoping I'd find Salieri alone. A stout, competent looking nurse stood guard, making notations on a chart. Her eyes tried to chase me away but I wasn't going anywhere.

"Riley King. I'm a friend of Father Salieri's."

"He needs his rest, sir. Why don't you check in with him in the morning."

Salieri coughed, more horribly than I'd heard before. A death rattle.

"It's all right nurse. Mr. King and I need the room for a moment," he said, his voice barely audible through the rasp.

"Five minutes. Although I doubt you'll be awake that long, after the Versed I just gave you" she said. She nodded

257

sternly and left the room; her disapproval of Riley King unvoiced but palpable.

"So, Riley, milad. Here for a final denouement from me?"

"No. I'll talk. You just listen, Father and interrupt if I have anything wrong."

He tried to laugh, but coughed instead. "I'll try," was his feeble reply.

"I think that Gazza was working with the government all along. I think that somehow these terrorists approached him about smuggling something in. He pretended to go along. But as the day neared you staged Gazza's death to save the bad guys the trouble of eliminating their middle men. Or at least make them think that. Tony's on a beach with his wife, somewhere safe. That about it?"

"*About.* Riley, I've already seen the archbishop --- confessed and received Extreme Unction. So let me finally speak forthrightly to you. Lean in and sit right by me now. It's hard for me to speak too loud."

I had been standing only a few feet away but even so, it was difficult to hear him. I pulled a metal chair up next to his bed and got as close as I could.

"Good. When Tony and I came back from Vietnam, we were both changed men. I was going through a crisis of faith." He tried to clear his throat and but only an asthmatic sigh emerged. "Could I trouble you for some water?"

I filled the glass on a nearby table and helped him drink.

258

I said, "So how did you resolve this?" On one hand, I was afraid to sacrifice these precious moments of consciousness to questions with no answers that he'd already expressed to me, but the man was dying and he deserved to tell the story his way.

"I was traveling to disadvantaged areas, seeking boys who could be lifted out of poverty through basketball. It became what businessmen call win/win these days. The better players I got, the more money for the school --- the more good works I could do and the more young men I could help. It expanded beyond basketball. We started giving out more and more academic scholarships."

He coughed again, this time more gently as the water had eased some of the harshness in his throat. His voice was weaker now as sleep or death approached.

"Well, between recruiting in Newark and Jersey City, I was exposed to many people of the Islamic faith, most of whom were good gentle folk. I learned about their religion and found much to admire in it. In any case, my travels led me to a particular young boy who showed a remarkable bent for science. He was in the seventh grade and already was doing work that would challenge college students. I took a great interest in him and became sort of a father figure to him, if you will."

"Single mom?"

"Oh, no. He had a father. In fact, that's where he got much of his talent for science. But he seemed afraid of his father, always hushed up when I asked about him. One day, I came to the boy's house to pick him up for a Science Fair.

259

I thought at first he wasn't there. The front door of the house was unlocked and I feared that something bad had happened, he'd always been so reliable. As I went in I heard some noise in the basement. The door to it was open. There the boy was—he'd lost track of time, engrossed in a project. But as I looked around the workshop, it became clear to me that someone was using the space to make bombs. The boy was startled, hustled me upstairs all apologetic for being late."

"So you uncovered a terrorist cell?"

"Now I told you how I came back from Southeast Asia a changed man. But so did my friend Tony. He worked undercover for the FBI from the day he got back. Pretended to be a don, all the while working against the mob from the inside. He legitimized his dad's old businesses, selling out to rivals rather than fight them. But he stayed in it enough to know what was going on and tip off the feds whenever something major was about to break. Can you imagine a life like that? Betraying people who thought they were your friends, but all the while being careful that nothing could be traced back to you?"

"All this time a snitch?"

"No one outside of his immediate handler could know. But I knew. Tony had confessed to me, and I carried his secret around. I must say, it was a heavy burden for us both. He helped the school so much, but still played the role of a criminal. Even the archbishop insisted that we maintain a distance from Tony. Oh, he was happy to accept his largesse, but when it came to publicly acknowledging his help, there was no way."

He was drifting. "So when you suspected the bomb maker, you told Gazza."

"Yes. And he told his handler. They came up with a plan to insinuate Tony into this cell. I was further amazed by the courage it took for him to do that."

"And yours too, Father. Any involvement with these people is a dangerous game."

His voice was growing fainter by the minute. I leaned in closer. "In any case, it was arranged that these young girls and later bomb components were to be smuggled into the states through one of the container docks Tony controlled in Newark. Through Tony's help, we arranged surveillance on the cells that would directly benefit. We knew there would be no way that we could hide our role in it after the arrests took place. So when everything was set up, we staged his assassination. The terrorists would have tried to kill him after they figured out that he betrayed them. You witnessing the killing was a little fillip I added so you'd stop digging into Tony's affairs at what I'm sure you'd now acknowledge was a sensitive time. The alternative was to let them arrest you for killing Ms. White and not release you until after the bust. I believed that we could trust you if we revealed the plan, but I was overruled. The fewer people who knew, the better. Even I didn't know the timing of the final phase until it was underway."

"And what about you? You weren't afraid that what was left of the cell would figure out you were involved and come after you?"

"My time is so brief they could leave that to Allah. But just in case, there are guards here. They must be pretty good if they avoided your notice."

"So you staged the murder with *me* as a witness?"

"You were beginning to snoop around Tony and some folks who knew you in the Bureau were afraid you'd mess up the sting. High praise on one hand, lack of trust on the other. Like I said, one faction wanted to arrest and hold you until it was all over. But I came up with an idea. I'd let you think that I was mad enough at Tony to kill him. An avenging angel for Paul or that unfortunate woman. All along we planned to fake his death at some point and move him into witness protection. The terrorists would think that a rival gang member or another part of their organization had done the job. In your case, we improvised so that you'd be a witness and drop your interest in Tony."

"Smart. Al Qaeda or whoever these guys are, would have gone to the ends of the earth to punish him."

"Very likely. He arranged to get a little work done on his mug. Soon, you probably wouldn't recognize him --- wherever he is."

"I'll let you rest Father."

I started out with a lump in my throat, but I still had one more thing. "Forgive me for doubting you. I wish I had a tenth of the guts you and Gazza showed defending your country. But why are they letting you trust me with this now?"

"I never had fears regarding your discretion. Now the operation has concluded there is really nothing you can do.

You were tested, by the way. You *could* have implicated me for shooting Tony when the heat was on you but you didn't buckle. You would have been arrested and held until after the sting had you acted otherwise. You would have been vindicated when the time came--- with help from our mutual friend Mr. Logan."

So old Dan knew all along. The tricky bastard.

"So Dan tried to wheedle the information out of me about Tony being dead and when I wouldn't tell him, he knew I was safe. Wow. Father, I need just one more thing from you. Did Gazza have anything to do with what happened to Paige White or Paul Geist?"

"On the eve of such a major operation, there's no way Tony would be concerned with some literary agent. Even if you still suspect the worst of him, knowing that he'd be vanishing within days and that my time was coming, why would we bother? Everything I told you about Paul was true. Tony paid him off and he vanished. I think you can see now, Tony had bigger fish to fry."

The undercover guys I knew in the bureau had courage beyond belief. One false move, one inappropriate word in the alternate universe they live in means instant death. Those types don't kill high school teachers who write dirty books.

I touched Father Salieri's hand gently and whispered my goodbyes into his ear. His eyes closed, in sleep I thought. As I took one lingering look at him, I was convinced it would be the last time I'd see him.

Forty four

Jaime Johansen sat across from me at the Red Oak Diner in Fort Lee. Dressed for business in a dark skirt and sleeveless chenille blouse instead of weekend casual, as I'd seen her last, she looked softer and more feminine. The auburn hair had grown out some, and the result was more pleasing to my eyes. She looked older: the death of her boss and the added responsibility that conferred had to be daunting.

I guided her into a booth, where we both ordered coffee. I felt apprehensive, not knowing if she held me accountable for my failure to protect her employer. I didn't know the acceptable way to describe what I assumed was their personal relationship. "I'm sorry about your boss. I wish I'd been able to do more to help her."

She tilted her head to one side. "My boss. Is that what she told you I was to her?"

If she was about to reveal her sexual proclivities, this was information I didn't really need to know. "She really didn't tell me much. Just that you were bright and capable and that she thought highly of you."

She shook her head. "She could tell other people that. Never me, though."

"Executives have different ways of motivating. Some like the carrot, others go for the stick."

"In parenting, too."

"Never had the chance to do that, I'm afraid. Lifelong bachelor."

She smiled, sipped her coffee and shrugged. "So why did you want to talk to me? To make me feel better about what happened to mother."

"Is that how the people in the agency referred to her?"

Again the awkward smile, this time with a sad little laugh. "No, just me. And even then it was strictly biological."

"Say what?"

"You didn't know? I'm not surprised. Paige didn't want any man she set her sights on to know she had a kid. Even a grown one of thirty six."

A breeze from an open door could have knocked me over just then. "Paige was your mother? No, I didn't know. Oh my God, I'm sorry. Here I was calling her a boss and.... jeez, I'm sorry."

"Not your fault. You see, Paige gave me away, literally. She and my dad got divorced when I was five and she insisted I go with him. Not like most moms, eh? There'd always be a card and a check on special occasions, maybe a weekend or two in the Hamptons in the summer. But I always felt like an encumbrance to her. There was always some new man in her life. I'm sure you knew she had the hots for you."

Not something I was going to acknowledge now.

She said, "Of course, I never wanted for anything. And when I got out of school, she hired me to work for her.

Although she didn't want the others in the agency to think she was playing favorites so she went out of her way to prove it. Harder on me than anybody else at work. But she got a little mellower as time went on and I proved myself. Even managed to tell me she loved me a couple of times near the end. I'm afraid it was too little, too late, though. I admired her as a businesswoman and I certainly wanted to emulate her career path. I'm running the agency now. But as a mother, well, let's just say there were better role models."

The one time I'd seen them together, it was seemed clear that Paige *was* trying to make up for the wasted years. I'd completely misread what I saw that day, knowing what I did about Paige's appetites. I felt bad for this kid, sorry that I couldn't fix the damage her childhood had visited upon her.

"You know, Jaime, she really thought the world of you. Even someone like me who barely knew her could see that. I guess she had a hard time expressing it to you directly. Maybe out of guilt at the way she abandoned you but she was sure proud of the way you turned out."

"I guess I knew that. I wish I could let it go but my dad was the only one who was there for me growing up. He made sure he was at my soccer games, my recitals, everything. A big author like him, you'd think he'd be too busy, but nope, he was always there for me."

"Is he still in your life?"

"Not as much anymore, not since I went to work for mom. Funny, they still had a professional relationship but I had to be the mediator with him. She couldn't. It was a pretty

big responsibility for a kid, handling contracts for someone
as big as John Peterson."

My day for surprises.

Johansen!

Some detective I was. I flashed back to McCullough
telling me who owned the Loveladies house and I only
thought of Buster Poindexter, not the young woman I'd been
introduced to earlier that day. A young woman who now
impressed me greatly with her maturity and intelligence.

"Look, I won't take up much more of your time. I
just wanted you to know whatever else, Paige did believe in
her work to the point she may have even died protecting it. I
told you that she hired me originally to track down the
author of a manuscript that she thought was special.
Unfortunately, I don't know if he's still alive either, but your
mom gave me a copy for safekeeping. I don't know who it
belongs to legally, but I'm returning it to you. I'm sure
you'll do the right thing. I wish I could tell you what that is."

She never took her eyes off me and barely
acknowledged the envelope I passed across the table, which
included the retainer.

She said, "I still don't understand why you wanted to
see me. You could have just fed-exed the card with a note."

"I was hired to do a job and I failed. I guess I needed
to apologize to someone and even though I didn't know she
was your mom, you were the person who came to mind."

"That's how you see it? You failed at your job?"

"Bad things happened. I didn't prevent them."

267

"No, I don't think things are simple. You were hired to find a missing person. And you had no inkling that my mother was in danger after the break-in?"

"I have to take responsibility for not seeing that. I let you both down."

I saw no benefit in reconstructing Paige's final hours for her daughter, or admitting that her mother and I had been intimate. I had to let this go, for everyone's sake. "Take care of yourself, Jaime. And try to think of your mom as someone who fought the good fight."

"So that's it? My mom's murder is a cold case now? Whoever did this gets away unpunished?"

"There's a good cop named McCullough who's on the case. I'll stay in touch with him and help where I can."

"Would you accept that if it was your mother?"

"No. I wouldn't."

She slit open the envelope with a long fingernail and extracted the card and the check. "What's this check for?"

"Your mom gave me a retainer. I think you can understand why I can't accept it."

"I get that you feel guilty about what happened. Look, I'm no wide eyed kid who believes in closure. My mother is gone and nothing is going to bring her back. But I can't let whoever did this go unpunished. I want justice, outside the law if necessary."

I'd felt the same way---I was ready to dispatch Gazza when I thought he was responsible, consequences be damned. But I couldn't counsel this young woman to take that path.

"You know what they say about revenge. *Dig two graves.*"

She slid the check back across the table. "Does that mean you won't help me?"

"Jaime, I'm not a hired killer."

"If you won't do this, I'll find somebody who will. I can't live with the thought that whoever killed my mother is still out there. No matter how she treated me when I was a kid, I won't let this stand."

"I don't want your money. I'll help you. But you have to promise me, if we find the guy, you'll let the system take care of it."

I shoved the check back. If she was going down this path, I couldn't let her do it alone or in the hands of some pro hitter.

She got up to leave and squeezed my hand. "If the system works the way it should, I can live with it. If it doesn't...."

The retainer check was still on the table after she departed. The SD card was gone.

269

Forty five

So throughout all of this, what had I accomplished? I'd managed to make no progress on the job I was hired to do --- find Paul Geist --- and in the meantime, I'd let my client be killed. The best that could be said was that my bumbling didn't screw up a massive FBI sting.

Two days after seeing Jaime, I arranged to meet McCullough at the end of his shift, which gave me time to go back home, take Bosco out, run three miles, and shower. All of the above were sorely needed.

I got to the restaurant a few minutes early and drank a cup of tea while I waited.

Diners were becoming my meeting place of choice these days, and after the dinner hour, the Starlight is a pretty dead place. The night crew is busy cleaning up after the day's bustle, and the short order cook isn't as adept or motivated as the prime time dudes. I figured there was nothing bad they could do to a tea bag.

McCullough slid into my booth at 9:15. "Busy day, detective?" I asked.

He looked tired. "Yeah. Sorry, but I've been chasing my tail putting out brushfires. Haven't had much time to think about what we talked about."

"Actually that's a good thing. Look, I checked into some things after seeing you and found some interesting stuff. I'm afraid I was sending your mind on a wild goose chase."

"Jesus, King just when I was starting to warm up to you a little you tell me this. Are you making this up as you go along or what?"

As usual, his perception was in sync with what was really happening. But I had to deflect that with an alternate version of the truth that closely tracked the few facts he could corroborate. Paradoxically, I was again playing the same role with him that Logan had with me.

"I know it looks like that. But I took a back door approach with an FBI forensics guy I used to be tight with. He got me in to see the body and I'm convinced now that Gazza is really dead. The dental records and DNA match, and what the fishies hadn't eaten sure looked like Tony Gazza. In any case, no more Tony Gazza."

"And the bureau wouldn't fake the dentals and DNA?"

"That's the first thing I looked for. Look, this spy stuff is a dirty business. Whatever role Gazza played, somebody couldn't afford to let him skate and maybe talk later. Maybe it was the terrorists themselves for all we know."

"But what about Gazza's family? His wife missing without a trace?"

"Give the government a little credit for mercy. Regardless of who really offed Gazza, they wouldn't make the wife pay for the sins of the husband. She's probably in a safe house awaiting relocation now. Assets from the house

271

sale and such will pay the freight. But she'll live out her life in comfortable obscurity, I'd imagine."

"You're satisfied with that? "

"I'm okay with it. I mean, he's dead, either way. But there *is* one thing."

"What's that?"

"Paige White. Salieri swore that Gazza didn't kill her or have it done. I don't think he'd lie about that. That means the real killer is out there somewhere."

McCullough took a long pull of coffee and winced at the bitterness of the rancid afterhours brew. "And since we're coming clean with everything, you don't want to confess that?"

"And here I thought you were warming up to me. No, I didn't do it and you know it. But I'd still like to know who did."

"You're still technically a suspect."

"I'm sorry you feel that way."

I started to gather my things up. I could see that McCullough would be little of help finding the real killer. He was reverting to his local cop mentality.

He said, "Wait a minute. Truth be told, I *don't* think you killed Paige White. In addition to my guilty pleasure of matching wits with you during our chats, all along I thought the timeline was too tight for you to have done it. Stone's version of your dinner timing checked with the restaurant staff's recollections. You would have had to kill her almost as soon as you walked in the door and that didn't make sense. But nonetheless, given how short we are with manpower and such, it's not likely we're going to find the killer on our own. If you want to get involved, I can't stop you. I'll try to get you a copy of the file. But no avenging Annie stuff. You find him first, he's mine."

That would do.

"Okay. It's a deal. What do you have so far? Anything useful?"

"Nothing much. Time of death was only approximate but best guess was within a half hour before you got there so you almost walked into it. Tire tracks. Your car. An SUV tire as well, probably a late model Ford Explorer. A couple of footprints, size nine. Your ten and a half's are there too."

"There was a green Ford Explorer parked near there. I thought it might be following me at one point. I gave you the plate number. You checked through DMV?"

"Of course. Stolen plates from some rich dentist's Lexus. No prints on the Lexus --whoever swiped the plates was careful. The Explorer could be the killer's vehicle but it's a dead end unless your boys have a tread they could compare it to."

I picked up the check a few minutes later and we agreed to keep in touch. McCullough seemed to have swallowed the story about Gazza being dead, but just in case, I called the hospital the next morning to warn the priest to back me up if the detective followed up.

Even though I half expected it, the news still jolted me. A nurse informed me that Father Salieri had left us during the night.

RICHARD NEER

Forty Six

The funeral was a simple, closed casket affair, held in the cathedral in Toms River since the parish church at Sacred Cross wasn't large enough to accommodate the mourners. The respect the man held in the community was on display, and it was never more deserved.

Patricia Murphy sought me out at the wake and handed me an envelope containing a handwritten note that he'd written moments before his death. In it, he said that as he prepared himself for the end, he felt a presence within that could only be that of the Christ. He hoped that someday I would find the peace and comfort he found there. He also wanted me to know that he had been truthful in our final conversation and that he knew that I could do more good with my life than chasing the phantom of Tony Gazza. It made me feel bad to have ever doubted him.

But my reasons for attending his wake and funeral were not *purely* to honor the man. I guess I was still hopeful that someone in attendance might unlock the key to Paige's murder. The ex-Mrs. Geist was the closest I got; surprisingly, she recognized me right away. Outside the church, she quietly took me aside and said that if I was free, she had discovered something that might be of interest if I could stop by her townhouse later.

274

When I arrived that afternoon, I was surprised to see her tidy home in disarray, U-Haul boxes scattered about the living room.

"Thanks for seeing me. Are you moving?"

She was dressed in jeans and a white blouse, and looked a bit slimmer. "Getting married. We're planning to go to Vegas over Christmas. I'm moving in with Gene next week. So I guess we'll be living in sin for a while first."

"Congratulations. Not on living in sin, I mean, well you know what I mean."

She smiled. Her whole being seemed different than the last time we'd met. Her eyes were bright and whereas she had seemed world weary before, now she seemed to eagerly anticipate her new life. This 'Gene' must be a good guy, although after Geist....

"I spoke to you on the off chance that you were still looking for my ex. In the process of moving, I uncovered a bunch of things in the attic that belonged to Paul. Nothing of any monetary value, only bad memories. I'd be happy to turn them over to you rather than just chuck it. Maybe as a detective, you might find something useful in there. I thought Paul had taken everything of his when he left, but he must have overlooked this."

The box was one of those translucent plastic mail containers, about a foot cubed. Peering in, I saw a mélange of loose papers, carelessly stuffed envelopes, and a few knick-knacks that one's desk accumulates over time.

I originally had hoped that her ex may have contacted her recently and that she was willing to point me toward him. My only interest in Geist at the moment was any tie he might still have to Paige. The contents of the box probably would be a colossal waste of time. Regardless, I thanked her and hauled it away. I'd get to it eventually.

I called Jaime Johansen the week after the funeral. We met for dinner in Ridgewood at a little Italian place called Mara's, and I told her everything I could about the book and the genesis of my suspicions regarding Gazza and Salieri. They were both gone and I was convinced that they were innocent. I said I'd keep looking and keep pushing the police to do the same.

She had read Geist's manuscript the night I'd passed it to her. In her professional opinion, it might find an audience, but she needed to establish legal rights to it. She wasn't as determined as her mother was to find the author. Given the fraudulent nature of Andolini publishing, I wasn't sure how to proceed, especially with Gazza now out of the picture. Did the rights revert to the ex Mrs. Paula Geist after a reasonable period? Could Jaime edit the manuscript to make the locale unrecognizable to protect Sacred Cross and release it under an assumed name (or John Peterson's) to see if anyone claimed the rights?

We spent the rest of the meal talking music, sports and New Jersey politics. We had a lot of common interests and it was a pleasant evening. I started to call Jaime more frequently after that night, ostensibly to apprise her of progress on the case although there wasn't much to report. I dispatched a couple of free-lancers to round up any video of Long Beach Island taken on that fateful Saturday ---

convenience stores, ATMs, security cameras, etc. We were hoping to catch a glimpse of Paige with the killer but there was nothing, not even tape of her with me. I interviewed the dentist whose license plates had been stolen. Nothing useful came of it.

The fact that there had been no forced entry led me to agree with the conclusion that Paige knew her killer. With Jaime's help, we compiled a list of friends, associates and rivals and systematically began establishing their whereabouts on the day in question. Without Jaime's knowledge, I even had Tommy Smith quietly check where her father was on the night in question and if he had anything to gain by eliminating Paige. Again, nothing promising turned up. I spent a couple Saturday nights interviewing bartenders and bouncers to see if anyone remembered Paige and if so, did they recall her being with anyone? Maybe an acquaintance with a grudge against Paige had stalked her, made it appear to her that he'd accidentally stumbled into the same bar, and created some pretext for going back to Johansen/Peterson's. Another blind alley.

Tommy hoped he might be able to suss out any industry enemies who would benefit from Paige's death. He found that although she wasn't the most popular woman in publishing, no one had any direct motive for capping her. His take was that promiscuity had finally caught up with her, that some sicko-spurned lover had reacted badly to being dismissed so casually from her bed. It would be nearly impossible to trace all the men she had slept with in the months leading up to her death. Frankly, I didn't have the time to try and I certainly wasn't going to lay that on Jaime. She reported that John Peterson was so appalled by his ex's murder that he immediately put the Loveladies house on the market. It was snapped up within days for twelve million, the notoriety enhancing rather than detracting from its value.

Jaime had come down on weekends to help out with some of the initial legwork, renting a room when she stayed overnight. After a couple of weeks, I summoned up the courage to suggest that she stay at my place. Hell, I had a spare bedroom and Bosco liked female company. She came to Bayville, but rather than bunk out in my guest room, she unpacked her things into the master chamber and our affair began.

It took me a while to shed my more paternal instincts and accept her as a grown woman but as time went on we spent less time chasing leads and more time chasing each other. I'll admit it was unsettling at first, the idea of making love to the daughter of someone I'd slept with. I was reluctant for another reason, given Stone's recent experience with a younger woman. But my relationship with her ultimately led to another issue.

Time spent with Jaime meant time spent away from Rick. He resented our involvement and didn't mince words expressing his distaste. He couldn't find much wrong with Jaime's character, so he attacked what she did for a living as parasitic and proceeded to minimize her in any way he could. I tried to be patient with him, understanding that his smoldering was a result of how he'd been burned. After a while, I found the easiest way around it was to avoid him, especially when he was drinking, which was more often than not these days. We did have a knock-down, drag-out battle over it one late night, which ended with me telling him that he needed some professional help. He threw it back in my face, insinuating that Jaime was my little red corvette, a mid-life plaything I'd soon weary of.

The argument settled nothing. We still got together when Jaime wasn't around, and I found that if I could steer the conversation toward sports or politics, he'd get involved in those subjects enough to leave my relationship with Ms. Johansen alone. But the free and easy times we had were becoming more infrequent, and he despised her all the more for stealing his pal.

She was great about it. She even set him up with an acquaintance of hers who was Rick's age and extremely attractive. We went as a foursome to a minor league game in Lakewood, but Stone was sullen the whole time and made an unfavorable impression on her friend. Afterwards, we decided that we'd best let Rick find someone on his own when he was ready but that even then, double dating would be awkward.

McCullough checked in every once in a while. He was turning up less than we were, and it wasn't long before other cases took priority over this one. He called in September to tell me that he was relegating it to the cold file, but that I shouldn't hesitate to call him if anything turned up. We chatted a bit about the terror sting and how the press still hadn't uncovered Gazza's or Salieri's role in it. For once, the FBI kept a tight lid on things. If he only knew the whole truth.

Of course my buddy Logan was cagey. We hooked up for drinks a few months after the bust and I told him what I knew. He merely smiled and said if he told me anything he'd have to kill me. I didn't think that remark was particularly amusing, but from the look in his eye, I could tell that Salieri's story was true. Logan was still holding something back, but by now I felt pretty safe from any reprisals. As an old friend, he seemed to trust me to keep what I knew under wraps. I was also sure that he wouldn't tell his queasier superiors about my advanced knowledge. Although after his promotion, he didn't have all that many superiors in the Bureau.

Life was settling into a nice routine. Business was better, and Jaime's weekend visits had expanded--- she'd drive down Thursday nights and stay until Sunday night or Monday morning.

But winter was closing in and I was getting restless again about being cooped up. I'd gotten down to my playing weight of 210 and didn't fancy putting any of it back on. I started surfing the web for warm places where I could relocate, sooner rather than later. I found myself trying to confine my search to big cities in hopes that there would be enough of a publishing hub there so Jaime might consider coming with me. I even fantasized that her agency could merge with Tommy Smith's. Southern California seemed the only place that might work for both of us, but if it was just to be me, there were a dozen spots that seemed comfortable. I wasn't sure how she'd respond if I broached the subject but I knew I'd have a hard time letting her go if she wasn't amenable.

On a cold early December afternoon with flurries swirling outside my window, I sat at my computer daydreaming of a golf resort near San Diego. Winter can be the ugliest time of year at the Jersey shore. Barren trees, brown marshlands and battered beaches can combine to create a desolate landscape. Warm autumn breezes off the ocean give way to arctic blasts from the northeast that can turn an otherwise mild day into a bone chilling hawk. But azure skies set against the bleached landscape, crystalline images of ice clinging to bare branches over a blanket of freshly fallen snow evoke a stark beauty on occasion, when the winds abate and the seas are calm as a millpond.

The phone interrupted my aesthetic musings. It was Jaime.

"Hey, your ears burning or something?" I said.

"Why's that?"

"I was just thinking about you."

"I like that you think about me. You manage to squeeze into my thoughts every so often. Like every five minutes."

"That's nice. What's up, girl? Just lonely?"

"No, something weird just happened."

I'm not a fan of weird. "What was it?"

"Have you seen the latest Vanity Fair?"

"I know you read it and tried to turn me on to it once but there's too much fashion and celebrity gossip in it for my taste."

"Mr. Meat and potatoes, eh? Careful you don't scrape your knuckles," she said, not entirely in jest.

"So what's the problem? Gwyneth Paltrow wearing the same dress you planned on for the Golden Globes?"

"It's not that simple. I'd just shoot the bitch. You've heard of Yvevgeny Strelnikov, right?"

The Russian again. "Never really read his stuff but sure, I saw the movie they made of his novel, what was it --- The Karmazov Letters? Years ago. Your mother said that Geist's book reminded her of him. He dropped out of sight, what, twenty five years ago. Commies had put him in prison on some trumped up rap. After the new regime freed him, he came here to the States. Lives up in New Hampshire like a hermit or something."

"Vermont, actually. Gave up his writing, lives off royalties somewhere in the woods. Supposedly grown a waist length beard and suspects the world is conspiring against him. Howard Hughes meets Rasputin."

"If you lived under the KGB, you might turn paranoid too. So why the interest in this guy now?"

"He's got a new book coming out and Vanity Fair is running an excerpt this month."

"Unless he owes you money on agent's fees, why would you care?"

"Riley, it's a major literary event. He never wrote many full length novels in his day, but a lot of people consider him the world's greatest living writer."

"Better than Clive Cussler?"

"I'll ignore that. He hasn't published in over three decades. This is huge. But there's a problem and you and I might be the only two people in the world who know about it."

"Okay. You've got my attention, woman of mystery. What is it?"

"I just finished reading the excerpt. Riley, it's almost word for word. It's a chapter of Paul Geist's book."

Forty Seven

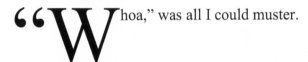"hoa," was all I could muster.

"You know what this means?"

My mind was overflowing with possibilities that defied articulation at the moment. I told Jaime that I'd be in the car within ten minutes and meet her at her apartment in ninety minutes. She said that would give her time to clean up some matters at the office.

She kept a small place on the river in Fort Lee overlooking Manhattan. It was a tidy one bedroom in a high rise her mother had helped her buy when she first came to work. Given the market in Northern Jersey, it was an investment worth many multiples of its purchase price. The view was its main attraction, and Jaime had kept the furnishings subordinate to it. Window treatments were minimal and she displayed no art on the Tuscan plastered walls. An entire side of the living room was lined with bookcases; its neatly arranged volumes stretching to the ten foot ceiling.

We were on her sofa, cradling glasses of a soft merlot and gazing out at the skyline. She had changed to a sweatshirt and jeans. She'd lit the gas fireplace, which filled the room with a rugged glow.

"So Strelnikov is a plagiarist?" I started. "Now he may be a weird guy, but I've never heard anyone impugn him on that score."

Jaime was one step ahead. "More likely the copier was Paul Geist. Somehow he stole a manuscript of the great man's work and tried to pass it off as his own."

"If that's the case, wouldn't Strelnikov find out about it and discredit Geist? It seems like he'd be found out in pretty short order if he tried that."

"That's if Strelnikov was in a position to know about it. They say that he lives like a hermit and that nobody's actually seen him for years. He might be dead for all anyone knows."

"This could have been something he wrote years ago, no? Somehow Geist got hold of it, made a couple of changes, and tried to pass it off as his own, knowing that an out of touch Russian couldn't or wouldn't refute the claim."

She sipped the wine and shrugged. "Or maybe Strelnikov is so crazy that he *gave* it to Geist, not wanting to accept the fame and media attention a new work would attract. All Geist would have to do is change the locale to Toms River from wherever the Russian had set it originally."

"Why would the Bolshevik do that?"

"Strelnikov, even in his salad days, hated glitz and glamour. He saw himself as just a working writer who should be given no more acclaim than a stonemason. There are probably only a half dozen interviews with the man ever published --- he never did radio or television. The only

285

pictures we have of him are almost three decades old. This would be totally in character, letting someone else take the credit for his words. He might have wanted the lion's share of the royalties, but it would be a hard offer for Geist to turn down."

"But why wouldn't Strelnikov just come up with a nom-de-plume and cut out the middle man?"

Jaime took a moment before answering. "That dog doesn't hunt. Literary experts would suspect that it was his. Look how they exposed J. K. Rowling on that book she wrote under a pseudonym years before."

I loved her voice. It was like music and sometimes, without even hearing the words, the sound of it could just carry me away. Do I have it bad or what?

"All right, but this is all academic and it proves nothing. The heart of the matter for us is this --- do we believe that someone killed your mom to get this manuscript back?"

That stopped her in her tracks. Her voice was thick with emotion. "That's back in play now, isn't it?"

"We tracked down all the Mr. Goodbar leads and they yielded nothing. The non-forced entry indicates premeditation and that she may have known her assailant. Geist might have told Strelnikov that he could get the book published under his name. When your mom didn't bite, maybe they went to plan B."

Jaime picked up the train. "Strelnikov might have needed money no matter how simply he lived in Vermont and needed to get this published for the royalties."

"So what if Strelnikov wanted it back and finally came to the conclusion that the only way to get the book the attention it deserved was to publish it under his own name. So he severs his arrangement with Geist, maybe promising him of a small piece for his troubles, and proceeds on his own. He contacts Vanity Fair and works a deal."

"But there were at least three people who believed it was the work of Paul Geist, not counting you. The priest, that gangster and my mother. All dead now. One of natural causes and two murders. And following that logic, maybe he killed Geist as well. Do you know what we're saying? That would mean that a major literary figure killed my mother to get his manuscript back. God, it's too horrible to think about."

I held her tighter. "Don't let it make you crazy. We don't know that any of this is true. There might be another explanation."

"But whatever it is, we need to find it. Are you still in?"

"You didn't need to ask. I hope you know that."

She looked up at me and said in a small voice, "I know. I love you Riley."

I then said the words I hadn't used in many years, not even to Liz Huntington.

"I love you, too."

Forty eight

I didn't want to leave Jaime alone to digest all of this so I called one of my men and asked him to take care of Bosco for the night. It saddened me that I didn't call Rick first as I had many times in the past, but I couldn't count on him for a favor if Jaime was in any way involved. As it was, I barely slept, leaving Fort Lee at 6 a.m., just ahead of New York's omnipresent rush hour. I managed to get back to the shore by seven thirty.

But Stone was still my go-to guy to bounce off on tough cases. I wasn't about to hit Flint McCullough again with wacky conspiracy theories until I had more proof. I hoped that my relationship with Rick hadn't cooled to the point where I couldn't rely on him for counsel.

He was a bit cold on the phone at first but then reminded me that he liked his coffee with half and half, and that two old fashioned Dunkin Donuts would work for him this morning. After a quick stop at the drive thru, I was in Mantoloking by eight, sustenance in hand.

"Sounds like we're going to Vermont," he said after I laid out the latest news about Strelnikov as we sat at his kitchen table. "I'll dust off the skis, just in case we have some down time."

"We? Hey Rick, I just wanted to get a fresh set of ears on this. You don't have any obligation to give anything more than advice."

"What's the matter? You don't want my company?"

"Not that at all. It's just that Jaime's coming. She speaks some Russian and she's got lots of literary contacts. I figured she might come in handy."

"Especially on those cold Vermont nights, huh? You need a belly warmer and the good old days of us finding one on the fly won't hack it anymore. The old poontang trumps friendship every time. I get the message."

Reducing Jaime's status to a convenient lay was typical of his disregard for her and it pissed me off. "No, you don't. I'd love to have you along but you've made no attempt to disguise your feelings about Jaime. I figured it'd be uncomfortable for you, that's all."

"For me? Or for her?"

I got up and walked to the window. The ocean was sprinkled with whitecaps, otherwise dark and foreboding. I wasn't in the mood to fight with my best friend but that seemed to be all we did lately. It was like being back in high school and he was asking me to choose between Jaime and him. I was fed up with his childish behavior and it was time to have it out again --- let the chips fall where they may.

"Look, Jaime really *wants* to like you. In fact, I think she actually does despite how hard you make it for her. She's really a great girl if you'd only give her a chance."

"Like you gave Lisa? You never really accepted her, did you?"

I rubbed my eyes. "If you're asking me if I liked Lisa, the answer is not really. I always thought she was someone more into herself and her career than in any kind of relationship."

He pounded his palm down on the table. "Why didn't you say anything at the time?"

"Because you were the one who had to deal with it. You seemed happy and that's all that mattered. The other stuff was none of my business."

"You could have saved me a lot of shit, man, if you'd opened your mouth."

"Come on Rick, would you have accepted it from me then? Don't you see it's what's happening now? Ever since Jaime, you and I haven't been the same and it's because you don't approve of her."

He said, "Do you think I want you to go through what I went through? It ripped my guts out. I still can't go a day without thinking about her. Wondering 'what if?' and second guessing everything I ever did with her."

"Ricky, you gave her everything any woman could ask for. You treated her like a princess. Damn man, even when I came over here for dinner, *you* were doing the cooking. Then you cleaned up while she sat on the deck, drinking wine and watching the waves."

I'd never seen him so despondent. Instead of recovering, he was slipping deeper into the morass, exacerbated by the deterioration of our friendship.

"Will you wake up? This is on her, not you. You may not want to hear this but Tommy Smith, the agent on the coast who's a buddy of mine, told me the other day that she's already ditched that producer she was going with and is taking up with the head of the network's news division. Who's married, by the way. Nobody's gonna be good enough for her until she hooks up with Warren Buffet."

"And you saw this coming?"

"Rick, I told you, if she made *you* happy, then so be it. All I heard from you was how great she looked or how she was doing on TV."

"And you don't see that with this chick Jaime?"

I chafed at him referring to her as "this chick" but it only supported what I already knew about his opinion of her. "No, I don't. Jaime's not like that."

"So you don't see she's using you to find out what happened to her mother?"

He was projecting what Lisa would do in the same situation and I was having none of it. "Stone, first off, we haven't really done anything about her mother for a few months now. This Strelnikov thing came out of the blue. And second, *I* want to find out what happened to Paige. The woman gave me a retainer to do a job I still haven't done. Not to mention the personal stuff. If this Ruskie had anything to do with offing Paige, I want to bring him down."

"Let me go to Vermont with you then. I want to."

His eyes were moist and downcast. "Riley, nothing matters to me anymore since Lisa left. I can't care about sports. I can't keep my head in my work. I sit through my show just waiting for it to be over. My heart isn't in it. I need something bigger to focus on. I need to get out of this house. Everything I see here reminds me of her."

291

He looked defeated --- desperate to pull out of the depression that had gripped him so utterly but he didn't know how. He was grasping at straws. "Maybe getting back in the action instead of being a spectator will help me. I'm feeling pretty useless these days. I want to come with you."

Would Stone be an aid or a burden? Best case, I could help rehab my friend and put his talents to use at unraveling this mess. Worst case, he could screw up my relationship with Jaime and divert our attention from Strelnikov.

I owed it to him to try. He'd helped me through some tough times, especially after Liz's death. "Okay. I'm not sure when we're going, maybe this weekend."

"No problem. I can take off any time. The station would probably be happy to see me go."

"Great. Now stop feeling sorry for yourself and get your shit together. We could be stalking a guy who's responsible for at least two murders. This isn't going to be a romp in the snow."

"I know. Thanks."

We finished our coffee and talked about Vermont for a bit, before he had to shower and get ready for his show. I went home to clean up and look in on Bosco. He was wagging his tail and licking my face as I came in, as if I'd been gone for years instead of just overnight. I gave him a Meaty Bone, wrestled with him for a while and took him for a short walk, during which he showed an uncommon interest in chasing some ballsy seagulls that dared encroach on *his* street.

292

But after I fed him and went into the bedroom to change, my warm feelings toward Bosco took a turn for the worse.

"Dammit, Bosco, I thought you were over this. Bad dog!"

Somehow, my best buddy had gotten into my walk in closet. Normally I keep the door closed so that he can't indulge his habit of stealing my shoes and chewing on the laces. Strewn about the closet were papers, some showing signs of Bosco's consideration, others mostly intact. I'd left the box that the ex Mrs. Geist had given me under my pants hangers and the dog had gotten into it and rooted around. I hadn't looked through the box in months after initially scouring the top layer and finding nothing of interest.

As I scooped up the mess and started to shovel the papers back into the box, a couple of crumpled slices caught my eye. Credit card receipts, dated just over two years ago. Vermont addresses.

I called Jaime at work. "It's me."

"Hey, Riles. You left pretty early this morning."

"I thought you could use the extra sleep."

"Thanks, it did help. Anyway, I called a friend of mine over at Vanity Fair. The long and the short of it is that they can't talk about Strelnikov. They said he contacted them from somewhere up north a while ago. They couldn't or wouldn't tell me exactly where or exactly when. They were suspicious at first but they scored what they believe is a chapter of fresh Yvevgeny Strelnikov."

"You didn't tell them about the Geist manuscript?"

293

"No, of course not. Strelnikov wanted no direct contact or any attempt to trace him. No e-mail. CIA type stuff. Contacts only at pre-arranged times, that sort of thing. The magazine folks were cautious, especially after the forgeries at CBS News that undermined Rather. They had experts go over the text. They asked for handwriting samples that were verified. They're convinced the work is authentic. But they have no way to contact him."

"What about the royalty checks?"

"Wired to offshore banks with strict privacy laws. Strelnikov said that if anyone made an attempt to find him, he'd know that someone at the magazine talked out of turn and he'd never work with them again. Said that if they earned his trust, he would give Conde Nast exclusive rights to the entire book. I imagine there'd be quite an auction if it was opened up for bidding. Their parent company could save a lot of advance money if they were the only one in the game."

"Sounds like he's taking great pains to cover his tracks. But I've stumbled onto something. Can you take a few days off? We might be headed north."

"You said it yourself, Vermont's a big state with a lot of wilderness."

"You know that box Geist's wife gave me? I found a bunch of credit card receipts... all from one area in Southern Vermont. They're a couple years old but it's a start."

"I'll pack my long underwear."

I said, "Just the thought of you in long underwear is pretty exciting."

"More exciting in a hot tub, without it."

"Down boy. Okay. Let me follow up on this. I'll call you later."

"Bye, babe. Love you."

"Call ya later." It still didn't come easy.

Richard Neer

Forty nine

We were in Jaime's Cherokee, headed north on the New York State Thruway, passing towns named after old Indian tribes. I drove, Stone riding shotgun, Jaime sprawled in the back seat, her laptop wired to the car's 12-volt DC source. We passed the site of the Woodstock Music and Arts Festival (three days of fun and music and nothing but fun and music) and Hunter Mountain, where *paisanos* from Brooklyn show off their skiing prowess by day and seduction skills by night.

So far, Stone and Jaime had been remarkably civil; in fact if I hadn't known their history, I'd say they were downright friendly. The design of the SUV made it hard for Jaime to hear from the back seat, so any comments directed to her had to be shouted. After a while, she gave up trying to be heard, eschewing small talk and only communicating when she had a question or a new idea on how to locate Strelnikov.

"Southern Vermont's got a lot of pretty desolate areas, Riles," Stone said, as a Range Rover zoomed by us as if our seventy-two mile an hour pace rendered us stationary.

"I know, but we've narrowed it down quite a bit."

"Awfully careless of Geist to leave that box behind if he truly wanted to disappear. Those credit card receipts could be misdirection."

296

"You've been reading LeCarre lately? You're assuming he planned this as long as two years ago. But just because Geist was there, it doesn't necessarily mean that Strelnikov is, too. But I'm thinking if we find one, he'll likely know where the other is, dead or alive."

The receipts showed how Geist had spent the summer before last in Townshend, West Dover, and Wilmington, Vermont at a number of hotels and motels. The majority of his time was spent in West Dover, the most prominent feature of which was Mount Snow, Vermont's southernmost major ski area. The mountain had also hosted the X Games for ESPN a number of times, but generally in the summer, only the natives and intrepid mountain bikers inhabit the nearly empty streets. The Dover Chamber of Commerce was constantly touting the area as a four season resort, and as pleasant as the town might be in the summer, autumn (incredible leaf peeping, the hills ablaze with maples) and winter, spring was short and muddy, with very little to do outdoors or in.

We took Route Seven just after Albany, which turned into Route Nine at the Vermont line. Jaime dozed in the back and Stone seemed barely conscious next to me. We'd made reservations for two rooms at a cozy bed and breakfast called the Deerhill Inn in West Dover, a place I'd always wanted to visit with a woman but had never been able to until now. It boasted a four star dining room, and the rooms all exuded early American romance. I looked forward to nights with Jaime much more than slogging through slush looking for Strelnikov. We hadn't given ourselves a hard

297

time frame but fortunately the inn was flexible until the week after Christmas. I figured if we didn't make any progress within a few days, we'd pack it in and try after the holidays, when the place got less congested again.

"Uhhn," Stone groaned from the passenger's seat. "Are we there yet?"

"That was funny the first three times you said it. Now it's getting tedious. We're just passing through Bennington, about forty minutes from the inn. Would you like me to stop for a coed?"

"Or two. Why not? *Young girl, get out of my mind.*"

As annoying as the song quotes are, it was a sign that he was healing. I glanced in the mirror to make sure Jaime was still asleep and not hearing our Neanderthal comments, but she smiled and winked at me before feigning slumber again. It was just another thing I loved about her. I could be completely tasteless in her presence and she'd laugh and understand it was just in fun.

The ride past Bennington took us over a small mountain that we'd dubbed the Enchanted Forest upon entering it for the first time years ago. It always had weather: thunderstorms in the summer, blizzards in winter, and floods in the spring. It seemed we never could negotiate the twenty miles up and over with some white-knuckled driving, often skidding downhill over slick and bending terrain. Today it was placid but we hurried through in acknowledgement of its nasty habit of suddenly turning cataclysmic. Snow was piled up at least three feet high along the side of the roadway, and the rock strewn stream that followed us most of the way was swollen and rising rapidly toward the top of its banks.

We reached the center of the village of Wilmington, where we turned north on 100 to Dover. Route 100 snaked through a valley up the spine of Vermont and on into Canada, passing many ski areas like Okemo and Killington along the way. Although the remnants of tropical storm Irene caused major flooding the year before Sandy, the hardscrabble natives had restored it to picture-postcard Vermont in the ensuing time: White clapboard churches, glowing yellow windows a la the late Thomas Kinkade, roofs heavy with snow, smoke billowing from rustic stone chimneys. There were barns with peeling red paint alongside rusted silver silos, split rails corralling spotted cows and brown horses. There were sagging old farmhouses, white with forest green shutters, and chic restaurants made to look like old farmhouses without the sag.

The Deerhill Inn might have hosted Crosby and Astaire a half a century ago as they sang and danced their way into Marjorie Reynolds's and Lila Dixon's hearts. We kicked the snow off our boots on the slate porch before entering the intimate vestibule to check in. An ageless white-haired lady in a gingham dress greeted us warmly and led us to our rooms after scanning our credit cards. Jaime loved the frilly canopy bed, set against the frosty windowpanes and heart pine floors and sighed appreciatively at the claw foot tub that adorned the small bath.

299

The trip had started wonderfully --- the sparks I anticipated from my two friends had been non-existent. I sensed it would be the calm before the storm and I was never more correct.

Fifty

After breakfast the next day we planned to split up --- Jaime and I would take the Cherokee while Stone would borrow one of the four-wheel drive Subaru's that the Inn rented as a courtesy for guests. Rick was off to see the local sheriff, a fellow named Ernie Novick, while we sought to mine whatever veins the local literary crowd might provide. Although cell phone coverage was spotty in the mountains, we agreed to stay in touch every two hours, on the half hour.

Our first stop was the town library, a small building in a sad state of disrepair. There was a mocked-up thermometer outside the brick and shingle structure, signifying a fund raising drive for renovations. The red line barely stretched halfway to the top of their modest expectations; the more prominent mark was left by the floodwaters that had risen almost to the first floor. The library's overheated interior smelled of damp wool as we creaked across the scarred pine floors toward the main desk, where a bespectacled young woman gave us a frosty smile reserved for unfamiliar visitors. She was a sturdy New England type, with an open face and dark eyes, magnified nearly double by her heavy prescription.

Jaime started by introducing herself as a literary agent who was trying to reach Yvevgeny Strelnikov in order to discuss royalties on the motion picture that had been made of the *Karmazov Letters*. She explained that the film had recently been released on bluray, and that the Writers' Guild had just negotiated new guidelines on compensation. It sounded more professional and credible than "we owe him some money. Tell us where he lives."

Either way, she wasn't buying. "I know there have been rumors that Yvevgeny lives in the woods around here but no one I know has ever seen him. They say he lives like a cave man --- complete with long fingernails and scraggly hair and beard. I can't say how much of that is urban legend and how much is true."

The term *urban legend* struck me as out of place in such rural country, but I couldn't come up with a more appropriate phrase. "Do you know anyone at all who might have any information as to his whereabouts? We might be talking about a substantial sum if the bluray sales take off," Jaime said.

"I guess you didn't hear me. I said that no one I know has ever seen him. Can't help. Wicked cold, isn't it?" She turned aside and began inserting cards into the little yellow pockets that were glued inside book covers. No modern scanners here.

If she did know anything more of Strelnikov she wasn't telling. Flinty Vermonters might seem curt to outsiders, but it's not personal, it's just their manner. They're more than willing to pass the time of day with you on subjects that interest them, but are quick to dismiss anything they consider a waste of their time, even if they have nothing better to do. Of course, part of her refusal to discuss the matter might have to do with the red thermometer outside the entrance. How much of that line might have been fueled by Strelnikov, if he was as devoted to the advancement of literature as he once had been?

We next drove into Wilmington to the only bookstore in town. It lay just east of the crossroads between Routes Nine and One Hundred in the center of the small village. It was a clapboard storefront with brick floors and battered oak stacks of mostly used books. A table near the entrance displayed a few current best sellers. It reminded me of a similar shop in Toms River, where people trade in old volumes for five per cent of their purchase price, usually in the form of credit. The good ones are then re-sold for ten times that amount. Most wind up *recycled*, as in ground into pulp to create new unsalable books.

The man who owned the store in Wilmington wore a plaid shirt with jeans held up by suspenders, which were probably necessary to keep his scrawny frame decent. A prominent Adam's apple protruded over pale leathery skin, which brought to mind the literary Ichabod Crane, not the handsome Limey who plays him on TV. Sparse gray hair was haphazardly arranged and hadn't experienced shampoo for several days.

Jaime repeated her story, which elicited a different reaction this time. I watched his eyes light up when she mentioned royalties.

"Might there be a finders' fee for information leading to his discovery?" he asked.

303

"We're not bounty hunters, sir. But who knows, Mr. Strelnikov may choose to show his gratitude in some fashion." Jaime was getting good at this game and there was no reason for me to chime in. Plus, Ichabod was clearly enthralled by her looks. As was I.

"Well, I don't know anything for sure but a friend of mine said that the great writer lives out in East Dover, a few miles off the county road towards Brattleboro."

"Anything more specific? That covers a lot of ground."

"No. I'm afraid not. But if you find him, you *will* mention my cooperation."

Jaime's smile could melt the icicles outside the shop. "Certainly. You wouldn't happen to know anyone else who might have more detailed information, would you?"

He considered this for a moment and then apparently decided he didn't want to share the spoils. "No, I'm sorry. No one comes to mind. Well, happy hunting. Remember me." He rummaged in his pocket and produced a tattered card.

'East Dover' did narrow things down a bit, but still left an area of at least fifty square miles to cover. Outside the storefront I called Stone. So far his morning had been as fruitless as ours.

"Novick was no help," he reported. "He said he doesn't read much. In fact, he'd never even heard of Strelnikov. Did give me an earful about the Patriots, though."

"Great. Look, I want you to head for Town Hall in Dover. They keep the property records in the basement there. He might have bought his place in East Dover under an assumed name, but check the tax rolls for anything that sounds promising."

"Okay. Where are you off to?"

"Not sure. I'll call you when we know."

Jaime had an idea. "Ever wonder where Strelnikov eats?"

"If he's as much of a hermit as they say, I doubt he eats out. Probably shoots squirrels and roasts them."

She said, "If he's that much of a mountain man, who says he cooks them first? But seriously, even if he hunts, which I doubt from reading his books, he'd need some basic provisions. Salt, flour, vodka. He *is* Russian. He'd need to get those things somewhere, right?"

"Jeez, you're smart. There's a Stop n' Shop in Wilmington, used to be a Grand Union, but that's not too convenient from East Dover. I bet there's a general store up there. Let's grab a bite and then and check it out."

After a delightful lunch at the Wilmington Inn's informal dining room, we drove north and branched off before we hit West Dover. The contrast between East and West Dover is palpable: the Western town is more modern, catering to the nightlife and conveniences of the affluent ski crowd, whereas the eastern part is authentic old Vermont. The countryside was dotted with threadbare farms scratched out amongst vast tracts of pine forest climbing toward snow-capped peaks. The town center was merely a brief strip on

305

the roadside featuring a gas station that sported an old Esso sign, a post office and a quaint general store. The front of the store was devoted to hardware while the back stocked groceries. There wasn't much selection, generally just one brand of each item and few frozen foods or similar perishables. The refrigeration case had just enough space for milk and eggs, a few packaged cheeses, and brown paper-wrapped cuts of beef, chicken and pork. As Jaime and I entered, we felt like we'd stepped back fifty years in time.

The only man in the entire store was wearing a white apron over his coarse woolen shirt and trousers so we took him to be the clerk. Jaime and I had worked out a different approach for this phase, and I began the gambit. Even though he seemed in his early forties and would no doubt be attracted to Jaime, this story favored a more masculine presence.

"Pardon me, sir, but we're here from New Jersey and we're looking for a cousin. He moved up here some years ago and he lost touch with the family. You see, my aunt just passed on and she left him with a small inheritance."

"What's this fellow's handle? You mean to tell me he doesn't know his own mother is dead? I don't understand."

I leaned in confidentially and lowered my voice. "They hadn't spoken in almost thirty years. You see, Vermont has a reputation as a tolerant state, if you get my meaning, and my cousin moved up here with his partner. His mother just couldn't accept the fact that her boy was, well you know. She was a devoted Christian woman and I'm afraid it was a conflict she couldn't resolve while living. But he was her only son, and in her will she forgave him and wanted him to have the house and the little money she'd accumulated."

"I understand. Poor woman. Don't know what I'd do if it happened to me. What's your cousin's name Mr.?"

"King, Riley King. You see, that's part of the problem. In one of the last letters he sent to my aunt, he said he was ashamed because she was so intolerant so he was taking his partner's name. It might be easier if I show you a picture,"

Jaime handed me an old publicity still of Strelnikov that we'd aged via Photoshop into looking like at 4x6 candid. "Understand, we didn't come up here just to deliver the news about Aunt Agnes. We ski at Mount Snow quite often and the rest of the family asked us to help out rather than have the estate bear the cost of a private detective to search for him. Besides, those guys are so sleazy they'd probably overcharge us double to find him. They're like lawyers, you know." I gave him the photo. "Does this man look familiar?"

Jaime elbowed me in the ribs and rolled her eyes in disbelief.

"I take your meaning. You probably have a lot of shysters in Jersey."

He polished his reading glasses with his breath and shirttail and stared at the photo. "Can't say I've seen this man recently but he does seem a bit familiar. I've only been here a year or so. Inherited the place myself."

307

"Well, on the off chance that his partner does most of the shopping, do you recognize this man?"

We'd done similar doctoring on some of Geist's yearbook pictures and handed over the one most recently taken.

Bingo.

"Now this man I know. Calls himself Peter Graves, like the actor on *Mission Impossible*. Don't make shows like that anymore. And those Tom Cruise movies were pure crap. Mr. Phelps as the bad guy, indeed. Anyway, this man has got long blonde hair now though I suspect it's a wig. And a beard. Wears thick glasses. Stops in every once in a while for provisions. Been after us to stock some more TV dinners and the like. Says he doesn't cook much and hates driving to that supermarket in Wilmington."

"That sounds like our cousin's partner. I have an older picture of him with blond hair. Here, does this look more like he does now?"

"That's him. That's old Peter. Funny, I never took him to be a fairy. No offense to your cousin."

"None taken. When was the last time he was in?"

"Let's see. It's been a few weeks at least. Used to be in every week or so." He furrowed his brow in thought. "Never talks about cooking for anyone back home. Never says much at all to be honest with you. Always in a hurry to get in and out, like somebody might actually say howdy to him. Strange duck— but queer? Gosh, you just never know."

"I'm not sure if he and my cousin are still, ahem, together. But even if they aren't, maybe this Graves fellow would know where he is now. Do you have an address?"

"Don't know addresses but I can give you directions. He's up in the hills, lives in an old cabin that some fisherman from Massachusetts owned years ago. I thought it was abandoned once he died but I guess your cousin and his friend must have bought it off the estate."

He rattled off directions, which Jaime quickly inscribed into her iPhone.

We were out of the general store as quickly as we could think of a gracious exit line, eager to be on our way. "Nice cover story, Riles," Jaime said as we slammed the Cherokee's doors closed. "But you had me in stitches when you were ripping your own profession. Was that a test of my poker face or what?"

"Sorry, kiddo. Struck me as comic relief."

"Well, funny but I'm beginning to wonder if part of your little fantasy isn't true. Do you think that Paul Geist and Yvevgeny are lovers? That could explain a lot."

"That'd come as a surprise to his wife, but hey, I bet Governor McGreevy's lady was a little shocked when he came out of the closet. Must be something in the water in New Jersey, I guess."

"Well, don't you drink any of it, big boy. I like you the way you are."

"Actually, hon, there's something I should tell you. You know Stone and I..."

She swatted my knee hard and snorted, "I know better, sweets. But seriously, are we walking into something dangerous here? Should we call in the police?"

"On what grounds? I mean, something weird is going on with this manuscript. I don't think the cops up here would view that as cause to get involved. Not yet, anyway."

"Granted. But if what we suspect is true, aren't we taking an awful chance?"

"I brought two friends to help out on that score. One is Stone ---who I'll call now and tell him to meet us at the cabin. The other is in my jacket pocket. He doesn't talk much, but when he does, people listen."

"You're scaring me now. You think it'll come to that?"

"I'll go in and you can stay in the car."

"No, if you go, I want to be with you. Strelnikov was quite the lady's man in Russia. Even if he *does* go both ways now, modesty aside, I think a pretty face might soften him up a bit. Besides, I speak the language."

"As I said, I'm carrying insurance."

I called Stone and told him what we'd learned and where we were headed. He thought he was about forty minutes away and said he'd leave immediately. Following the shopkeeper's directions, we took the county road about a mile west and then pulled off onto a pitted gravel road that soon rose to a steep grade. After a half-mile's incline, it leveled off onto a clearing at the base of a craggy mountain cliff. There stood a small rough-hewn log cabin, its stone chimney belching white smoke.

Someone was there.

Alongside the house, a wide frozen stream flowed silently beneath the ice. From this plateau at three thousand feet up, there was nothing but forest visible for miles in every direction --- a perfect spot to nest if one wanted to drop out of civilization.

But as we pulled around to park, I spotted something against the white snow that sent an electric chill through my gut.

Nestled in the driveway behind the cabin sat a dark green Ford Explorer.

Fifty one

The sight of the SUV made me think twice about entering the cabin. There were hundreds of green Explorers in Vermont alone, but it was too much of a coincidence to shrug off. It *had* to be the same one that had been parked on Long Beach Island this spring, stolen tags aside.

"Should we wait for Rick before we go in?" Jaime didn't appear frightened, although there would be no shame if she were. In a moment, we might come face to face with the man or men who killed her mother. The nearest help was miles away.

"I think we're better off taking our chances sooner rather than later. They might have spotted us coming in. Stone will be here soon. Here's my spare gun. It's a twenty-two. You know how to use it?"

"Daddy insisted. Went to the regional finals in target shooting one year."

"It's quite a bit different with a live target. This gun doesn't have a lot of stopping power so aim for the chest. Just put it in the pocket of your parka and keep your hand on it. I'm still not sure you should come in."

"Women can have a calming influence in tense situations. At least that's what I've read."

I kissed her cheek. "I suppose in some ways that might be true, but it's dangerous to generalize. Just stay cool, and in a couple of hours we'll be soaking in a hot tub back at Deerhill."

"If I needed any more incentive to keep going, that would be it."

I kissed her again and we got out of the car. I pulled the bulky sleeve of my down parka over my right hand, which was holding the gun. That way, it was concealed yet ready to fire at a moment's notice. We approached the cabin, keeping an eye on the windows for flashes of sudden movement. So far, all was quiet.

This wasn't the rustic, rundown shack I had visualized. This place had two satellite dishes: one facing southwest for television, and another due south, for high-speed Internet access. Armed with these, there was no way that Strelnikov could be so out of touch as to be unaware of his book's release. He had to be a collaborator, willing or unwilling.

We circled around the building once to make sure no one was hiding outside. There were tracks in the snow leading in every direction: human tracks—different boots but roughly the same size. Still nothing stirred from within the house, so we moved around front.

The exterior had been freshly chinked and sealed and the red metal roof was clearly a recent addition. The windows were high tech triple-insulated glass casements, again not what would have been installed originally in an old fisherman's cabin. Jaime and I stepped quietly onto a wide porch decked with Brazilian Ipe, a wood not in common use when the house was built.

A sturdy mahogany door graced the front entry and I knocked on it softly. No answer. I tried the latch—it was unlocked.

"You stay back against the porch wall," I whispered to Jaime. "I'll go in first and you wait for me to signal before you come in. Okay? Wait."

The door opened noiselessly and I stepped into the dimly lit main room. A wood fire was flickering in a massive stone fireplace. There were stairs leading to a loft above the main room and an alcove just to the right of the fireplace, which I guessed contained the eating area. There was another doorway to the left—a bedroom or study. Opposite the fireplace sat a high definition TV with a Bose surround system and bluray player. All in all, it was a pretty modern and comfortable set up.

"Okay, Jaime, coast looks clear. Come in."

I barely heard her enter. "Somebody had to be here Riley," she said. "They wouldn't leave the fire on like that, unattended."

"It's different out here in the country," I said.

"Not that different," came a high pitched, slightly accented voice from behind. "You should have listened to your girlfriend. If that's a gun in your right hand, I'd advise you to set it on the table now. Do that and turn slowly. In case you haven't guessed, I've got a gun on you."

I did as I was told, catching Jaime's eye as I turned, hoping she'd read my expression to keep her hand in the pocket holding my .22. She was smart enough to do so without my instruction.

The voice had the trace of an accent, I presumed it to be Russian. I put my piece on the coffee table and turned slowly to see Yvevgeny Strelnikov, pointing a small pistol in our direction.

Fifty two

"Comrade Strelnikov, I presume. It's a pleasure to meet you. What an unexpected honor," I said, turning on all the charm I could muster.

He picked my gun off the table tucked it into his waistband. "Hardly unexpected, Mr. King."

"Pardon the grade B dialogue, but how do you know who I am?"

He sniffed and gestured with the gun. His face was red with windburn and as he pulled off his ski cap, he revealed closely clipped dark hair. He certainly wasn't the unkempt mess he'd been rumored to be by the townspeople. For a man over sixty, he looked at least a decade younger. His gray beard was the one aspect they'd gotten right --- it was bushy and six inches too long unless you were in ZZ Top or modeling for a cough drop package. Although he was slender and not very tall, he reminded me of what Garth Hudson used to look like in the sixties.

"You don't think I read the papers on the Internet?"

"I didn't know I was so famous."

That seemed to catch him a bit off guard and I could see the wheels turning. "Your involvement in a few murder cases in New Jersey caught my eye, Riley King. The internet is a marvelous thing for research and inspiration. And who might this lovely young lady be?"

316

"Her name is Jaime Johansen. She's from the Paige White Agency, Fort Lee, New Jersey. Since you know who I am, I'm sure you realize you have nothing to fear from us. We only came armed because we were concerned about wolves. You could put the gun down and offer us a cup of tea."

I read nothing from Jaime's face. I didn't know whether she was shocked into passivity or was coldly planning her next move.

Strelnikov cleared his throat. "Wolves, eh? Very inventive. You think I keep wolves as pets? But your little pretense aside, you may as well be comfortable. Sit on that sofa together and please take off your coats."

Jaime spoke to him for the first time, her voice small at first but growing stronger as she walked toward the expansive leather couch. "I'm still cold. I'll leave mine on if you don't mind."

Smart girl.

"As you wish." He backed toward the fireplace --- the gun and eyes still trained on us. He slid a couple of split logs from their cradle into the blaze, which flared instantly at the addition of dry oak. "It will warm up quickly I promise you. But I'm afraid you won't be around long enough for tea."

"We hoped you'd give us a warmer reception. If our presence is unwelcome, we'll leave now," Jaime said.

I might have used the same line. As quick as Jaime was however, I doubted she'd ever faced down a loaded gun before.

Strelnikov wasn't buying it. "I don't think that will be possible. Not until you've answered some questions."

"We're all yours, Mr. Strelnikov." Always be accommodating whenever possible, granting permission gives you a degree of perceived control.

"Good. As long as you answer truthfully, things will go much smoother."

The bare trace of accent seemed to fade in and out. He had been in this country nearly thirty years and with the satellite dish, even Putin would have seen enough American television to assimilate.

He leaned against the wall facing us, some fifteen feet away. "Now first, tell me why you're here."

I started tentatively. "We came to give you a heads-up. We both are big fans of yours from way back and we wanted to warn you of a possibly embarrassing situation."

"I'm way past the point of being embarrassed, if you care to know the truth."

I slowly slid my arm around Jaime. She sat on my right and the gun was in her right pocket. "You see, my friend Jaime got wind of the fact that some blogger is doing a piece on the release of the chapter of your new book to Vanity Fair. Apparently working on the premise that the work isn't authentic, and the folks at Vanity Fair are getting a bit nervous. They need more proof that the work is original."

"Are you telling me that the magazine sent you up here to find me? We had a prearranged contact scheduled for a week from now."

"The Vanity Fair people thought that there may not be enough time."

I could tell he was intrigued by my story but wasn't sure. "Who from Vanity Fair sent you?"

Jaime bailed me out. "The publisher, Daniel Welles. He's a family friend."

He recognized the name and nodded. Jaime was aware that I didn't know much about Vanity Fair. Not long ago I would have said she once sang with Prince.

"I understand why you would be dispatched in that case, King. But Ms. Johansen, why you? What would your interest be in this?"

Jaime blurted it out before I could intercede. "I'm not sure if you're cognizant of it, but your life is shrouded in mystery to most of us. There are rumors that you were dead, or that you had gotten cabin fever, or had become an eccentric who lived like some kind of feral beast. Daniel wasn't sure how much English you now spoke and sent me along to be sure. I speak some rudimentary Russian."

"Nice try Ms. Johansen but you'll have to do better. Mr. Welles and I have spoken extensively over the last months. He had no problem with my English. I never speak Russian anymore."

"All right Strelnikov, I'll come clean. Jaime was afraid to admit this, but you're right. Vanity Fair didn't send us. Jaime's late boss had a manuscript that is almost word for word the same as the chapter you sent to the magazine. But it was allegedly written by someone else."

I thought that my little speech covered all the bases, surrendering ourselves to his superior perception while admitting a venial sin, albeit one in his greater interest.

He seemed revolted by my explanation. "You want to know why I live alone up here in the mountains? You've just precisely illustrated why. It is obvious you came to blackmail me."

Jaime again spat out something in Russian, something that sounded angry. Strelnikov reacted with a blank stare. Jaime had miscalculated badly again, I thought. There was no point inflaming the man, not when he pointed a gun at us.

I tried to be more soothing. "My apologies if my friend overreacted. But our motives are pure and she's offended that you'd think we are blackmailers."

"Save your breath, Riley," Jaime interjected. "This isn't Yvevgeny Strelnikov. He didn't understand a word I just said. You never forget your native tongue that completely. I just called him a third rate hack who copied the ramblings of a pitiful schoolteacher because he's an impotent old man who was overrated to begin with. This isn't Strelnikov."

She smiled, but there was no amusement in her eyes. "We finally get to meet Paul Geist. You can drop the phony accent, pal. We're onto you."

Fifty three

Strelnikov/Geist raised his weapon and pointed it at Jaime.

"You know ever since saw you coming up my road, I've been contemplating if there was any way I could turn you away alive. But since this conniving twat had to play amateur detective, I'm afraid I have no alternative."

"Hold on," I said. "Think about this for a minute. Don't paint yourself into a corner you'll never be able to get out of."

He lowered the gun and spat into the fire. "You know King, I really do regret that you got caught up in this. I lived in Toms River for a long time and I couldn't help admiring your exploits. You know, there was even a time when I thought of approaching you about writing a book about your life and adventures. I envisioned myself becoming Doctor Watson to your Holmes. What I need to do now will give me no pleasure."

That explained his knowledge and interest in New Jersey matters. There was no way that a native Russian would be aware of a minor figure like me. That should have tipped us off from the get-go. My only hope now was to engage him long enough for Stone to get here.

"Don't you see Geist, it's over? Kill us and others will follow. People know where we are and who we were looking for."

He shook his head. "That may or may not be true, but you underestimate me. It'd be a shame to give up this little hideaway. Over the years, I've embellished it with all the comforts a man could desire. But don't think for a minute that I didn't anticipate that this day might come. I knew that I might be forced to vanish again." He chuckled at his own cleverness. "How many little cabins in the woods do you think there are in Vermont? Or Canada. Like a chess grandmaster, I'm several moves ahead of you. By the time anyone knows you're missing, the great Strelnikov will be long gone. A phoenix will rise from his ashes somewhere, though."

Until Jaime had spoken Russian and exposed his deception, I had been convinced that we were talking to Strelnikov and that Geist was dead or out in the woods somewhere. But where was Strelnikov?

"Your book will die along with it." Jaime said. "We were telling the truth. The police back home know we're here and so do the feds. I told them where a full copy your manuscript was hidden if anything was to happen to us."

"Nice try. So like your boss, the late Ms. White. Make up any crazy story to save her skin. You are an emasculating bitch, just like she was. Wouldn't even return my calls. She was too important, so busy churning out cheap trash for money."

"She was my mother. You killed my mother. And she turned out to be the only one who believed in you. You murdered the one person who was willing to help you."

"I wasn't aware that she was your mother. But it hardly changes things, does it?" He looked down at the gun.

I tried to stall. "Geist, why don't you try your hand at being Doctor Watson? I'm not Sherlock Holmes and I can't piece this all together. How did you get Strelnikov involved in this and where is he now?"

He smiled ironically. "As a writer, I've always hated those scenes where the bad guy spills his guts and explains his nefarious plot to the hero. It never made sense --- as in all those Bond movies where a simple bullet to the brain would have thwarted 007 and let SPECTRE take over the world. But no, the villain had to tie up all the loose ends and then devise some elaborate death scheme that gives the cavalry time to ride in and save the day. Why should I tell you anything?"

He'd unwittingly sketched out our only hope, which was to stay alive until Stone could rescue us. I was trying to tempt him into falling into the trap he'd just described --- appealing to his vanity. Even bad guys want to be appreciated, at least make us lower creatures understand how brilliant they are.

"So as a writer, Paul, can I call you Paul? Paul, you must have planned this years in advance. However this ends, don't you want somebody to know how hard you worked and how dazzling your plotlines were? A writer needs an audience or he's not really a writer, is he?"

323

"Well, Riley, since we're using first names now, that's really the crux of it. I *am* a writer and a damn good one. But because of the way this country is caught up in greed and bullshit, my work was unpublished. Maybe years ago it was different, when editors weren't afraid to take chances, when they had the stones to believe in something and commit their full energies toward making it happen. But now all anybody cares about is money and their own security, and with these mega-corporations running things, rarely does anything that couldn't be categorized as pulp fiction or some mindless political screed ever see the light of day. Unless of course, the author had already proved his merit before the flood. Thus, the John Peterson's of the world get their garbage published and I struggle."

Jaime remained silent. The man who had killed her mother had just ripped into her father. I couldn't imagine how much loathing was roiling within her.

Geist seemed to enjoy telling his story. "I know I'm better than ninety nine per cent of the drivel that's out there. So I started submitting my work to Paige White. It was odd in that I'd never actually met the woman, but we'd have conversations on the phone about my work and she'd tell me that she'd submit it to editors when she thought I was ready. She said that I was very, very close but that for one reason or another, she couldn't close a deal. But at least she responded. Then I gave her *Julie and James* and nothing happened. I called and she didn't return my calls. I knew that this was my best work and that even the most tone-deaf editor would see that. But Paige White was silent. She'd gone Hollywood on me. Become so big time with all her other projects that she didn't have time for Paul Geist anymore."

Jaime had to defend her mother, as pointless as it seemed now. "You're so wrong. Paige was always a friend to new authors. She saw the commercial stuff as a way to subsidize the quality work. She read a little bit of everything that was sent her, maybe not right away, how could she? But she hired Riley to find you so she could get your novel published, and as thanks, you killed her for it."

"That's the same line of bullshit she tried to lay on me."

"It happens to be true," I said. "Why the hell do you think I'm here? Paige paid me out of her own pocket to find you. And that's why your actions make no sense. If Paige was finally going to help you reach your dream, why did you kill her?"

His face sagged as he shrugged. "Like the great comedians say, it's all a matter of timing. If Paige White had come to me two months earlier, we'd be toasting each other with champagne at my book party now. But by the time she did, things had already spiraled out of control. It was too late."

"Meaning you'd already killed Strelnikov."

He waved the gun carelessly, but there was too much space between us to make a move. I had eased my hand into Jaime's right pocket and pried her fingers away from the gun. She resisted at first, bent on killing Geist herself. I feared that even if she tried to get off a shot, the odds were

325

that he'd be able to respond and kill us both. I needed control of the gun, in hopes that something might distract the man long enough to get off a clean shot without reprisal. I was counting on Stone to be that distraction and calculated that he couldn't be more than five minutes away. It could be the longest five minutes of our lives, if our lives lasted that long.

Geist wiped his lips and with his left hand, the gun now trained on us again. "You know, Riley there is a bit of Sherlock Holmes in you. But you're not exactly right about my old friend and mentor Yvevgeny. His appearance had changed since leaving Russia and most of the folks up here didn't even know who he was to begin with. But I did.

"I started coming up here about six or seven years ago. Strelnikov had always been an idol of mine and one night by chance, he and his wife happened to be having dinner at the same Chinese place I was. Somehow, I managed to stifle my hero worship and engaged him in conversation. We became friends, maybe because he missed sophisticated literary company. I'd visit him whenever I came up here."

His rambling gave me time to plan what I might do to stay alive. I could shoot once through Jaime's pocket, then roll over her onto the floor while extracting the gun for the kill shot. It would take some athleticism but with luck, all we'd suffer would be some bruises if we hit the edge of the coffee table.

That's with luck. If things went badly, the gun would get caught in the nylon lining of her pocket and Geist would empty the pistol into us both.

He continued his story. "Times were good those summers. Yvev was an inspiration. He was a font of knowledge and encouraged me to write. He'd critique my short stories and he really seemed to believe that I had talent."

"So why didn't he help you get published? And why didn't he write anything other than *Julie and James*?" Jaime asked, stalling to create an opening for me to shoot.

"He didn't write that, *I did*. I won't deny his influence and how he polished it, which I suppose made it read like he wrote it himself. Yvev didn't write anymore. You see, he never thought of himself as all that great a writer. He told me it was almost as if someone else was dictating the words and he was just transcribing them. Then sometime years ago, that voice inside his head stopped and he couldn't write. He emigrated here and became just an ordinary citizen. He was always uncomfortable being treated like a prophet or some kind of voice of his generation. He lived in fear that he couldn't give people the answers they sought and that he'd be exposed as a fraud."

"So why didn't he just help *you* get published?" Jaime persisted.

"Strelnikov became a different man three years ago. His wife was killed. She was walking in the woods and she just collapsed. Heart attack. Losing her unhinged him. She was his life. Other than me, he had almost no friends. He

327

started drinking more, became a hopeless alcoholic. He let himself go, got sick. He'd go weeks without bathing. He was awful to be around. I was about to give up on him when I came into some money."

"Tony Gazza's money."

"Again Riley, I commend you. If we had more time, I'd be interested in hearing how you uncovered that little nugget. Yes, it was the notorious gangster Tony Gazza who set me free. I showed the book to my principal, Father Salieri. Despite my estimation of him as an open minded man, he was shocked by the content. So much so that he told his benefactor, Tony Gazza about it. I guess rather than rub me out, as the old mob would have done, they bought me off. Tony Gazza comes to me and asks how much it would take to kill the book forever. It was enough money for me to leave my job and come up here to write."

He'd just confirmed what Salieri and Gazza had insisted all along, leaving out the part where Gazza scared the piss out of him to get him to go along with the scheme. But I still didn't follow it. "So *Julie and James* was dead. Why kill Paige?"

"You know Riley, as much as I admire you, you haven't been fooling me one bit. Why is your hand in Ms. Johansen's pocket? Please extract it and place both of your hands in plain sight. And Ms. Johansen, it strikes me that you might have a weapon concealed in that jacket. Please take it out slowly and place it on the table. I'm willing to talk about your late mother's unfortunate demise to satisfy your final morbid curiosity, but if you make any kind of sudden movement, I'm afraid I'll have to terminate my story rather abruptly."

Damn. All this time I'd been stringing him along, just waiting for the chance to strike, and he'd had his eye on my hand. "Do as he says, Jaime," I said.

"Why? You're going to kill us anyway, aren't you?"

Damn, Jaime don't force his hand. The more time we stall, the better chance we have.

"I imagine with your background in the FBI, Riley, you know how painful multiple gunshot wounds can be. On the other hand, done properly, it can be over quickly with a minimum of discomfort. It's up to you."

"He's right, Jaime. This guy has us *stone* cold now. Lay the gun down on that *rickety* table."

He might think my choice of words peculiar, but Geist wouldn't pick up the reference to Stone. I hoped Jaime would. We were playing for time until help arrived. She laid the .22 on the table. Rick was our only hope now and I prayed he hadn't gotten lost in the Vermont woods or in a bottle somewhere.

"All right, Paul, let's hear the rest. No more tricks up our sleeve."

"I'm glad that's settled. In any case, I agreed to bury *Julie and James* to avoid a scandal at Sacred Cross. But as sophisticated as Gazza thought he was, he knew nothing. Once I saw they were trying to buy me out, I played them, rather skillfully. All along, I could have changed the names, the locale, even the country in which it was set for that matter. The genius of the work was in the characters and the writing, Yvev's embellishments on my creation. But Gazza was offering me money, not that much at first. So I kept saying no, delaying, until he upped the ante to enough money that could support me for a few years while I wrote another book, or rewrite this one without altering what made it great. Hell, *Lolita* could have been set in California instead of New England and who would have cared? So I took the money, cashed in my other assets and moved up here with my mentor."

"Even though Strelnikov was a hopeless drunk by now?"

"I thought I could save him but Yvev was slipping fast. I watched the man waste away before my eyes until one day in March, he just didn't get up one morning. Liver, heart, lungs, who knows? --- all were in such bad shape that anyone could have been the reason he died. There was a late season storm. We got twenty inches of wet snow and I was stranded in the cabin with the body. The realization came to me that no one had seen the famous Strelnikov in years. I was doing the shopping for him. I was taking care of him. He was hardly a public figure anymore and nobody knew what he really looked like. So I became him. We were about the same height and coloring. A little makeup, a wig, a beard. I'd picked up some rudimentary Russian just being around him and planned to study the language a little more. It would have been enough to get me by in time had you not tricked me with it today. I envisioned an entire campaign --- Yvevgeny Strelnikov's first novel in thirty years. I contacted Vanity Fair and sent a sample chapter under the strictest terms of secrecy. They flipped and offered me tons of money for first dibs."

"So now you had to dispose of the body without anyone knowing he had died, which I imagine was pretty easy in these woods."

"Some days the bear eats you. *A grizzly end*, pardon my pun. After hibernation, those creatures are famished. Poor Yvev was so soaked in vodka that those animals must have wandered around the forest intoxicated for days."

I said, "So after Strelnikov was gone, you had to silence anyone else who'd seen the manuscript and knew that it wasn't his. I imagine you discovered that Salieri was near death so he wasn't a concern.

"And Gazza was in no position to challenge the great Strelnikov like he had a poor teacher. So that left Paige. But she finally did read the original draft and thought it was great. She tried to contact you. Why not just let her find you a publisher?"

"Again, bad timing --- a cosmic tragedy that places us where we are now. The woman thought that she had no way to get in touch with me but she was wrong. I kept that e-mail account alive but didn't reply to her inquiries when she said that she had read the book and wanted to rep it. You see, by then --- it was too late. I had already contacted Vanity Fair with the sample chapter as Strelnikov."

I'd come to the conclusion that Geist *was* insane. Whether it was there in his genes, or whether the long winter in Vermont cooped up with a disturbed Russian genius had tipped him over, Geist had lost it. Like most madmen, he hadn't thought his delusional schemes through to their logical end.

Where was Stone?

The .22 was on the coffee table where Jaime had laid it. His story was nearing its completion and my only chance now was to dive for the gun. I figured that I would get hit at least once and maybe twice before I reached it, but at least I could stay alive long enough to put a couple of shots into Geist. That way Jaime would be spared and with any luck, Geist's inexperienced aim would cause him to miss or only wound me. I'd wait until he flinched or sneezed or anything that would give me an extra split second.

I kept him talking. "But why did you have to kill her? Paige might have kept your secret or found a way to give you credit. Or even perpetrated the ruse that you were Strelnikov. There were ways, other than murder."

"You don't think I thought of that? Killing her was not my first choice. I knocked on the door, introduced myself. She said that she'd been looking for me --- gave me the whole line about how she had thought the manuscript was great. I offered her terms similar to what you outlined --- just go along and pretend I was Strelnikov. I had enough short stories and an unpublished novel of his. I could sprinkle in my own work in his style. Staying low profile, no one need be the wiser. But alas, she wouldn't hear of it. Her own career would be ruined it if came out that she faked a Strelnikov original. I admit I found killing her strangely exhilarating. All that rejection, those years of being told I wasn't good enough. It made it easier to keep plunging that knife in until she was silenced for good."

I said, "How could you be sure that no other copies existed? Copies could be all over the world. She had given me one, and I digitally reproduced it several times."

"Interesting. She lied to protect you, said that no one else had seen it. Had I known, I'd have had to kill you as well --- make it appear to be murder/suicide. I had the opportunity but I merely knocked you out instead. You showing up when you did was rather convenient. There was a good chance they'd blame you for the killing. In a way, she saved your life by lying that no other copies existed.

"And Mr. King ---- if you had just let things go? The priest died of natural causes. Gazza was mercifully taken, so I read. Paige White would have been the only casualty. As it is, I think you both know the sad dénouement to the story. I'll dispose of your bodies. Luckily for you, the bears are already asleep so your final resting place will be where I buried what was left of Yvevgeny. Then, if your weak threats have any substance, I'll wipe away any trace that I've been here and be off to cabin number two."

"But the police will expose the whole sordid mess when they get the manuscript and even Strelnikov's name will be poison."

"A bluff on your part, I think. But if not, there's enough greed in publishing that someone would put it out despite the scandal and it might sell even more as a result of the notoriety. As I said, I have enough of Yvevgeny's life in a little trunk--- his diaries, notes, original manuscripts, etc.

that I can convince any expert that the work is his. Even preserved some tissue and blood for DNA analysis. And with money, I can become anybody I want. I have an inspiration --- I'll write under the name Riley Johansen --- a lasting memorial to the two of you."

"How sick is that?" Stone's voice boomed from across the room. "Drop it, Geist."

Fifty four

G eist didn't drop it. He didn't shoot either. He stood his ground.

"We seem to have a Mexican standoff here, don't we?" he said, his gun aimed squarely at Jaime's chest. "I'm sure whoever you are, you're fully capable of killing me. But then I'd be killing the girl and most likely King, as well. So let me propose a bloodless solution."

Stone was edging toward the couch where we were sitting.

"Stop right there," Geist commanded. "Move any closer and I'll shoot the girl and then King."

Stone froze in his tracks and I spoke. "Are you ready to die, Geist? The man with the gun is Rick Stone, former Marine. He's holding a gun of nearly twice the caliber and muzzle velocity of the one you've got. You're outnumbered and out-gunned. The only *bloodless solution* available to you is to give up. You'll be arrested and tried in New Jersey, where no one's been executed since the seventies. Worst case for you, you'll spend the rest of your life at Rahway. Although knowing New Jersey, maybe some great defense lawyer like Jack Furlong could get you acquitted. You shoot any of us now and the others will surely kill you. Bad as the prisons may be, you'll be alive and you might even be able to write. Seems to me your best alternative is to drop the gun like my friend says."

Geist promptly rejected the offer. "Not interested. My proposition is this: You let me go now. I'm not naïve enough to ask that you give me a ten-minute head start. Just let me get to my car. I'll disable yours on the way out. I'll cut the satellite dish wires. No cell reception here as you may know. You can walk out to the main road in half an hour maybe. If you're lucky a motorist will happen by and you can call the authorities. Maybe they'll catch me, maybe they won't. But no matter what, the odds are in your favor for survival. You have thirty seconds.

"If you refuse, I'll shoot the girl and whoever else I can before you get to me. Chances are I'll be dead, but one or two of you will be too. I knew it might come down to something like this someday. Nothing for me to lose now. I'm ready to face the end. Are any of you?

When we didn't respond immediately, he said, "Thirty seconds, clock's ticking."

Letting Jaime die to avenge her mother was not a trade I was willing to make. Stone was an expert marksman but who knows who'd be hit in the crossfire. I'd lost Liz. Paige was killed under my watch. I wasn't about to risk that with Jaime.

Stone pre-empted my desire to cave into the Geist's proposal. "Geist, listen hard. I've been here for a while. I heard you say how Strelnikov never woke up one morning. And when I first got to the porch and saw you holding a gun on my friends, I called 911. Satellite phones like mine do

336

work here. The police will be blocking your only exit point in minutes. You won't get far. Drop the gun now and like Riley says, you'll have a chance."

Geist's lips curled into a thin sneer. "Satellite phone. Maybe, maybe not. Ten seconds."

What happened next will haunt me as long as I live. It began as a low rumble from deep within Stone, rising in volume and intensity like a football team breaking huddle. It crested as an all out battle cry. He bull-rushed the smaller man, his gun blazing.

Instinctively, Geist turned his weapon from Jaime to meet the coming onslaught, firing directly at his charging adversary. He may have already been dead as he squeezed off two rounds in Stone's direction.

A tight cluster of three shots were grouped around the English teacher's heart and a torrent of blood erupted from his mouth as he collapsed. Although momentarily stunned by how quickly it happened, I quickly seized the twenty-two from the coffee table and pressed it to his temple. There was no movement from Geist as his sightless eyes stared ahead, wide with disbelief.

His mission accomplished, Stone pivoted and staggered towards Jaime, crimson seeping through his white ski sweater just above the waist.

"I had nothing to lose either," came his guttural gasp before falling to the floor.

RICHARD NEER

Fifty five

D aredevils often say that they never feel more alive than at the moment they experience a close encounter with death. Risk takers who jump from airplanes and wait until the last possible moment to open their chutes, mountain climbers, trapeze artists who work without a net, cliff divers, those who cheat death --- I've never understood the rush and certainly never wanted to experience it.

You can't cheat death ---- when your number's up, it's sayonara. If somehow luck intervenes and a potentially deadly situation breaks in your favor, a wise man doesn't re-up to give the reaper another shot. It borders on insanity to push the odds until the law of averages favors the other side.

There are notable exceptions. Policemen, career militarists, and missionaries may lay their lives on the line every day but what differentiates them from daredevils is that they have an overarching cause they believe is more important than their life. While one may not share that faith, it's surely laudable to risk you own neck for the benefit of mankind. But to endanger your life for cheap thrills or some made-up world record that no one cares about is an indictment of how shallow we have become.

The deep-seated impulse that caused Rick to place himself in harm's way to protect Jaime and me was noble. But the immediate catalyst was despair – a lengthy

338

depression that had made him feel his own life wasn't worth continuing. It would have been easy to blame Lisa Tillman for his condition, but not all spurned lovers recklessly throw themselves into the line of fire. The fault lay within him, somewhere deep.

The point became academic. We knew that he had lied about having a satellite phone. We rushed him down the long mountain trail until our cell phones worked, Jaime pressuring the wounds as best she could to slow the bleeding. From there, it was a race to a well-equipped EMS vehicle that we rendezvoused with near Brattleboro in time to stabilize his condition. It was touch and go for two days, but he pulled through.

To my amazement, the near death experience that his body suffered gave his mind an affirmation of life. Almost as soon as he regained consciousness, he seemed grateful for the second chance that fate had given him. He wanted to know everything about Paul Geist and his transformation into Strelnikov. He wanted the New York papers brought to him so he could follow the Jets run to the playoffs. Rather than lament how the injuries he'd suffered might impair his athletic abilities, he looked forward to time in the gym to get tougher than ever.

Within a week, Rick was strong enough physically to be transferred to the Toms River Medical Center. Jaime and I had gone ahead to welcome him back, decking out his private room with flowers, fruit baskets and letters of encouragement from his listeners. The medical staff chased us from the suite briefly as they set him up in bed, with the requisite tubes and monitors.

Standing outside his door when we emerged was Lisa Tillman.

"Hello, Lisa." I said, not bothering to introduce her to Jaime. Lisa's image had been omnipresent on billboards as the network launched her daytime program.

"Riley," she said, extending a slender hand that I took, against my initial instincts.

"I'm not sure that it's a good idea for Rick to see you just now."

"Why don't we let him decide that?"

Had I misjudged Lisa, since she had taken obvious pains to be here? Had she realized what she had in Rick and rushed to be by his side in his time of need? Just as he seemed to be getting over her, did she want to rekindle their relationship?

"Lisa, I don't know if he's up to it today. Why don't we wait until he's settled in a little? That ride from Vermont had to be rough."

"Riley, it's pretty clear you don't understand television. I can't hold the camera crew over another day. That would cost the network thousands and our budget is not unlimited."

"Your camera crew?"

"Well, of course. The whole story of Strelnikov's death and that fake Geist and how Rick saved the day is national news. Rick's a hero. Who better to give him his first national TV exposure than me? I've already worked up a very flattering profile of him using some video we shot from our vacation last year. Who knows, this could catapult him into big time television and I don't mean some piddling cable shit down here. I'm thinking network. Maybe even LA where we could be together."

I was incredulous and I thought Jaime was going to haul off and deck her right then.

"Riley, he saved your life," Lisa went on. "You owe him this chance at the brass ring while he's hot. His moment could pass quickly, you know how that is. I'm going in."

I stepped in front of the door and grabbed her arm. "No, you're not."

"What right do you have to stop me?"

Jaime intervened. "She's right, Riley. I think Rick's strong enough."

She gave me a look I'd come to know well over the last few months, one that usually meant she knew something I didn't. I yielded to her intuition and let Lisa pass.

She was in the room for less than two minutes before stomping out. "Screw you, King. You saw me coming and got to him first, didn't you, you son of a bitch?"

I was about to protest but she had bolted out of earshot already.

Jaime winked at me. "Let's see Rick. I'm dying to hear what he said to her."

Stone was sitting up in bed, seemingly no worse off than if he were recovering from the flu. He was smiling, opening his fan mail.

341

"Do you believe this, Riles? If every one of these folks got a people meter, I'd have the number one talk show in the country. Did they run a special train from Florida to carry all this fruit? How did all this stuff get here? Is this your doing?"

"Much as I'd like to take credit, every paper and TV network in the country ran the story and mentioned that you were being moved down here soon. I guess your adoring fans did the rest. I just might have to give that unlistenable radio show of yours another chance."

"I sure won't be talking about your exploits at Georgetown any time soon. Count on that. *Meet the new boss.*"

"So…" I said, mainly to keep Jaime from exploding in anticipation, "what did Lisa want?"

"Lisa? I think she wanted to scoop Katie Couric and Diane Sawyer and do the first network interview with her bullet ridden ex."

"And?"

"You know that country song by Dierks Bentley, *Drunk on a Plane*? I told her to take her camera crew and kiss my ass."

Jaime smiled. "Always the gentleman, Rick."

"Was it me, or has she put on some weight?" he asked, and we all had a good laugh.

"Hand me that box of mail, will you, Riles? McCarver told me that if I wanted to respond to some of these cards, he'd send a couple of secretaries over." He winced as he shifted in the bed, evidence that it would be a while before we'd be shooting hoops together.

"Hey man, relax. Let me read you some of it. Jaime, could you do me a favor? I'm really dry, this hospital air and all. Grab me a soda. There's a machine just down the hall."

"Sure. I know you boys want to be alone and talk about manly things. Just don't go comparing my ass to Lisa's, okay? I don't have two hours a day to work out like she does."

She smiled and left us.

"She's a keeper, my friend," Stone said after the door swung shut. "I'm sorry I gave her such a hard time."

"I think you made up for it. Here, let me read you some of these postcards."

There were probably two hundred cards and envelopes in a box the hospital had provided. Stone would probably be there long enough to reply to them all, if another torrent didn't arrive in the next day's mail. I rifled through them quickly, reading him ones from people he knew or that originated from outside the region. There were a few from southern Florida, where some of his New York listeners had migrated. I left the sealed letters for him to read privately. They had doubtless taken more time to organize their thoughts and deserved more than my passing mention.

"Jeez, Stone, here's one from Mexico. Your fans can't reach all the way down there, can they?"

"Maybe it's from someone who used to live here and moved south of the border. Internet radio. WJOK streams, you know. Probably listen online or something."

"Yeah, that makes sense. It just says, '*Great work solving a vexing mystery. Regards to Mr. King. God be with you both.*' No signature. Well, nice of them to include me, anyway."

"Lucky they didn't know you're agnostic or whatever you are."

There was something familiar about the writing on the back of the card. It was very neat, precise script, like a female schoolteacher's hand --- perhaps a nun's. Or maybe someone who had been taught by them. It was postmarked San Miguel, Mexico, a small village that I'd heard housed quite a few American émigrés.

"When those bullets started flying, I think I saw God," I said, half serious. The card had started me thinking, but I wasn't sure exactly what. "Mind if I keep this one since it mentions me?"

"Not at all. At least you have one fan who isn't left over from your sorry college basketball career."

"Yeah. Hey, man, it's good to have you back. I mean, really back."

"I understand. There was an imposter living in my body the last few months, too."

Jaime came back with a couple of Diet Dr. Peppers and we chatted for a few more minutes until Rick got tired. We went out to dinner after leaving the hospital and she stayed over at my place that night. Christmas was just a week away, and with all the craziness, I'd yet to set up a tree. Maybe we'd get one tomorrow.

At about two in the morning, something woke me. I first thought it might have been Jaime stirring, although she seemed to be fast asleep now. It turned out to be Bosco, who had wedged himself between us at bedtime and was having a doggie dream, chasing rabbits or Milk Bones or whatever dogs dream of. His legs were twitching and kicking me in the side.

I tried to get back to sleep. I turned on the television with the sound off, activating the closed captions so as not to awaken Jaime. The two thirty SportsCenter came and went but still my eyes were wide open. I decided to get up and read a little in the next room. The novel Jaime had brought me was pretty dull so far, maybe it would lull me to sleep.

As I got up, I noticed the postcard I'd borrowed from Stone lying on the dresser. I figured it would make a better bookmark than the folded-over dust jacket I was currently employing, so I took it with me and plopped down on the sofa with my book. I was about to slip the postcard into the book, a few pages past the slow progress I'd made so far.

But the writing on the unsigned card caught my attention again. In the cold silence of the night, my brain clear of distraction, I remembered where I'd seen it before. The letter that bore the same handwriting was tucked away in another book.

From my bookcase, I extracted my Georgetown graduation gift, my father's prized early edition King James Bible. As I opened it, Salieri's final missive to me fell to the floor.

ABOUT THE AUTHOR

"Something of the Night" is Richard Neer's first work of fiction featuring detective Riley King and his talk radio ally Rick Stone, as they investigate crime along the eastern seaboard.

His work of non-fiction entitled "FM, the Rise and Fall of Rock Radio", (Villard 2001), is the true story of how corporate interests destroyed a medium that millions grew up cherishing.

Neer has worked in important roles both on and off the air at two of the most prestigious and groundbreaking radio stations in history--the progressive rocker WNEW-FM for almost thirty years, and the nation's first full time sports talker, WFAN, over the past twenty-eight.

The follow-up to "Something of the Night", entitled "The Master Builders" was released in May of 2016. The next novels were in the King series were *Indian Summer, The Last Resort, The Punch List, An American Storm* and *Wrecking Ball*. There are also two short Stories, *King's Christmas* and *Spirits in the Night*.

Made in the USA
Middletown, DE
23 June 2020